Mr. Wayt's Wife's

Marion Harland

Alpha Editions

This edition published in 2023

ISBN : 9789357957908

Design and Setting By
Alpha Editions
www.alphaedis.com
Email - info@alphaedis.com

Contents

MR. WAYT'S WIFE'S SISTER.

CHAPTER I.

ONE breezy May day, such a little while ago that it is hardly safe to name the year, a New Jersey ferry "car-boat" was so far behind her time that the 12.30 train for Fairhill left without waiting for her.

Ignorant, or incredulous of the untoward happening, the passengers rushed for and through the station to find egress discouraged by the impassive official whose stentorian tones were roaring through the building the name and stopping places of the next train. Among the foremost in the pell-mell run was a hazel-eyed young man with a gripsack in his hand, and the olive bronze of a sea voyage upon a very good-looking face. He was always persuaded that he could have eluded the great-voiced doorkeeper and boarded the last platform of the moving cars, had he not run afoul of a wheeled chair midway between the seats and inconveniently set radiators in the waiting room, and narrowly escaped a "header." He did not actually fall; neither did he overset the vehicle. Avoiding both calamities by vaulting the dashboard and front wheels, he yet dropped his hat and valise in different directions, and brought up at an obtuse angle by catching at one of the marble-topped radiators. The first use he made of his hat, which was picked up by a smiling bystander, was to lift it to a woman who was propelling what he had mistaken for a baby's perambulator.

"I beg your pardon, I am sure!" he said, in manly fashion. "I hope the"—he was about to say "baby," but changed the phraseology just in time—"that nobody was hurt!"

A glimpse of the occupant of the chair had showed him a wan face too old for a child's, too small for that of a grown person. Before the woman addressed could reply, elfish accents, husky and precise, said, "Not at all— thank you!" and there was a cackle of shrill, feeble laughter.

The young fellow had lost the train that should have returned him in forty minutes to the family he had not seen in six months; he was just off shipboard, and felt the need of a bath and toilet upon steady ground, with plenty of elbow room. He had come near having a bad fall, and had not missed making a ludicrous spectacle of himself for the entertainment of a gaping crowd. But he laughed in a jolly, gentlemanly way, and again raising his hat passed on without a second glance at the mute personage who had pushed the wagon directly across his track.

Like the rest of the disappointed wayfarers he walked quite up to the outlet of the station, and peered anxiously through at the empty rails, still vibrating from the wheels of the vanishing train, yet he neither frowned nor swore. He did not even ask: "When does the next train go to Fairhill?" The time-table in his pocket and that upon the wall, set at "2 P. M.," told him all and more than he wanted to know. The excitement and suspense over, his inner man became importunate. He had had an early breakfast on the *City of Rome*, and was far hungrier now than then. Doubling upon his tracks, he repaired to the restaurant in the same building with the vast waiting room and offices. The place was clean, and full of odors that, for a wonder, were fresh and savory, instead of hanging on the air and clinging to the walls like a viewless "In Memoriam" of an innumerable caravan of dead-and-gone feasts. The *menu* was promising to an unsated appetite, and having given his order to a waiter the even-tempered customer sat back in his chair and surveyed the scene with the air of one whose mind was, as the hymnist aptly puts it, "at leisure from itself."

This lack of self-consciousness underlay much that made March Gilchrist popular in his set. He was a clever artist, and wrought hard and well at his profession, although he had a rich father. His position in society was assured, his physique fine, and education excellent—advantages fully appreciated by most of the men, and all the women he knew. If he recognized their value he was an adroit dissembler. Simple and frank in manner, he met his world with outstretched hand. When the hand was not taken he laughed in good-humored astonishment, went about his business, and forgot the churl. His schoolmates used to say that it did not pay to quarrel with him; his parents, that he and his sister May should exchange names. That his amiability was not the result of a phlegmatic temperament was apparent in the quick brightness of the eyes that roved about the dining room, leaving out nothing—from the lunch counter in the adjoining room, set with long ranks of salvers with globular glass covers that gave the array the expression of a chemist's laboratory, to the whirligig fans that revolved just below the ceiling with the dual mission of cooling the atmosphere and chasing away flies. Our returned traveler seemed to find these harbingers of summer weather and summer pests amusing. He was watching them when a voice behind him accosted a hurrying waiter.

"There is a young girl over there who cannot walk. Will you lift her out of her chair and bring her in? It is just at the door, and she is very light."

"Busy now, miss! Better ask somebody else!" pushing past.

The baffled applicant stood in the middle of the floor, irresolute, seeming the more solitary and helpless because young and a woman. Thus much, and not that she was comely and a lady, March saw before he sprang to his feet and faced her respectfully.

"I beg pardon! but can I be of use? It will give me pleasure if you will allow me." Catching sight in the doorway of the one in whose behalf she had spoken, an arch smile—respectful still—lighted up his honest countenance. "If you will let me make amends for my awkwardness of a while ago!"

He was a society man, and might have been aware how unconventional was the offer. He palliated the solecism, in describing the incident at home, by saying that he saw in every elderly woman his mother, in a young one, his only sister.

"Thank you! if you will be so kind"—accepting the proposal as simply as it had been made. "I could bring her in myself, but she does not like to have me do it here."

"I should think not, indeed! One of the best uses to which a man's muscles can be put is to help the weak," rejoined March heartily.

A gleam crossed the unchildish visage of the cripple when he stooped to lift her. She recognized him, but offered no verbal remark then, or when he deposited the light burden in the chair set for her by a waiter more humane, or less driven than his testy comrade.

"You are very good, and we are much obliged to you," the guardian said, with a little bow of acknowledgment which he took as dismissal also, withdrawing to his own place.

"Set the table for seven, please," he heard her continue to the waiter, businesslike and quiet, "and reserve another seat at that table"—designating one remote from the larger—"for a gentleman who will come in by and by. There is a man, too, for whom I wish to order luncheon at the counter in that room. He can get a good meal and be comfortable there, I suppose?"

"A traveling party of nine!" thought March, apparently intent upon the depths of his soup tureen. "With this girl as courier. Yet she mentioned two men!"

The family filed in while he speculated. Twin boys of twelve or thirteen, dressed exactly alike in gray jackets and knickerbockers, except that the red-haired one wore a blue necktie and the brown-haired a scarlet; a pretty, blue-eyed girl of eight, and a toddler of two, led by a sweet-faced mother, with fair hair and faintly tinted complexion, of the china shepherdess school. The "courier," assisted by the waiter, seated them all without bustle, before addressing an individual who had followed at a respectful distance and now hung aloof, chewing the brim of a brand-new straw hat.

"Homer!" said the young lady gently and distinctly, as she might direct a child, "you will get your dinner in the next room. Come!"

By shifting his position slightly, March could see her point the man to a stool and give orders for his refreshment. He was undersized, lean, and sandy haired, small of feature and loutish in carriage. His eyes had red rims, and blinked incessantly, as if excessively weak or purblind. When he began operations upon coffee and sandwiches, he gobbled voraciously, gnawing off mouthfuls like a greedy dog. His clothes were so distressingly ready-made, and accentuated his uncouthness so unmercifully, as to leave no doubt that the wearing of coat and vest was a novelty and an equivocal boon.

"An odd fish!" commented March mentally. "Why should a civilized family haul him after them like a badly made kite tail? And they are not vulgarians, either!"

His eyes strayed discreetly back to the table set for seven. The mistress of ceremonies sat at the head, and was studying the printed *menu*. It lay flat on the cloth that the crippled girl at her right might read it with her. Their heads were close together, and the gravity upon the countenance of the elder was reflected by the shrewd elfin face. Presently they began to whisper, the bare, thin finger of the younger of the two tracing the lines to the extreme right of the *carte*. It was plainly a question of comparative expense, March perceived with a pang of his kind heart. For he had been a boy himself, and the children were hungry.

"Hurry up—won't you, Hetty," called the redheaded twin impatiently. "Give us the first thing you come to so long as it isn't corned beef, pork and beans, or rice pudding. I'm *starved!*"

"Me, too!" echoed his fellow.

"You needn't make mincemeat of your English on that account!" piped the crippled sister tartly. "It is no little matter to order just the right things for such a host. Mamma, you must have a cup of tea, I suppose?"

The young lady interposed, writing while she talked:

"Of course! And all of us will be the better for some good, hot soup. This is luncheon, not dinner, recollect. We only need something to stay our appetites until six o'clock," she added, putting the paper in the waiter's hand.

She did not look like one who did things for effect, yet there was meaning in her manner of saying it. If she was obliged to cut her coat according to her cloth, she would just now make the scantiness of the pattern seem a matter of choice and carry out the seaming gallantly.

"How much further have we to go?" queried eight-year-old, somewhat ruefully.

Six o'clock was to her apprehension a long time ahead.

"We are within half an hour of home. We might have been there by now, but we thought it better to wait over a train to rest and get rid of the dust we brought off the cars."

"And to let *him* get shaved and barbered and prinked up generally!" shrilled the cripple malevolently.

"Hester!" The mother's voice was heard for the first time.

"Well, mamma?"

"That is not respectful, my love. You are tired, I am afraid."

The shrewd face jerked fretfully, and the lips were opened for a retort, checked by a gloved hand laid upon the forward child's. There was only a murmur, accompanied by a pettish shrug.

March was ashamed of the impulse that made him steal a look at the tray bearing the result of the whispered consultation. Three tureens, each containing two generous portions of excellent English gravy soup with barley in it, a pot of tea, bread and milk for the baby and plenty of bread and butter were duly deposited upon the board.

"I'll take the rest of your order now," said the waiter, civilly suggestive.

"This is all. Thank you!" in a matter-of-course tone that was not resentfully positive.

The "courier" understood herself, and having taken ground, how to hold it. This was luncheon. March caught himself speculating as to the dinner bill of fare.

The spokeswoman may have been two-and-twenty. She was slightly above the middle height of healthy womanhood, had gray, serious eyes, with brown shadows in them when the lids drooped; well-formed lips that curled roguishly at the corners in smiling; a straight nose with mobile nostrils, and a firm chin. There was character in plenty in the face. Such free air and sunshine as falls into most girls' lives might have made it beautiful. The pose of her head, the habitual gravity of eyes and mouth, the very carriage of the shoulders and her gait testified to the untimely sense of responsibility borne by this one. She was slight and straight; her gown of fawn-colored cloth fitted well, and a toque of the same material with no trimming, except a knot of velvet ribbon, was becoming; yet March, who designed his sister's costumes, was quite certain that gown and hat were homemade and the product of the wearer's skill. Both women were unmistakably gentle in breeding, and the children's chatter, although sometimes pert, was not rude or boisterous.

A man entered by the side door while the chatter was stilling under the supreme attraction of the savory luncheon, and, after a word to a waiter, took the chair which had been tilted, face downward, against the far table at the "courier's" order. He was tall, and had an aquiline, intellectual cast of countenance. His hands—the artist had an appreciative eye for hands and fingers—were a student's; his linen was irreproachable; his chin and cheeks were blue-shaven, and his black hair was cut straight across at the back, just clearing the collar of his coat, instead of being shingled.

"A clergyman!" deduced Gilchrist, from the latter peculiarity. "That—not the white choker—is the trade-mark of the profession. Did barber or preacher establish the fashion?"

After inspection of the *menu*, the newcomer ordered a repast which was sumptuous when compared with the frugal one course of the seven seated at the table in the middle of the room. He took no notice of them nor they of him. His mien was studiously abstracted. While waiting for his food he drew a small blotting pad from his pocket and wrote upon it with a stylographic pen, his profile keener as his work went on. In pausing to collect thoughts or choose words the inclination of his eyes was upward. After his entrance profound silence settled upon the central table. Not even the baby prattled. This singular taciturnity took on significance to the alert wits of the unsuspected observer when he saw a swift interchange of looks between the cripple and her left-hand neighbor, attended by a grimace of such bitter disdain directed by the junior of the pair at the student as fairly startled the artist.

The unconscious object of the shaft put up paper and pen, and addressed himself with deliberate dignity, upon the arrival of his raw oysters, to the lower task of filling the material part of him. He was discussing a juicy square of porterhouse steak, as March bowed respectfully on his way out to the girl at the head of the board, a smile in his pleasant eyes being especially intended for the dwarfed cripple beside her.

Homer had bolted the last fragment of a huge segment of custard pie, washed down the crust with a second jorum of coffee, and sat, satiate and sheepish, upon the tall stool, awaiting orders.

"The most extraordinary combinery, taken in all its parts, it was ever my luck to behold," declared March Gilchrist at his father's dinner table that evening. "Intensely American throughout, though. I wish I knew whether or not the man who appropriated the reserved seat was a usurper. If he were, that spirited little economist of a courier was quite capable of dispossessing him, or, at least, of calling the waiter to account for neglect of duty. And what relation did blind Homer bear to the party?"

"Dear old March!" said his sister affectionately. "Story weaving in the old fashion! How natural it sounds! What jolly times you and I have had over our amateur romances and make believes! Which reminds me of a remarkable sermon preached Sunday before last by our new pastor. (I told you we had one, didn't I?) The text was: 'Six waterpots of stone, containing two or three firkins apiece!'"

"Absurd!"

"True; but listen! The text was only a hook from which he hung an eloquent discourse upon the power of faith to make wine—'old and mellow and flavorous,' *he* called it—out of what to grosser souls seems insipid water. It was a plea for the pleasures of imagination—*alias* faith—and elevated our favorite amusement into a fine art, and the fine art into religion. I came home feeling like a spiritual chameleon, fully convinced that rarefied air is the rightful sustenance of an immortal being. According to our Mr. Wayt, what you haven't got is the only thing you ought to be sure of. Life is a sort of 'Now you see it and now you don't see it' business throughout. Only, when you don't see it you are richer and happier than when you do. Did you ever think to hear me babble metaphysics? Now, where are those portfolios?"

"Make believe that you have overhauled them, and be blest," retorted her brother. "There's a chance to practice your metaphysical cant—with a new, deep meaning in it, too, which you will detect when you inspect my daubs. I did some fairish things in Norway, however, which may prove that your rule has an exception."

The Gilchrists freely acknowledged themselves to be what the son and daughter styled "a mutual admiration square." March's portfolios were not the only engrossing subject that drew them together in the library, where coffee and cigars were served.

May and her father turned over sketches and examined finished pictures at the table, passing them afterward to the mother, who was a fixture in her easy-chair by reason of a head, covered with crisp chestnut curls, lying upon her lap. May was her companion and co-laborer, dutiful and beloved, despite the impetuosity of mood and temper which seemed inharmonious with the calmer nature of the matron. The mother's idol was the long-limbed fellow who, stretched upon the tiger-skin rug, one arm cast about her waist, submitted to her mute fondling with grace as cheerful as that with which she endured the scent of the cigar she would not let him resign when he threw himself into his accustomed place. She was a good wife, but she never pretended to like the odor of the judge's best weed. March's cigars, she confessed, were "really delightful." Perhaps she recognized in his affluent, joyous nature something hers lacked and had craved all her life; the golden side of the iron shield. Assuredly, her children drew the ideality in which they reveled from the father.

The tall, dignified woman who queened it in the best circles of Fairhill society, and was the chiefest pillar in the parish which had just called Mr. Wayt to become its spiritual head, was the embodiment of what is known as hard sense. Mind and character were laid out and down in straight lines. Right was right; duty was duty, and not to be shirked. Wrong was wrong, and the shading off of sin into foible was of the devil. She believed in a personal devil, comprehended the doctrines of the Trinity, of election and reprobation, and the resurrection of the physical body. Twice each Sabbath, once during the week, she repaired to the courts of the Lord with joys unknown to worldly souls. The ministry she held in the old-fashioned veneration we have cast behind us with many worse and a few better things. Others might and did criticise the men who wore white neckties upon weekdays and had their hair cut straight behind. The hands of the presbytery had been laid in ordination upon them. That was a sacred shield to her. In spirit she approached the awful circle of the church with bared feet and bent brow. Within it was her home. To her church her toils were literally given. For it her prayers continually ascended.

She had looked grave during May's flippant abstract of the new preacher's discourse anent the six stone waterpots. Her family might suspect that she could not easily assimilate spiritual bread so unlike that broken to his flock by a good man who had been gathered to his fathers six months before, after a pastorate of thirty years in Fairhill. Nobody could elicit a hint to this effect from her lips. Mr. Wayt was the choice of a respectable majority of church and parish. The presbytery had accepted his credentials and solemnly installed him in his new place. Henceforward he was her pastor, and as such above the touch of censure. He had been the guest of the Gilchrists for a week prior to the removal of his family to the flourishing suburban town, and received such entertainment for body and spirit as strengthened his belief in the Divine authority of the call he had answered.

He left Fairhill four days before March landed in New York, to meet his wife and children in Syracuse and escort them to their new abiding place. During these days the mothers and daughters of the household of faith had worked diligently to prepare the parsonage for the reception of the travelers, Mrs. Gilchrist being the guiding spirit. And while she drew the shining silk of her boy's curls through fingers that looked strong, yet touched tenderly, the Rev. Percy Wayt, A. M. and M. A., with feet directed by gratitude and heart swollen with pastoral affection, was nearing the domicile of his best "member."

A long French window upon the piazza framed the tableau he halted to survey, his foot upon the upper step of the broad flight leading from the lawn. It was a noble room, planned by March and built with his proud father's money. Breast-high shelves filled with choice books lined the wall; above them were a few fine pictures. Oriental rugs were strewed upon the polished floor; lounging and upright chairs stood about in social attitudes. The light of the shaded reading lamp shone silvery upon Judge Gilchrist's head and heightened the brightness of May's face. March's happy gaze, upturned to meet his mother's look of full content, might have meant as much in a cottage as here, but they seemed to the spectator accessories of the luxurious well-being which stamped the environment.

He sighed deeply—perhaps at the contrast the scene offered to the half furnished abode he had just left—perhaps under the weight of memories aroused by the family group. He was as capable of appreciating beauty and enjoying ease as were those who took these as an installment of the debt the world owed them. The will of the holy man who preaches the great gain of godliness when wedded to contentment, ought to be one with that of the Judge of all the earth. Sometimes it is. Sometimes——

"Ah, Mr. Wayt!" Judge Gilchrist's proverbially gracious manner was never more urbane than as he offered a welcoming hand to his wife's spiritual director. "You find us in the full flood of rejoicing over our returned prodigal," he continued, when the visitor had saluted the ladies. "Let me introduce my son."

Mr. Wayt was "honored and happy at being allowed to participate in the reunion," yet apologetic for his "intrusion upon that with which strangers should not intermeddle."

While saying it he squeezed March's hand in a grasp more nervous than firm, and looked admiringly into the sunny eyes.

"Your mother's son will forgive the interruption when he learns why I am here," he went on, tightening and relaxing his hold at alternate periods. "I brought my wife and babies *home* to-day. I use the word advisedly. I left a desolate, empty house. Merely walls, ceilings, doors, windows, and floors. A shell without sentiment. A chrysalis without the germ of life. This was on last Monday morning."

By now the brief sentences had come to imply depth of emotion with which March was unable to sympathize, and he felt convicted of inhumanity that this was so.

"I advised Mrs. Wayt of what she would find. Hers is a brave spirit encased in a fragile frame, and she was not daunted. You, madam," letting go the son's hand and facing the mother, "know, and we can never forget what we found when, weary and faint and travel-stained, we alighted this afternoon at the parsonage gate."

With all her native aplomb and half-century of world knowledge Mrs. Gilchrist blushed, much to the covert amusement of husband and son. If the judge had manner Mr. Wayt had deportment, and with it fluency. His weighty words pressed her hard for breath.

"Please don't speak of it!" she hastened to implore. "We did very little—and I no more than others."

"Allow me!" Gesture and tone were rhetorical. "You—or others under your command—laid carpets and set our humble plenishing in order. There is not much of it, but such as it is, it has followed our varied fortunes so long that it is endeared by association. You arranged it to the best advantage. You stocked larders and made up beds, and kindled the fire upon the household altar, typified by the kitchen range, and spread a toothsome feast for our refreshment. You and your sister angels. If this be not true, then benevolent pixies have been at work, for, although we found the premises swept and garnished, not a creature was to be seen. Generosity and tact had met together; beneficence and modesty had kissed each other. I assure you, Mr. Gilchrist"—wheeling back in good order upon March—"that in seventeen years of the vicissitudes of a pastoral life that has had its high lights and depressing shades, such delicacy of kindness is without a parallel."

"Let me express my sympathy in the shape of a cigar," said March, taking one from the table. "I brought over a lot, which my father, who is a connoisseur in tobacco, pronounces fit to smoke. Should you agree with him, I shall esteem it a compliment if you will let me send a box to the parsonage to-morrow."

Mr. Wayt's was an opaque and not a healthy complexion. It was mottled now with a curious, dull glow; the muscles of his mouth twitched. He waved aside the offering with more energy than courtesy.

"You are good, sir—very good! But I never smoke! My nervous system is idiosyncratic. Common prudence inhibits the use on my part of all narcotics and stimulants, if principle did not. To be frank"—inclusively to all present—"I am what is known as 'a temperance crank.' You may think the less of me for the confession; in point of fact, I lost one charge in direct consequence of my peculiar views upon this subject; but if I speak at all, I must be candid. Believe me nevertheless, Mr. Gilchrist, your grateful debtor for the proffered gift. If you will now and then let a kindly thought of me mingle with the smoke of your burnt offering, the favor will be still greater."

"May I trouble you to say to Mrs. Wayt that the cook you asked me to engage for her cannot come until next Monday morning?" said the practical hostess. Mr. Wayt's sonorous periods always impelled her to monosyllabic commonplaces. "Perhaps she cannot wait so long?"

"I take the responsibility of promising for her, madam, that she *will*. Apart from the fact that her desire to secure a servant recommended by yourself would reconcile her to a still longer delay, her household, as at present composed, has in itself the elements of independence. We have a faithful, if eccentric, servitor, who has an abnormal passion for work in all its varieties. He is gardener, house servant, cook, groom, mason and builder, as need requires. He mends his own clothes, cobbles his shoes—and I am not without a suspicion of his proficiency as a laundryman."

He rendered the catalogue with relish for the humor of the situation. The exigencies of parsonage life which had developed the talents of his trusty retainer seemed to have no pathos for the master.

"Where did you find this treasure? And is he a Unique?" asked May laughingly.

"I believe the credit of raking the protoplasmic germ out of the slums of Chicago, where we were then sojourning, belongs to my wife's sister, Miss Alling. The atmosphere of our home has warmed into growth latent possibilities, I fancy. It was a white day for poor Tony when the gutter-wash landed him at our door. Even now he has physical weaknesses and mental deficiencies that make him a striking object-lesson as to the terrible truths of heredity."

"How many children have you, Mr. Wayt?" questioned March, with irrelevance verging upon abruptness.

"George W. Cable's number—five. You may recall the witty puzzle he set for a Massachusetts Sunday School. 'I have five children,' he said, 'and half of them are girls. What is the half of five?' 'Two and a half,' came from the perplexed listeners. It transpired, eventually, that the other half were girls also."

He was an entertaining man, or would have been had he been colloquial instead of hortatory. Yet what he said was telling rather from the degree of importance he evidently attached to it than from the worth of the matter. In a smaller speaker, his style would have been airy. Standing, as he did, six feet in his slippers, he was always nearly—occasionally, quite—imposing. Men of his profession seldom converse well. The habit of hebdomadal speech-making runs over and saturates the six working days. Pastoral visitation is undoubtedly measurably responsible for the trick of talking as for duty's sake, and to a roomful. The essential need of the public speaker is audience, and to this, actual or visionary, he is prone to address himself. Mr. Wayt could not bid an acquaintance "Good-morning," in a chance encounter upon boat or car, without embracing every passenger within the scope of his orotund tones, in the salutation. A *poseur* during his waking hours, he probably continued to cater to the ubiquitous audience in his dreams.

"Come out for a turn on the piazza, May!" proposed March, after the guest had taken his leave.

The night was filled with divine calm. The Gilchrist house surmounted a knoll from which the beautiful town rolled away on all sides. In the distance a glistening line showed where the bay divided Jersey meadows from the ramparts of the Highlands. The turf of the lawn was ringed and crossed by beds of hyacinths and tulips. The buds of the great horse-chestnut trees were big with promise; the finer tracery of the elms against the moonlit sky showed tufts of tender foliage. Faint, delicious breaths of sweetness met brother and sister at the upper end of their walk, telling that the fruit trees were ablow.

"East or West, Hame is Best!"

quoted March, taking in a mighty draught of satisfaction. "Not that I brought you out here to listen to stale Scotch rhymes. Don't annoy the precious mother by letting her into the secret, May, but Mr. Wayt is the man I saw in the restaurant to-day, and I believe that was his family!"

CHAPTER II.

THE almost unearthly stillness of the fragrant May night was, as often happens at that lovely, uncertain season, the precursor of a rainy day.

Hetty Alling, awakening at four o'clock to plan for the work that lay before the transplanted household, heard the first drops fall upon the tin roof of the piazza under her window like the patter of tiny, stealthy feet scaling the eaves and combing, then advancing boldly in rank and rush until the beat was the reverberant roar of a spring flood.

It awoke nobody else under the parsonage roof-tree. Hester slept soundly beside her. She never slept quietly. In addition to the spinal disease which warped the poor girl's figure she suffered from an affection of the throat that made her respiration in slumber a rattling snore, interrupted at regular intervals by a gurgle that sounded like strangulation. So audibly distressing was it that her father could not sleep within two rooms of her, and the healthy occupants of the intervening nursery complained that "nothing was done to break Hester of making such a racket. If she wanted to stop it she could."

Her young aunt and roommate knew better. Hester had shared her bed for almost nine years. Mrs. Wayt's orphaned sister was but fourteen when she came to live in the parsonage, then situated in Cincinnati. It had been a hard winter with the pastor's wife. While her mother lay dying in Ithaca, N. Y., her then only daughter, the first born of her flock, a beautiful, vivacious child of eight, met with the accident which crippled and dwarfed her for life. The telegram announcing Mrs. Alling's illness was answered by one saying that Hester was at the point of death. She had just passed the first doubtful stage upon the return journey lifeward, when Hetty, in her new black frock, insisted upon relieving the grief-worn watcher over the wreck that could never be put together again.

Lying in strange quarters in a strange town at the dreariest hour of the twenty-four, Hetty recalled that as the date when the load of care, now an integral part of herself, was first fastened upon her. She had before this likened it to a needle she had once, in childish wantonness, run under the bark of a young willow, and seen disappear gradually from view as the riven bark grew over it, until, at the end of a year, no vestige of the steel remained, except a ridge which was never smoothed away. She was not exactly penniless. The portion left her by her mother was judiciously invested by her guardian, and yielded her exactly four hundred dollars a year. It was transmitted promptly, quarterly, until she was of age, by which time she was so rooted and grounded in prudence that she continued to draw the like amount at equal periods.

"It is enough to dress her," Mrs. Wayt had said to her husband, in seeking his sanction to her offer of a home to one who stood alone in the world save for her sister, and an uncle who had lived in Japan for twenty years. "And she is welcome to her board—is she not, Percy, dear?"

"Welcome, dear love? Can you ask the question with regard to your only sister—poor motherless lamb! While we have a roof between us and the sky and a crust of bread between us and starvation, she shall share both. Let *me* write the letter!"

The epistle was almost tattered with many readings when Hetty became an inmate of her brother-in-law's home. She had not kept it until now. That was not strange, Fairhill being the latest in a succession of "settlements" to which the brilliant gospeler had accepted calls, generally unanimous and almost invariably enthusiastic. There were three children at Hetty's coming—her own and her mother's namesake, Hester, and Percy and Perry, the twin boys. Four had been born since, but two had not outlived early infancy. Mr. Wayt would not have been a preacher of the period had he not enriched some of his most effective discourses with illustrations drawn from these personal bereavements.

His celebrated apostrophe to a six-months old daughter, beginning—"Dear little Susie! She had numbered but a brief half year of mortal life, but she was loving and beloved! I seem to feel the soft strain of her arms about my neck this moment"—is too familiar to my readers, through newspaper reports, to need repetition here. The sermon embodying this gem of poetic and rhetorical emotion is known to have won him calls to three churches.

It was still dark when Hetty's ear caught the muffled thud of feet upon the garret stairs. Wherever providence and parish preferences cast the lot of the Wayts, Homer's bedroom was nearest the heavens that were hot by summer and cold by winter.

"I don't set no store by ceilin's," he told Hetty when she "wished they could lodge him better." "Seems if 'twas naturaler fur to see the beams purty nigh onto my nose when I fus' wake in the mornin'. I'm kind o' lonesome fur 'em when I caan't butt me head agin the top o' me room when I'm a mind ter."

At another time he confided to her that it was "reel sociabul-like to hear the rain onto the ruff, clus' to a feller's ears o' nights."

He was on his way down to the kitchen now to light the fire. Unless she should interfere, he would cook breakfast, and serve it upon the table she had set overnight, and sweep down the stairs and scrub the front doorsteps while the family ate the morning meal. He called himself "Tony," as did all the family except Hetty and Mrs. Wayt. The former had found "Homer Smith, Jr.," written in a sprawling hand upon the flyleaf of a songbook which formed the waif's entire library. Hetty had notions native to her own small head. One was that the—but for her—friendless lad would respect himself the more if he were not addressed by what she called "a circus monkey's name." For this reason he was "Homer" to her, and her sister followed her example because she considered the factotum and whatever related to him Hetty's affair, and that she had a right to designate her chattel by whatever title she pleased.

Tony had come to the basement door one snowy, blowy day of a particularly cruel winter, when Hetty was maid of all work. He stood knee-deep in a drift when she opened the grated door and asked, hoarsely but without a touch of the beggar's whine, for "a job to keep him from starvin'." He was, as he "guessed," twenty years of age, emaciated from a spell of "new-money," and so nearly blind that the suggestion of a "job" was pitiably preposterous. Hetty took him into her neat kitchen, made him a cup of tea, and cut and plied him with bread and butter until he asserted that he was "right-up-an'-down chirpy, jes' as strong's enny man. Couldn't he rake out the furnace, or saw wood, or clear off the snow, or clean shoes, or scrub the stairs, or mend broken things, or wash windows, or peel pertaters, or black stoves, or sif' ashes, or red-up the cellar—or—or—somethin', to pay for his dinner? I aint no beggar, ma'am—nor never will be!"

Hetty hired him as a "general utility man," at ten cents a forenoon and his breakfast, for a week—then, for a month. He lodged wherever he could—in stable lofts, at the police station, under porches on mild nights, and when other resorts were closed, in a midnight refuge, and never touched liquor or tobacco in any form. At the month's end, his girlish patroness cleared a corner of the attic between the sharp angle and the chimney, set up a cot, and allowed him to sleep there. Mr. Wayt had no suspicion of the disreputable incumbent of the habitation honored by his name and residence, until one memorable and terrible March midnight when a doctor must be had without the delay of an instant revealed the secret, but under circumstances that strengthened the retainer's hold upon his employers. Since then, he had been part and parcel of the establishment, proving himself as proficient in removals and settlings-down as in other branches of his business.

Mr. Wayt liked to allude to him as "Hetty's Freak." At other times he nicknamed him "Kasper Hauser." Once, and once only, in reference to Hetty's influence over the being he chose to regard as half-witted, he spoke of him as "a masculine Undine," whereupon his sister-in-law turned upon him a look that surprised him and horrified his wife, and marched out of the room.

Mrs. Wayt followed her presently and found her gazing out of the window of the closet to which she had fled, with livid face and dry eyes that were dangerously bright.

"Percy hopes you were not hurt by his harmless little jest," said the gentle wife. "You know, Hetty, it would kill me if you and he were to quarrel. He has the kindest heart in the world, and respects you too sincerely to offend you knowingly. You must not mind what sounds like extravagant speech. We cannot judge men of genius as we would ordinary people. And, dear, for my sake be patient!"

The girl yielded to the weeping embrace of the woman whose face was hidden upon her shoulder.

"Mr. Wayt"—she never gave him a more familiar title—"cannot hurt me except through you, Fanny. You and he must know that by now. I will try to keep my temper better in hand in future."

Hetty was young and energetic, and used to hard work. She had put the children to bed early on the evening of their arrival in Fairhill; sent her sister, who had a sick headache, to her chamber before Mr. Wayt returned from the Gilchrists'; given Hester's aching limbs a hot bath and a good rubbing, and only allowed Homer to help her unpack boxes until half-past ten, not retiring herself until midnight. The carload of furniture, which had preceded the family and been put in place by the neighborly parishioners, looked scantily forlorn in the roomy manse. The Ladies' Aid Association had asked the privilege of carpeting the parlors, dining room, stairs, and halls, and Judge Gilchrist, instigated by his wife, headed a subscription that fitted up the pastor's study handsomely. The sight of this apartment had more to do with Hetty's short speech last night and her down-heartedness this morning than the newness of quarters and the knowledge of the nearly spent "housekeeping purse."

"The people will expect us to live up to that study!" she divined shrewdly, staring into the blackness that began to show two gray lights where windows would shape themselves by and by. "And we cannot do it—strain and save and turn and twist as we may. We are always cut out on a scant pattern, and not a button meets without starting a seam. How sick and tired I am of it all! How tired I am of *everything!* What if I were to lie still as other girls—as *real* young ladies do—and sleep until I'm rested out—rested all through! I should enjoy nestling down among the pillows and pulling the covers about my head, and listening to the rain, as much as the laziest butterfly of them all. What's the use of trying to keep things on their feet any longer when they must go down with a crash sooner or later?

"I'm *awfully* sorry for Hetty Alling!" This was the summing up of the gloomy reverie. In saying it inwardly, she raised herself to pinch the pillow savagely and double it into a higher prop for her restless head. "She is lonely and homesick and hasn't a friend in the world. She never can have an intimate friend for reasons she knows so well she is sometimes ready to curse God and die.

"There! Hester, dear! I only moved you a little to make you lie easier. No! it is not time to get up. Don't talk, dear, or you'll wake yourself up."

She was never cross with the afflicted child, but in her present mood, the moan and gurgle of her obstructed respiration went through her brain like the scraping of a saw. The change of position did not make the breathing more quiet, and Hetty got up with the general out-of-tune-ativeness best expressed by saying that "one's teeth are all on edge." She dressed by candlelight, to save gas, and groped her way down the unfamiliar backstairs to the kitchen.

It was commodious and well-appointed, with a pleasant outlook by daylight. In the dawn that struggled in a low-spirited way through the rifts in the rain and refused to blend with the yellow blink of her candle and Homer's lantern, no chamber could be less than dismal.

Homer was on his knees in front of the flickering fire, at which he stared as if doggedly determined to put it out of countenance.

"Now"—his way of beginning nine out of every ten sentences—"this ere's a new pattern of a range to me, an' it's tuk me some time fur ter git holt on it. Most new things comes awk'ard to most folks."

Hetty blew out her candle, and, dropping into a chair in physical and mental languor, sat watching the grotesque figure clearing away ashes and cinders. His wrestle with the new pattern had begrimed his pale face and reddened his weak eyes. His matutinal costume of a dim blue flannel shirt, gray trousers, and a black silk skull cap cast off by Mr. Wayt, pushed well back upon the nape of the neck and revealing a scanty uneven fringe of whitey-brown hair, did not provoke the spectator to a smile.

"There is no bringing *him* up to the tone of that study!" she meditated grimly. "He and I are hopeless drudges, but he is the happier of the two. Homer! I believe you really *love* to work!" she broke forth finally.

Homer snickered—a sudden spurt that left him very sober. His laugh always went out like a damp match.

"Yes'm, cert'nly, ma'am! Ef 'twant fur work, there wouldn't be nuthin' to live fur!"

He shambled off to the cellar with the ashpan, and in a few minutes, she could distinguish in the sounds rumbling and smothering in the depths beneath her feet the melancholy tune of his favorite ditty:

"On the banks of the Omaha—maha!

'Twas there we settled many a night.

As happy as the little bird that sparkled on our block

On the banks of the Omaha!"

Hetty raised the window and leaned out, gasping for breath. A garden lay behind the house and on one side of it. It was laid out in walks and borders, and was rather broad than deep. Beyond this were undefined clumps of trees that looked like an orchard. Roofs and chimneys and spires and lines of other trees, marking the course of streets, were emerging from the soaking mists. Five o'clock struck from a tower not far away, and then a church bell began to ring gently—a persuasive call to early prayers.

The warm, sweet, wet air that aroused her to look over the sill at a row of hyacinths in full bloom, the slow peal of the bell, the hush of the early morning, did not comfort her—but the soft moisture that filled her eyes drew heat and bitterness out of her heart. When she went up to awaken Hester she carried a spray of hyacinth bells, weighted with fragrant drops. Fine gems of rain sprinkled her hair, her cheeks were cool and damp, the scent of fresh earth and growing things clung to her skirts. She laid the flowers playfully against the heavy lids lifted peevishly at her call.

"'There's richness for you,'" she quoted. "A whole bed of them is awaiting your inspection in the garden. And such lovely pansies—some as big as the palm of your hand. You and I and Homer, who is wild with delight over them, will claim the flowers as our especial charge and property."

"Thank you for the classification!" snapped Hester. "Yet we do belong to backyards as naturally as cats and tomato cans. At least Homer and I do. You'd climb the fence if you could."

"With the other cats?" said Hetty lightly. "See! I am putting the hyacinths in your own little vase. I unpacked your china and books last night. Not a thing was even nicked. You shall arrange them in this jolly corner cupboard after breakfast. It looks as if it were made a-puppose, as Homer says. He has bumped his head against strange doors and skinned his poor nose against unexpected corners twenty times this morning. He says: 'Now—I s'pose it's the bran-new house what oxcites me so. I allers gits oxcited in a strange place.'"

The well-meant diversion was ineffectual.

"His oxcitement ought to be chronic, then! Ugh! that water is scalding hot!" shrinking from the sponge in Hetty's hand. "For we've done nothing but 'move on' ever since I can recollect. I overheard mother say once, with a sort of reminiscent sigh, that our 'longest pastorate was in Cincinnati.' We were there just four years. We were six months in Chillicothe, and seven in Ypsilanti. Then there was a year in Memphis, and eighteen months in Natchez, and thirteen in Davenport. The Little Rock church had a strong constitution. We stayed there two years and one week. It's *my* opinion that *he* is the Wandering Jew, and we are one of the Lost Tribes."

She smiled sour approbation of her sarcastic sally, jerking her head backward to bring Hetty's face within range of her vision. The deft fingers were fastening strings and straps over the misshapen shoulders. The visage was grave, but always kind to her difficult charge.

"You think that is irreverent," Hester fretted, wrinkling her forehead and beetling her eyebrows. "It isn't a circumstance to what I am thinking all the time. Some day I shall be left to myself and my bosom devil long enough to spit it all out. It's just bottling up, like the venom in Macbeth's witches' toad that had sweltered so long under a stone. But for you, crosspatch, all would have been said and done long ago."

"You wouldn't make your mother unhappy if you could help it," Hetty said cheerily. "And it isn't flattering to her to compare her daughter to a toad."

Hester was silent. As she sat in Hetty's lap, it could be seen that she was not larger than a puny child of seven or eight. The curved spine bowed and heightened the thin shoulders; she had never walked a step since the casualty that nearly cost her her life. Only the face and hands were uninjured. The latter were exquisitely formed, the features were fine and clearly cut, and susceptible to every change of emotion. That the gentle reproof had not wrought peaceable fruits was apparent from her expression. The misfit in her organization was more painfully perceptible to herself early in the day than afterward. She seemed to have lost consciousness of her unlikeness to other people while asleep, and to be compelled to readjust mental and physical conditions every morning. Hetty dreaded the process, yet was hardly aware of the full effect upon her own spirits, or why she so often went down to breakfast jaded and appetiteless.

"I often ask myself," resumed Hester, with slow malignity, repulsive in one of her age and relation to those she condemned—"if children ever really honor their parents. We won't waste ammunition upon *him*—but there is my mother. She is a pattern of all angelic virtues, and a woman of remarkable mental endowments. You have told me again and again that she is the best person you ever knew—patient, heroic, loving, loyal, and so on to the end of the string! You tell over her perfections as a Papist tells her beads. The law of kindness is in her mouth; and her children shall arise and call her blessed, and she ought not to be afraid of the snow for her household while her sister and her slave Tony are to the fore. Don't try to stop me, or the toad will spit at you! I say that this, one would think, impossible She, the modern rival of Solomon's pious and prudish wise woman—is weak and unjust and——"

Hetty interrupted the tirade by rising and laying the warped frame, all a-quiver with excitement, upon the bed.

"You would better get your sleep out"—covering her up. "When you awake again you will behave more like a reasonable creature. I cannot stay here and listen to vulgar abuse of your mother and my best friend."

She said it in firm composure, drew down the shades, and without another glance at the convulsed heap sobbing under the bedclothes, left the chamber. Outside the door she paused as if expecting to be recalled, but no summons came. She shook her head with a sad little smile and passed down to the breakfast room.

Father, mother, and four children were at the table. Mr. Wayt, in dressing jacket, slippers, and silk skull cap, a cup of steaming chocolate at his right hand, was engrossed in the morning paper. A pair of scissors was beside his plate, that he might clip out incident or statistics which might be useful in the preparation of his wide-awake sermons. He made no sign of recognition at the entrance of his wife's sister; Mrs. Wayt smiled affectionately and lifted her face for a good-morning salute, indicating by an expressive gesture her surprise and pleasure at having found room and meal in such attractive order. Long practice had made her an adept in pantomime. The boys nodded over satisfactory mouthfuls; pretty Fanny pulled her aunt down for a hug as she passed; even the baby made a mute rosebud of her mouth and beckoned Hetty not to overlook her.

Mr. Wayt's digestion was as idiosyncratic as his nervous system. While the important unseen apparatus carried on the business of assimilation, the rest of the physical man was held in quiescent subjugation. Agitation of molecular centers might entail ruinous consequences. He reasoned ably upon this point, citing learned authorities in defense of the dogma that simultaneous functionation—such as animated speech or auricular attention and digestion—is an impossibility, and referring to the examples of dumb creatures to prove that rest during and after eating is a natural law.

He raised his eyes above the margin of his newspaper at the clink of the chocolate pot against the cup in Hetty's hand. The questioning gaze met a goodly sight. His wife's sister wore a buff gingham, finished at throat and wrists with white cambric ruffles, hemmed and gathered by herself. Her dark brown hair was in perfect order; her sleeves were pushed back from strong, shapely wrists. She always gave one the impression of clean-limbedness, elasticity, and neatness. She was firm of flesh and of will. The prettier woman at the head of the table was flaccid beside her. The eyes of the younger were fearless in meeting the master's scrutiny, those of his wife were wistful, and clouded anxiously in passing from one to the other.

"For Hester," said Hetty, in a low voice, looking away from Mr. Wayt to her sister. "She is tired, and will take her breakfast in bed."

"I remonstrate"—Mr. Wayt's best audience tones also addressed his wife— "as I have repeatedly had occasion to do, against the practice of pampering an invalid until her whims dominate the household. Not that I have the least hope that my protest will be heeded. But as the child's father, I cannot, in conscience, withhold it."

Light scarlet flame, in which her features seemed to waver, was blown across Hetty's face. She set down the pot, poured back what she had taken from it, and with a reassuring glance at her sister's pleading eyes, went off to the kitchen. There she hastened to find milk, chocolate, and saucepan, and to prepare a foaming cup of Hester's favorite beverage; Homer, meanwhile, toasting a slice of bread, delicately and quickly.

Hester's great eyes were raised to her aunt from lids sodden with tears; her lips trembled unmanageably in trying to frame her plea.

"Forgive me! please forgive me!" she sobbed. "You know what my morning fiend is. And I am not brave like you, or patient like mother!"

Hetty fondled the hot little hands.

"Let it pass, love. I was not angry, but some subjects are best left untouched between us. Here is your breakfast. Homer says that I 'make chawkerlette jes' the same's they did for him in the horspittle when he had the new-money.' They must have had a French *chef* and a marvelous *menu* in that famous 'horspittle.' It reminds me of Little Dorritt's Maggie and her "evenly chicken,' and 'so lovely an' 'ospittally!'"

She had the knack of picking up and making the most of little things for the entertainment of her hapless charge. Mrs. Wayt was much occupied with the other children, to whom she devoted all the time she could spare from her husband. It happened occasionally that he would eat no bread she had not made, and oftener that his craving was for certain *entrées* she alone could prepare to his liking. She brushed his coat and hat, kept the run of missing papers and handkerchiefs, tied his cravats, sat by him in a darkened room when he took his afternoon siesta, wrote letters from his dictation, and, when he was weary, copied in a clear, clerkly hand or upon his typewriter, sermons and addresses from the notes he was wont to pencil in minute characters upon a pocket pad. At least four nights out of seven she arose in the dead of darkness to read aloud to him for one, three, and four hours, when the baleful curse, insomnia, claimed him as her prey. His fad, at this date, was what Homer tickled Hester into hysterics by calling "them horsephates." Horsford's acid phosphate, if the oracle were to be believed, ought to be the *vade mecum* of ailing humanity. He carried a silver flask containing it in his pocket everywhere; dropped the liquid furtively upon a lump of sugar, and ate it in the pulpit, during anthem, or voluntary, or offertory; mixed it with water and drank it on the cars, in drugstores, in private houses, and at his meals, and Mrs. Wayt kept spirit lamp and kettle in her bedroom with which to heat water for the tranquilizing and peptic draught at cock-crowing or at midnight. If she had ever complained of his exactions, or uttered an ungentle word to him, neither sister nor child had heard her. She would have become his advocate against himself had need arisen—which it never did.

"My ministering angel," he named her to the Gilchrists, his keen eyes softened by ready dew. "John Randolph said, in his old age, of his mother: 'She was the only being who ever understood me.' I can say the same of my other and dearer self. She interprets my spirit intuitions when they are but partially known to myself. She meets my nature at every turn."

She met it to-day by mounting guard—sometimes literally—before the door of his study—the one room which was entirely in order—while he prepared his discourses for the ensuing Sabbath. The rest found enough and more than enough to do without the defended portal. Fanny was shut up in the dining room with the baby Annie, and warned not to be noisy. The twins carried bundles and boxes up and downstairs in their stocking-feet; Homer pried off covers with a muffled hammer, and shouldered trunks, empty and full, leaving his shoes at the foot of the stairs. Hester said nothing of a blinding headache and a "jumping pain" in her back while she dusted books and china. Hetty was everywhere and ever busy, and nobody spoke a loud word all day.

"You might think there was a corpse in the study instead of a sermon being born!" Hester had once sneered to her confidante. "I never hear him preach, but I know I should be reminded of the mountain that brought forth a mouse."

One of her father's many protests, addressed *at* Hetty and *to* his wife, was that their eldest born was "virtually a heathen."

"Home education in religion, even when administered by the wisest and tenderest of mothers—like yourself, my love—must still fall short of such godly nurture and admonition as are contemplated in the command: 'Forsake not the assembling of yourselves together.' There is didactic theology in David's holy breathing: 'A day in thy courts is better than a thousand.'"

"Better than a thousand in the same place? I should think so," interposed Hester's tuneless pipe. "He needn't have been inspired to tell us that! Family worship suffices for my spiritual needs. That must be the porch to the 'courts,' at least."

In speaking she, too, looked at her mother, although every word was aimed at her father.

"It is a cruel trick that we have!" Hetty had said of the habit. "Every ball strikes that much-tried and innocent woman, no matter who throws it."

"Of course!" retorted the sarcastic daughter. "And must while the angle of incidence is equal to that of reflection."

In the discussion upon family *versus* church religion she carried her point by a *coup d'état*.

"Pews and staring pewholders are all well enough for straight-backed Christians!" she snarled. "I won't be made a holy show of to gratify all the preachers and presbyteries in America!"

Anything like physical deformity was especially obnoxious to Mr. Wayt. The most onerous duties pertaining to his holy office were visitation of the sick and burial of the dead. Hester's beautiful golden hair, falling far below her waist, veiled her humped shoulders, and her refined face looking out from this aureole, as she lay in her wheeled chair, would be picturesquely interesting in the chancel, if not seen too often there. The coarse realism of her refusal routed him completely. With an artistic shudder and a look of eloquent misery, likewise directed at his wife, he withdrew his forces from the field. That night she read "Sartor Resartus" to him from three o'clock until 6 A. M., so intolerable was his agony of sleeplessness.

It happened so often that Hetty was the only responsible member of the family who could remain at home with the crippled girl, that neither Mr. nor Mrs. Wayt seemed to remark that her churchgoing was less than nominal. Hester called Sunday her "white-letter day," and was usually then in her best and most tolerant temper, while her fellow-sinner looked forward to the comparative rest and liberty it afforded as the wader in marshlands eyes a projecting shoulder of firm ground and dry turf.

It was never more welcome than on the fair May day when the Fairhill "people" crowded the First Church to hear the new pulpit star.

"The prayer which preceded the sermon was a sacred lyric," said the Monday issue of the *Fairhill Pointer*. "In this respect Rev. Mr. Wayt is as remarkably gifted as in the oratory which moved his auditors alternately to tears, and smiles, and glows of religious fervor. We regret the impossibility of reporting the burning stream of supplication and ascription that flowed from his heart through his lips, but a fragment of the introduction, uttered slowly and impressively, is herewith given verbatim, as a sample of incomparable felicity of diction:

"'THOU art mighty, merciful, masterful, and majestic. *We* are feeble, fickle, finite, and fading.'"[A]

March Gilchrist had his say anent the sample sentence on the way home from church. He was not connected with the press, and his criticism went no further than the ears of his somewhat scandalized and decidedly diverted sister.

In intuitive anticipation of the reportorial eulogy, he affirmed that the diction was *not* incomparable.

"I heard a Georgia negro preacher beat it all hollow," he said. "He began with: 'THOU art all-sufficient, self-sufficient, and *in*-sufficient!'"

"March Gilchrist! How dreadful!"

They were passing the side windows of the parsonage, which opened upon a quiet cross street. May's laugh rippled through the bowed shutters of the dining room behind which sat a girl in a blue flannel gown, holding upon her knee and against her shoulder a hunchbacked child with a weirdly wise face. They were watching the people coming home from church.

"A religious mountebank is the most despicable of humbugs," said March's breezy voice, as he whirled a pebble from the walk with his cane, and watched it leap to the middle of the street.

Hester twisted her neck to look into Hetty's eyes.

"They are discussing their beloved and eloquent pastor! My heart goes out to those two people!"

CHAPTER III.

"HETTY! do you ever think what it would be like to be engaged?"

"Engaged to do what?" said Hetty lazily.

She lay as in a cradle, in a grassy hollow under an apple tree—the Anak of his tribe. The branches, freighted with pink and white blooms, dipped earthward until the extreme twigs almost brushed the grass, and shut in the two girls arbor-wise. The May sun warmed the flowers into fragrance that hinted subtly of continual fruitiness. Hester said she tasted, rather than smelled it. Bees hummed in the boughs; through the still blandness of the air a light shower of petals fell silently over Hetty's blue gown, settled upon her hair, and drifted in the folds of the afghan covering Hester's lower limbs.

Homer had discovered in the garden fence a gate opening into this orchard, and confidentially revealed the circumstance to Hetty who, in time, imparted it to Hester, and conspired with her to explore the paradise as soon as the boys and Fanny were safely off to Sunday School.

"Engaged to do what?" Hetty had said in such good faith that she opened dreamy eyes wide at the accent of the reply.

"To be married, of course, Miss Ingenuous! What else could I mean?"

"Oh-h-h!" still more indolently. "I don't know that I ever thought far in that direction. Why should I?"

"Why shouldn't you, or any other healthy and passably good-looking girl, expect to be engaged—and be married—and be happy? It is time you began to take the matter into consideration, if you never did before."

"There is usually another party to such an arrangement."

"And why not in your case?"

"Where should he come from? Is he to drop from the moon? Or out of the apple tree"—stirred to the simile by the flick of a tinted petal upon her nose. "Or am I to stamp him out of the earth, *à la* Pompey? And what could I do with him if he were to pop up like a fairy prince, at this or any other instant?"

"Fall in love with him, and marry him out-of-hand! I *wish* you would, Hetty, and take me to live with you! That is one of my dearest dreams. I have thought it all out when the backache keeps me awake at night, and when I get quiet dreamy hours by day, when *he* is off pastoraling, and the boys and Fan are at school, and baby Annie is asleep, and I can hear Tony crooning 'Sweet Julia' so far away I can't distinguish the frightful words, and you are going about the house singing to yourself, and blessing every room you enter like a shifting sunbeam."

"Why, my pet, you are talking poetry!"

Hetty raised her head from the arms crossed beneath it, and stared at the child. The light, filtered through the mass of scented color, freshened her complexion and rounded the outlines of her face; her solemn eyes looked upward; her hands lay together, like two lily petals, upon the coverlet. Unwittingly she was a living illustration of her father's theory of the Reality of the Unseen.

"No!" she answered quietly. "Not poetry, for it may easily come to pass that you should have a husband and home of your own. I do dream poems sometimes, if poetry is clouds and sunsets and music nobody else hears, and voices—and love words—and bosh!"

Hetty could not help laughing.

"Tell me some of the glory and the bosh! This is a beautiful confessional, Hester; I wish we had nothing to do for a week but to lie on the grass, and look at the blue sky through apple blossoms."

"Amen!" breathed her companion softly, and for a while they were so quiet that the robins, nesting upon the other side of the tree, began to whisper together.

"Bosh and my poetry dreams are synonyms," resumed Hester, her voice curiously mellowed from its accustomed sharpness. "Other people may say as much of theirs. I *know* it of mine. There's the difference. All the same they are as sweet as the poisoned honey we were reading about the other day, which the bees make from poppy fields. And while I suck it, I forget. My romance has no more foundation than the story of the Prince and the Little White Cat. Mine is a broken-backed cat, but she comes straight in my dreams after her head is cut off. You don't suppose she minded *that!* She must have been so impatient when the Prince hesitated that she was tempted to grab his sword and saw through her own neck. You see she recollected what she had been. The woman's soul was cooped up in the cat's skin. And I was eight years old when the evil spell was laid upon *me!*"

The tears in Hetty's throat hindered response. Never until this instant, with all her love for her dependent charge, her knowledge of her sufferings, and the infinite pity these engendered, had the deprivations Hester's affliction involved seemed so horribly, so atrociously cruel. The listener's nails dug furrows in her palms, she set her teeth, and looking up to the unfeeling smile of the deaf and dumb heavens, she said something in her heart that would have left faint hope of her eternal weal in the orthodox mind of her brother-in-law.

Hester was speaking again.

"Every painter has his models. I have had mine. I dress each one up and work the wires to make him or her go through the motions—my motions, mind you! not theirs, poor puppets! When the dress gets shabby, or the limbs rickety, I throw them upon the rubbish heap, and look out for another.

"I got a new one last Thursday. The man who jumped over me in the station, and afterward carried me into the restaurant (such *strong*, steady arms as he had!) is a real hero! Oh, I am building a noble castle to put him in! He lives near here, for he passes the house three times a day. His eyes have a smile in them, and his mustache droops just like Charles I.'s, and he walks with a spring as if he were so full of life he longed to leap or fly, and his voice has a ring and resonance like an organ. The pretty girl that called him 'Mark' to-day, is his sister."

"Why not his wife?"

"Wife! Don't you suppose I know the cut of a married man, even on the street? He hasn't the first symptom of the craft. He doesn't swagger, and he doesn't slink. A husband does one or the other."

Hetty laughed out merrily. There was a sense of relief in Hester's return to the sarcastic raillery habitual to her, which made her mirth the heartier.

A man crossing the lower slope of the orchard heard the bubbling peal, and looked in the direction of the big tree. So did his attendant, a huge St. Bernard dog. He tore up the acclivity, bellowing ferociously. Before his master's shout arose above his baying he was almost upon the girls. At the instant of alarm, Hetty had thrown herself before the wheeled chair and the helpless occupant, and faced the foe. Crouching slightly, as for a spring, her face blenched, eyes wide and steady, she stood in the rosy shadow of the branches, both hands outthrown to ward off the bounding assailant.

"What a pose!" was March's first thought, professional instinct asserting itself, concerned though he was at the panic for which he was responsible. In the same lightning flash came—"I'll paint that girl some day!"

"Don't be frightened!" he was calling, as he ran. "He will not hurt you!"

Hester had shrieked feebly, and lay almost swooning among her cushions. Hetty had not uttered a sound, but, as the master laid his hand on the dog's collar her knees gave way under her, and she sank down by the cripple's chair, her head resting upon the edge of the wicker side. She was fighting desperately for composure, or the semblance of it, and did not look up when March began to apologize.

"I am awfully sorry," he panted, ruefully penitent. "And so will Thor—my dog, you know—be when he understands how badly he has behaved. He is seldom so inhospitable."

The words brought up Hetty's head and wits.

"Are we trespassing?" she queried anxiously. "We thought that this orchard was a part of the parsonage grounds, or we would not have come. It is we who should beg your pardon."

"By no means!" He had taken off his hat, and in his regretful sincerity looked handsomer than when his eyes had smiled, concluded Hester, whose senses were rapidly returning. "My name is Gilchrist, and my father's grounds adjoin those of the parsonage. He had the gate cut between your garden and the orchard, that the clergyman's family might be as much at home here as ourselves. I hope you will forgive my dog's misdemeanor, and my heedlessness in not seeing you before he had a chance to frighten you."

Summoning something of his father's gracious stateliness, he continued, more formally:

"Have I the pleasure of addressing Miss Wayt?"

Bow and question were for Hetty. Hester's voice, thin and dissonant, replied with old-fashioned decorum of manner, but in unconventional phrase:

"*I* have the misfortune to be Miss Wayt. This is Mr. Wayt's wife's sister, Miss Alling."

It was a queer speech, made queerer by the prim articulation the author deemed proper in the situation. March tried not to see that the subject of the second clause of the introduction flushed deeply, while her mute return of his bow had a serious natural grace he thought charming. When he begged that she would resume her seat, the little roguish curl at the corner of her lips, which he recollected as archly demure, came into play.

"We have no chairs to offer, but if you do not object to the best we have to give"—finishing the half invitation by seating herself upon a grass-grown root, jutting out near the trunk of the tree.

"The nicest carpet and lounge in the world," affirmed March, sitting down upon the sward. "Odd, isn't it, that American men don't know how to loll on the turf as English do? Our climate is ever so much drier and we have three times as many fair days in the year, and some of us seem to be as loosely put together. But we don't understand how to fling ourselves down all in a heap that doesn't look awkward either, and be altogether at ease in genuine Anglican fashion. Even if there are ladies present, an Englishman lies on the grass, and it is considered 'quite the thing, don't you know?' They say the imported American never gets the hang of it, try as he will. A man must be born on the other side or he can't learn it."

"There may be something in your countryman's born reverence for women that prevents him from mastering the accomplishment," said Hetty, a little dryly.

March bowed gayly.

"Thank you for the implied compliment in the name of American men! I am glad you are getting the benefit of this perfect May day. There, at any rate, we have the advantage of the Mother Country, if she *has* given us the Maypole and 'The Queen of the May.' This is a sour and dubious month in Merry England."

"You have been there, then?"

Hester said it abruptly, as she said most things, but the eagerness dashed with longing that gave plaintive cadence to the question, caught March's ear.

"Several times. I sailed from Liverpool twelve days ago. I was just off the steamer, and may be a little unsteady on my feet, when I collided with your carriage last Thursday, and you generously forgave me."

The girl was regarding him with frank admiration that would have annoyed an ultra-sensitive man, and amused, while it flattered, a vain one.

"It must be *heavenly* to travel in the country of Scott and Dickens!" she said, quaintly naïve. "How you must have enjoyed it!"

"I did, exceedingly, but less on account of 'David Copperfield' and 'Nicholas Nickleby' than because, as a boy, I reveled in English history, and that my mother's father, for whom I was named, was English. You should hear my sister talk of her first journey across England. She would say every little while in an awed undertone: 'This is just *living* Dickens!' You have not met her yet, I think?" to Hetty.

"No."

The tone was reserved, without being rude. He could have fancied that sadness underlay civil regret. Perhaps May had been mistaken in postponing her call until the parsonage was in perfect order.

"She means to call very soon. She thought it would be unneighborly to intrude before you had recovered from the fatigue of removal and travel. Mr. Wayt was my father's guest for a day or two, you know, before your arrival, and I have since had the pleasure of meeting him several times and of hearing him preach this morning."

In the pause that succeeded the speech the church bell began to ring for afternoon service. Under the impression that he had lost caste in not attending upon the second stated ordinance of the sanctuary he offered a lame explanation.

"I am afraid I am not an exemplary church-goer. But I find one sermon as much as I can digest and practice from Sunday to Sunday. My mother doesn't like to hear me say it. She thinks such sentiments revolutionary and uncanonical, and no doubt she is right."

"Anybody is excusable for preferring to worship 'under green apple boughs' to-day," observed Hester, with uncharacteristic tact. "You see we have always lived in cities, great and small. We have been used to brick walls and narrow, high houses, with paved backyards, with cats on the fences"—disgustfully—"and wet clothes flapping in your eyes if you tried to pretend to ruralize. Everybody hasn't as much imagination as Young John Chivery, who said the flapping of sheets and towels in his face 'made him feel like he was in groves.'"

"Fairhill has preserved the rural element remarkably well, when one considers her tens of thousands of inhabitants, her water supply and electric lights," said March; "and luckily one doesn't need much imagination to help out his enjoyment of the world on this Sunday afternoon."

His tone was so respectfully familiar, his bearing so easy, the girls forgot that he was a stranger.

"It wasn't your Dickens who said it, but you can, perhaps, tell me who did write a verse that has been running in my unpoetical brain ever since I entered your fairy bower," he said by and by.

"The orchard's all a-flutter with pink;

Robins' twitter, and wild bees' humming

Break the song with a thrill to think

How sweet is life when summer is coming.

"That is the way it goes, I believe. It is a miracle for me to recollect so much rhyme. The robins and bees must have helped me out."

"I wish I knew who did that!" sighed Hester. "Oh! what it must be to write poetry or paint pictures!"

March's glance of mirthful suspicion changed at sight of the knotted brow and wistful eyes.

"One ought to be thankful for either gift," he said quietly. "I was thinking just now how I should like to make a picture of what I saw as I ran up the hill. May I try some day?"

Hetty drew herself up and looked inquiry. Hester's hands fluttered, painful scarlet throbbed into her cheeks.

"Can you draw? Do you paint? Are you an *artist?*" bringing out the last word in an excited whisper.

March was too much touched to trifle with her agitation. "I try to be," he answered simply, almost reverently.

"And would you—may I—would it annoy you—Hetty! ask him. You know what I want!"

"My darling!" The cooing, comforting murmur was passing sweet. "Be quiet for one moment, and you can put what you want to say into words." As the fragile form quivered under her hand, a light seemed to dawn upon her. "You see, Mr. Gilchrist, my niece loves pictures better than anything else and— she never has met a real, live artist before," the corners of her mouth yielding a little. "She has had a great longing to know how the beautiful things that delight her are made—how they grow into being. Is that it, dear?"

Hester nodded, her eyes luminous with tears she strove to drive back.

March struck his hands together with boyish glee.

"I have it! I will make a study of 'orchards all a-flutter with pink,' and you shall see me put in every stroke. May I begin to-morrow? Blossom-time is short. How unspeakably jolly! May we, Miss Alling?"

The proposition was so ingenuous, and Hester's imploring eyes were so eloquent, that the referee turned pale under the heart-wrench demur cost her.

"Dear!" she said soothingly, to the invalid, "it would not be right to promise until we have consulted your mother. Mr. Gilchrist is very kind. Indeed"— raising an earnest face whose pallor set him to wondering—"you must believe that we do appreciate your goodness in offering her this great happiness. But—Hester, love, we *must* ask mamma."

March had seen Mrs. Wayt in church that forenoon, and been struck anew with her delicate loveliness. Could she, with that Madonna face, be a stern task-mistress? With the rise of difficulties, his desire to paint the picture increased. That this unfortunate child, with the artist soul shining piteous through her big eyes, should see the fair creation grow under his hand had become a matter of moment. As poor Hester's effort to express acquiescence or dissent died in a hysterical gurgle, and a shamed attempt to hide her hot face with her hands, the tender-hearted fellow arose to take leave.

"I won't urge my petition until you have had time to think it over. But I don't withdraw it. May I bring my sister over to see you both? She is fond of pictures, too, and dabbles in watercolors on her own account. Excuse me—and Thor—for our unintentionally unceremonious introduction to your notice, and thank you for a delightful half-hour. Good-afternoon!"

Hetty looked after him, as his elastic stride measured off the orchard slope—a contradiction of strange mortification and strange delight warring within her. It was as if a young sun-god had paused in the entrance of a gruesome cave, and talked familiarly with the prisoners chained to the walls. With all her resolute purpose to oppose the intimacy which she foresaw must arise from the proposed scheme of picture-making, she could not ignore the straining of her spirit upon her bonds.

"Oh!" wailed Hester, lowering her hands, "I didn't mean to be so foolish! I will be brave and sensible, but you know, Hetty, I have never had anything like this offered to me before. It is like dying with thirst with water before one's eyes, to give it up. And when he said: 'Blossom-time is short,' it rushed over me that I never had any—I can never have any. I am just a withered, useless, ugly bud that will never be a flower."

An agony of sobs followed.

"My precious one!" Hetty's tears flowed with hers. "Do I ever forget your sorrows? Are you listening, dear? If possible, you shall have this one poor little pleasure. You must trust your mother's love and mine, to deny you nothing we can safely give. If we must refuse, it is only bearing a little more!"

The going out of the May day was calm as with remembered happiness, but the chill that lurks in the imperfectly tempered air of the newborn season, awaiting the departure of the sun, was so pronounced by seven o'clock that Hetty called upon Homer to build a fire in the sitting room, where she and Hester were sitting. The children were sent to bed at eight o'clock. Mrs. Wayt was lying down in her chamber with one of her frequent headaches, rallying her forces against her husband's return from the long walk he found necessary "to work off the cumulative electricity unexpended by the day's services."

"I belong to the peripatetic school of philosophy," he said to a parishioner whom he met two miles from home.

"He was forging ahead like a trained prize-fighter," reported the admiring pewholder to a friend. "Nothing of the sentimental weakling about *him!*"

March and May Gilchrist, pausing upon the parsonage porch, at sound of a voice singing softly and clearly within, saw, past a half-drawn sash curtain, Hetty rocking back and forth in the firelight, with Hester in her arms. The cripple's head was thrown back slightly, bringing into relief the small, fine-featured face and lustrous eyes. Her wealth of hair waved and glittered with the motion of the chair like spun gold. It might have been a young mother crooning to her baby in a sort of chant, the words of which were distinctly audible to brother and sister, the nearest window being lowered a few inches from the top. Hester loved heat and light as well as a salamander, but could not breathe freely in a closed room. To-night was one of her "bad times," and nothing but Hetty's singing could win her a moderate degree of ease.

"Blow winds!" [sang Hetty]

"And waft through all the rooms

The snowflakes of the cherry blooms!

Blow winds! and bend within my reach

The fiery blossoms of the peach!

"O Life and Love! O happy throng

Of thoughts whose only speech is song!

O heart of man! canst thou not be

Blithe as the air is, and as free?"

March moved forward hastily to ring the bell. He felt like an eavesdropping spy upon the unconscious girls. Without any knowledge of the isolation and mutual dependence of the two, the visitors perceived pathos in the scene— in the clinging helplessness of one and the brooding tenderness expressed in the close clasp and bent head of the other.

The singing ceased instantly at the sound of the gong. "By George! what an alarm!" muttered March, discomfited by the clang succeeding his touch. "And I gave it such a genteel pull!"

His attitude was apologetic still, when Mr. Wayt's wife's sister opened the door.

"I seem fated to be heralded noisily!" he said regretfully. "I had as little idea of the tone of your doorbell as you had of the power of Thor's lungs. Miss Alling, let me introduce my sister! She gave me no peace until I brought her to see you."

May extended her hand with unmistakable intention of good fellowship.

"I scolded him for stealing a march upon me this afternoon while I, like a dutiful Christian, was in church," she said. Her smile was her brother's, her blithe, refined tones her own. "But I mean to improve my advantages the more diligently on that account."

The genial persiflage had bridged over the always awkward transit from front door to drawing room when the host is the conductor. It was the more embarrassing in this case because the two meagerly furnished parlors were unlighted except as a glimmer from the hall gas added to the sense of space and emptiness.

"Allow me!" March took from Hetty's fingers the match she had lighted, and reached up to the chandelier. The white illumination flashed upon a pleasing study of an up-looking manly face, with honest, hazel eyes, drooping mustache, and teeth that gleamed in the smile attending the question: "I hope your niece is none the worse for her fright?"

"Thank you! I think not. She is rather nervous than timid, and not usually afraid of dogs."

"I hope we can see her to-night?" May took up the word. "My brother says she is such a dainty, bright little creature that I am impatient to meet her."

Hetty's eyes glowed with gratitude and surprise. No other visitor had ever named the afflicted daughter of the house in this tone. The frank, cordial praise kept back no implication of pitying patronage. Mr. Wayt's wife's sister had knocked about the world of churches and parishes long enough to know that the perfect breeding which ignores deformity without overlooking the deformed is the rarest of social gifts. In any other circumstances, she would have refused steadfastly to subject Hester to the scrutiny of a stranger. As it was, she hesitated visibly.

"She is seldom able to receive company in the evening. But I will see how she is feeling to-night."

She had remarkable self-possession, as March had noted already. She got herself out of the room without mumble or halt. She walked well, and with a single eye to her destination, with no diffident conjectures as to how she moved or looked. March had keen perceptions and critical notions upon such points.

"What an interesting looking girl," observed May, in an undertone.

And March, as cautiously—"I hope she will let us see the little one! She is the jolliest grig you can conceive of."

Both tried not to look about them while waiting for the hostess' return. The place was forlornly clean, and the new carpets gave forth the ungoodly smell of oily wool that nothing but time and use can dissipate. Plaintive efforts to abolish stiffness were evident in chairs grouped in conversational attitudes near the summer-fronted fireplace, and a table pulled well away from the wall, with books and photographs lying about on it. March could fancy Hetty doing these things, then standing disheartened, in the waste of moquette, under the consciousness that there was not one-fifth enough furniture for the vast rooms. At this point, he spoke again subduedly:

"What possessed the church to build these desolate barns and call them family parlors?"

May was a parish worker, and looked her surprise.

"A parsonage must have plenty of parlor room for church sociables."

"Then those who use them ought to furnish them. Or, say! it wouldn't be amiss to keep them up as show places are abroad—by charging a shilling admission fee."

Hetty's return saved him from deserved rebuke.

"My niece will be very happy to see you," she reported, rather formally, her eyes darkling into vague trouble or doubt as she said it. On the way across the hall she added hurriedly to May: "We never overpersuade her to meet strangers. In this case there was no need."

May's gloved hand sought hers with a swift, involuntary gesture. It was the merest touch that emphasized the low "Thank you!" but both struck straight home to Hetty's heart. The Gilchrist tact was inimitable.

Hester lay upon a lounge, propped into a sitting posture with pillows. Her hair and drapings were cunningly disposed. A casual eye would not have penetrated the secret of the withered limbs and curved spine. A red spot like a rose-leaf rested upon each cheek, her eyes shone, and her silent smile revealed small, perfect teeth like a two-year-old baby's. She was so winsome that May stooped impulsively to kiss her as she would a pretty child.

"I came to tell you how angry we all are—my father, mother, and I—with my brother and his dog for scaring you to-day," she said, seating herself on an ottoman by the lounge, and retaining hold of the wee hand until it ceased to twitch and burn in hers. "I did think Thor knew better! His tail committed innumerable apologies to me when I told him I hoped to see you this evening."

March and Hetty, chatting together near the crackling wood fire, caught presently sentences relative to colors and pencils and portfolios, and slackened their talk to listen. May had elicited the confession that Hester's brush was a solace and the only pastime she had "except reading and Hetty's music."

"But it's only trying with me," said the tuneless voice. "I have had no teacher except Hetty."

"My dear Hester!" cried the person named. "Be candid, and say 'worse than none!'"

Hester colored vividly at this evidence that her confidences to her new friend were shared by others, but rallied gallantly to support her assertion.

"She doesn't think she has any talent for drawing, but she took lessons for three months that she might teach me how to shade and manage perspective, and use water colors. She and I amuse ourselves with caricatures and all that, and I make drawings—very poor ones—to illustrate poems and stories, while she reads to me, and I do a little—you can't imagine *how* little and how badly!—in color. Just bits, you know—grass and mossy sticks, and brambles running over stones, and frost-bitten leaves—and such things. Hetty is always on the lookout for studies for me. I cannot sit up long enough to undertake anything more important if I had the skill. And I shouldn't dare venture to copy anything really beautiful—such as apple blossoms," with a short-lived smile at March that left a plait between her eyes.

Intercepting Hetty's apprehensive glance, he smiled in return, but forbore to introduce the petition left with them that afternoon. May had been stringent on this point.

"Don't allude to it this evening!" she enjoined upon him. "Nothing is in worse taste than to use a first call as a lever for selfish ends. I'll run in to-morrow morning, and try my powers of persuasion. Meantime, get your canvas and palette ready."

Hetty's spirits rose when she perceived that the exciting topic was avoided. The four were in the swing of merry converse when the clock struck nine, and, as if he had waited for the signal, Mr. Wayt walked in. March, who sat by Hetty, saw her stiffen all over, and her eyes sink to the floor. Hester began to cough irrepressibly—a hard, dry hack, to quiet which Hetty went to get a glass of water. The pallor of the pastor's face had a bilious tinge; his eyes were sunken, his whole appearance haggard and wild. Yet his greeting to the guests was effusive, his flow of language unabated. Neither daughter nor sister-in-law offered to second him. Hester's roses faded, the ever present fold between her eyebrows was almost a scowl. Hetty was coldly imperturbable, and the Gilchrists soon made a movement to go.

Mr. Wayt stepped forward airily to accompany them to the door, Hetty falling into the rear and parting from them with a grave bow upon the threshold of the sitting room.

"My regards to your estimable parents," said the host on the porch, his pulpit tone carrying far through the night. "A clerical friend of mine dubbed Judge Aaron Hollingshed of Chicago, an active elder in his church, and his wife, who was a true mother in Israel—'Aaron and *her*.' I already, in spirit, apply the like titles to Judge and Mrs. Gilchrist. It is such spirited support as theirs that upholds the hands of the modern Moses against the Amaleks of the day. Thank you for calling, and good-night to you both."

CHAPTER IV.

MAY GILCHRIST had not overestimated her persuasive powers. A call on Mrs. Wayt, undertaken as soon as she had seen, from her watch window, the tall, black figure of the clergyman issue from his gate, and take his way downtown, won his wife's sanction to the presence of her sister and daughter in the orchard that afternoon to watch Miss Gilchrist's brother upon a sketch he proposed to begin before the apple blossoms fell.

"I shall be there, of course," the young diplomatist mentioned casually. "I am studying art in an amateurish way, under my brother's direction. I dearly enjoy seeing him paint. His hand is so firm and rapid, and his eye so true! Your daughter tells me she is fond of drawing. March and I would be only too happy to render any assistance in our power to forward her studies in that line."

"My sister has spoken to me of your kindness and his," Mrs. Wayt answered thoughtfully. "She told me also that she had referred the question of accepting Mr. Gilchrist's generous proposition to me. Hesitation seems ungracious, but my poor child is very excitable, and in nerve so unfit to work long at anything that I have doubted the expediency of allowing her to become interested in her favorite pursuit to the extent necessary for the acquisition of any degree of skill."

Nevertheless May went home victorious, and Mrs. Wayt, disquiet in eye and soul, sought her sister and detailed the steps of the siege and the surrender.

"Refusal was impossible without risking the displeasure of influential parishioners, or exciting suspicions that might be more hurtful," she concluded.

Hetty was cleaning silver in the dining room. Over her buff gingham she wore a voluminous bib apron; housewifely solicitude informed her whole personality. Her hair was turned back from her temples, and the roughened roll showed rust-red lights in a bar of sunshine crossed by her head as she moved. The lines of her face had what Hester called "their forenoon *sag*," a downward inclination that signified as much care as she could bear. She rubbed a tablespoon until she could see each loosened hair and drooping line in it, before unclosing her thinned lips to reply. Even then her speech was reluctant.

"The child is yours, Frances—not mine, dearly as I love her. I understand as well as you how cruel it seems to deny her what is, in itself, a harmless pleasure. Still, we have agreed up to this time that it is inexpedient to give people the run of the house, and this looks like a straight road to that."

She did not glance up in speaking, or afterward. Her accent was unimpassioned, her thoughts apparently engrossed in the business of bringing polish out of tarnish.

"There are circumstances that may alter cases—and premises," returned Mrs. Wayt deprecatingly. "I cannot but feel that we may begin to argue and determine from a different standpoint. I wish you could be a little more sanguine, dear."

"You don't wish it more than I do, sister! I wasn't built upon the 'Hope on, Hope ever' plan. My utmost effort in that direction is to make the best of what cannot be bettered. And since you have said 'Yes' to this painting scheme we will think only of what a boon it will be to Hester. The new cook is a more imminent difficulty. This house is large, and the salary excellent, I admit, but it would have been wise to wait until our arrival before engaging her."

She knew that her sister was as much surprised as herself at Mr. Wayt's commission to Mrs. Gilchrist, also that the wife would not plead this ignorance in self-defense.

"Homer, you, and I could have divided the housework, as we did in other places," continued Hetty, attacking a row of forks, now that the spoons were done with, "and we could hire a woman by the day to wash and iron. The cook may justify Mrs. Gilchrist's recommendation. I dare say she will. Only—but I'll not utter another croak to-day! You are an angelic optimist, and I am given over to pessimism of the opposite type. We will accept Mary Ann and the rest of the goods the Fairhill gods provide, including the open-air studio, eat, drink, and be merry, and make up our minds that to-morrow we *won't* die! I'd seal the covenant with a kiss if I were quite certain that I am not silicon-ed up to the eyes."

Mrs. Wayt bore a pained and heavy heart to the nursery and her mending basket. She loved Hetty fondly, and with what abundant reason no one knew so well as the heroic wife of a selfishly eccentric man. She trusted her sister's sterling sense, and in most instances was willing to abide by her judgment, but there were radical differences in their views upon certain subjects. The very pains Hetty took to avert open discussion of what lay like a carking blight upon the spirits of both caused friction and rawness, and the feigned levity with which she closed the door upon the topic would have been insult from anyone else. She had no alternative but to submit, no help but in the Refuge of all pure souls tempted almost out of measure by the sins and perversities of those dearest to them. Upon the knees of her heart she besought wisdom and comfort, and—sweet satire upon the pious duty of self-examination!—forgiveness for her intolerance of others' foibles!

Baby Annie was building block houses upon the floor, and filling them with dandelions. Homer had brought a small basketful up to her just before Mrs. Wayt was summoned to her visitor, and had helped the child erect a castle while the mother was below. Upon her entrance, he shuffled out as sheepishly as if she had detected him rifling the pockets of her husband's Sunday clothes. These lay over a chair by her work table. While she prayed, her fingers plied the needle upon a ripped lining and two loose buttons.

"See, mamma," entreated the little one. "So many dandeyions! Annie make house for dee papa!" The mother stooped to kiss her; a tear splashed upon the mass of wilting golden disks packed into papa's treasure chamber. At the same age Hester had prattled of "dee papa," and was his faithful shadow wherever he would allow her to follow. He had been too busy of late years and too distraught by various anxieties to take much notice of the younger children, but he had made a pet of little Hester. He used to call her "Lassie with glory crowned," as he twined and burnished her sunny curls around his fingers. Annie was a loving little darling, but neither so sprightly nor so beautiful as her first-born at the same age. She worshiped her father, and he was beginning to recognize and be pleased by her preference.

"Poor Percy!"

"Papa sick?" asked the child, startled by the ejaculation.

"No, my darling. Papa is very well. Mamma is only sorry! sorry! *sorry!*"

"Sorry! sorry! *sorry!* Mamma sorry! sorry! *sorry!*" While she crammed the yellow flowers into the castle, the baby made the words into a song, catching intonation and emphasis as they had escaped her mother's lips.

Dandelions dying were as fair to her as dandelions golden-crisp in the meadow grass. A drop of blood, red from the heart, would mean no more than a coral bead.

At three o'clock, Hester's chair was drawn by Homer into the orchard. The painter, his sister, his dog, and his easel were already in place. March had sketched in the arbor, and indicated the figures sufficiently to reveal the purpose of the picture.

Blossom-time is short, but fortunately the weather that week was phenomenally equable for May. In eight days the painting was finished. The reader may have noticed it at the Academy exhibition the next winter, where it was catalogued as "The Defense." Hetty's portrait and pose were admirably rendered, and the bound of the big St. Bernard was fiercely spirited. But the wonder of the group was the occupant of the low wicker carriage.

"My baby daughter!" faltered Mrs. Wayt, on first seeing it, and no more words would come.

To herself and to March, later and confidentially, Hetty spoke of it as "Hester glorified." At times, she was almost afraid to look at it. It was the face of an infant, but an infant whose soul had outleaped the limitations of years. The filmy gold of her hair lay, cloudlike, about her, her perfectly molded hands were clasped in the fearless delight of ignorance as she leaned forward to welcome the enemy her custodian was ready to beat off. It was Hester in every lineament.

Even the baby knew it. But it was Hester as her brothers and sisters would never see her unless among the fadeless blossoms of the world where crooked things will be made straight.

March Gilchrist was not poetical except with his brush. It was his tongue, his song, his story. Through it Hetty Alling first learned to know him, yet they were never strangers after that earliest meeting in the orchard. She was a capital sitter, and he lingered over her portrait as he dared not over Hester's for fear of wearying her. While Hetty posed, and he painted, May and Hester became warm friends. Miss Gilchrist had her own sketchbook, and March improvised an easel for it, which was attached to the wheeled chair, in desk fashion. Under May's tutelage Hester made a study of apple blossoms, and another of plumy grasses which the overlooker praised with honest warmth, and promised to keep forever as souvenirs of the "pink-and-white week." The robins were so used to the sight of the social group that they exchanged tender confidences freely overhead, as to summer plans and prospective birdlings. Thor's massive bulk crushed, daily, the same area of sunny turf, and he may have had canine views as to the folly of working when the sun was warm and the sod softest. The orchard, where every tree was a mighty bouquet, was an impervious screen between the party and the streets and such windows as commanded the slope.

"It is paradise, with rows upon rows of shining, fluffy angels to keep out the rest of the world!" said Hester, on the afternoon of the last sitting. "I'm glad it is we who are inside! And not another soul!"

March was dabbling his brushes in a wide-mouthed bottle of turpentine, preparatory to putting them up.

"Nothing exclusive about her—is there?" he laughed to Hetty, in mock admiration.

She answered in the same vein:

"She was always an incorrigible aristocrat!"

"Say a beggarly aristocrat, and free your mind!" retorted Hester good-humoredly. "I don't care who knows it. Who doesn't prefer a select coterie to a promiscuous 'crush'? I'd like to dig out this orchard just as I would a square of turf, and set it down in the middle of the South Seas (wherever they may be) where the trees wouldn't shed their blossoms the whole year round, and we four—with the robins and Thor thrown in ornamentally—might paint and talk and live forever and a day. I used to wonder what answer I would make to the fairy who offered three wishes—but I am quite ready for her now. I'd fuse them all into one!"

"Are you sure? Going! Going! the last call! *Gone!*" cried March, bringing down his biggest brush, *à la* auctioneer's hammer, upon Thor's head.

"Gone it is!" responded Hester, folding her tiny hands upon her heart, and closing her eyes in an ecstasy of satisfaction. "Let nobody speak for five minutes. (Look at your watch, Mr. Gilchrist!) For five minutes we will make believe that the deed is done, and we are translated. I hear the surf on the shores of the

"Dear little isle of our own,

Where the winds never sigh, and the skies never weep.

"Hush!"

They humored this one of her caprices, as they had others. She was full of fancies, some odd, some ghastly, some graceful. Even practical May yielded obedience to the mandate, and, laying her head against the bole of the tree, met the bright eye of the mother robin peering over the edge of her nest with what May chose to interpret as a wink of intelligent amusement.

"She asked me as plainly as dumb show could ask, who would provide three meals a day for the happy exclusives, and, when I alluded to breadfruit trees and beefsteak geraniums, wanted to know where ovens and gridirons would come from," said May afterward; "That formed the basis of *my* five-minute reverie."

My soul, to-day,

Is far away,

Sailing the Vesuvian bay;

My winged boat,

A bird afloat,

Swims 'round the purple peaks remote.

So runs the poem, between the lines of which might be written the exultant, "*Absent from the body!*" Hester's soul had the poet's power of "drifting" into absolute idealization. She was used to building with dream stuff. In the time she had allotted, she lived out a lifetime, to tell of which would require hours and many pages. That she paid for the wide sweep into the remote and the never-to-be, by reaction bitterer than death, never dissuaded her from other voyages of the "winged boat."

For perhaps sixty seconds Hetty, sitting upon the turf by the recumbent Thor, and idly pulling his shaggy hair, reflected regretfully upon this certain reflex action; then, as if uttered in her ear, recurred the words: "Where we four might paint, and talk, and *live* forever!"

"We four!" Involuntarily, her eye sped from one to another of the group; from May's placid visage and smile upraised to the robin's nest, to the face framed about by pale blue cushions—colorless as wax, the pain lines effaced by the sweet exaltation oftenest seen upon the forehead and mouth of a dead child—consciousness, rising into majesty, of having compassed all that is given to the human creature to know, the full possession of a happy secret to be shared with none who still bear the weight of mortality. Hetty's heart slackened its beat while she gazed upon the motionless features. Her "child" was, for the time, rapt beyond her reach. Yet it was only "make believe" after all, that snared her into temporary bliss!

Before the pang of the thought got firm hold of her she met March Gilchrist's eyes, full, and fixed upon hers.

He lay along the grass, supporting himself on his left elbow, his cheek upon his hand, the other hand, still holding the big brush, had fallen across Thor's back. His eyes were startled, as by an unexpected revelation, and as her glance touched them, sudden, glad light leaped from depth to surface. He would not release her regard—not even when the glow that succeeded the numbness of the thrill stole from limb to limb, and suffused her face, and all the forceful maiden nature battled with the magnetic compulsion. The sough of the spring breeze in the flower-laden branches, likened by Hester to the whispering surf upon island sands; the humming bees and twittering birds; the sun-warmed scent of apple blooms and white clover and the sweetbrier growing just without the canopy of the king apple tree; the faint flush of light strained through locked masses of blossoms, were, for those supreme moments, all the world—except that this man—God's most glorious creation—spoke to her, although his lips were moveless, and that the stir of a new and divine life within her heart replied.

"I am sure the time must be up!" said May yawningly. "Poor Hester is fast asleep, and my tongue aches with holding it so long."

Hester unclosed her eyes slowly, smiled dreamily, and essayed no denial. March was on his knees, collecting brushes and tubes into his color box. Hetty was folding a rug so much too heavy for her wrists that May sprang to seize the other end.

"Why—are you chilly? Your fingers are like ice!" she exclaimed, as their hands met. "And how you shiver! I am afraid we have been selfish in keeping you out of doors so long!"

The ague shook the mirth out of the nervous laugh with which Hetty answered:

"Now that the strain of the week's suspense and sittings is over, and the result of our joint labors is a pronounced success, I am a little tired. The spring is a trifle crude as yet, too," she subjoined, speaking more glibly than usual. "By the time the sun reaches the tops of the trees, we begin to feel the dew fall. Hester, we must go in!"

March took the handle of the wheeled chair from her. "That is too heavy for you on the thick grass. May, will you abide by the stuff until I come back?"

On every other afternoon, Homer had come down at five o'clock to roll the carriage up the ascent. Hester lay among the pillows, her eyes again shut, and the reflection of the happy secret upon her face. Hetty walked mutely beside her.

March liked the fine reserve that kept her silent and forbade her to risk another encounter of glances. She was all womanly, refined in every instinct. Crushing the young grasses with foot and wheel, and bowing under the stooping branches, they made their way to the gate in the parsonage fence. Homer shambled hurriedly down the walk to meet them.

"Now"—he stammered, laying hold of the propeller of the chair—"I'd 'a bin yere sooner, but I had to go downtown on an arrant——"

"That's all right!" said March good-naturedly. "I was happy to bring Miss Wayt up the hill. Good-by, Queen Mab! May I have the honor of taking you to my home studio to see the picture when it is varnished and framed?"

She replied by a gentle inclination of the head, and the same joyous ghost of a smile. She was like one lost in a dream, so deep and delicious that he will not move or speak for fear of awakening.

March raised his hat and stood aside to let the carriage pass. As Hetty would have followed, his offered hand barred the way.

"One moment, please!" he said, in grave simplicity. "I have to thank you for some very happy hours. May I, also, thank you for the hope of many more? I should be sorry if our acquaintanceship were to fall to the level of social conventionality. We have always been intimate with our pastor's family, and mean, unless forbidden, to remain true to time-honored precedent."

If he had alarmed her just now, he would prove that he was no love-smitten boy, but a purposeful man, who understood himself and was obedient to law and order. Hetty gathered herself together to emulate his tranquillity.

"I especially want to thank *you*, out of her hearing, for the great kindness you and your sister have showed to my dear little invalid. She will never forget it, nor shall I. It has been the happiest week of her life. I think but for your offer to lend her books, and Miss Gilchrist's promise to keep on with her painting lessons, that the end of our sittings would be a serious affliction to her. Please say this from me to Miss Gilchrist, also. Good-evening!"

He ran lightly back to May and "the stuff." He had not obtained permission to call, but neither was it refused. He liked dignity in a woman. As he phrased it, "it furred the peach and dusted the plum." He was entirely willing to do all the wooing.

May innocently applied the last touch to his unruffled spirit in their family confabulation in the library that evening.

"That Hetty Alling is one of the most delightful girls I ever met!" she asseverated emphatically.

"In what respect?" inquired her judicial parent.

"She has individuality—and of the best sort. She is intelligent, frank, spirited, and with these sterling qualities, as gentle as a saint with poor little Hester, who must be a great care to one so young as Hetty. I mean to do all I can to brighten the monotonous existence the two girls must lead. From all I can gather without asking impertinent questions, they are thrown almost entirely upon one another for entertainment and happiness. It is an oddly assorted household, taken as a whole."

"Talking of originality," observed March after a meditative puff or two, "you have it in the niece. It is fearfully sad that such a mind should be crowded into the body of a dwarf. She dotes upon books. If you will look up a dozen or so that you think she—or Miss Alling—would enjoy, I will take them over to-morrow."

His mother's attitude changed slightly, although her face was unaltered. She seemed to hold her breath to listen, her whole inner being to quicken into intensity of interest. March, stretched luxuriously upon the rug, in his usual post-prandial attitude, felt her sigh.

"Do I tire you, mother, dear?" he asked.

"Never, my boy!"

Nor ever would, although within the hour and with a throe that tested her reserves of fortitude, she had surrendered the first place in his heart. The blow was unexpected. The orchard paintings and her children's interest in them had seemed entirely professional to her. March had sketched dozens of girls, and fallen in love with none of them. With all his warmth of heart and ready sensibilities, he was not susceptible to feminine charms. As a boy, he became enamored of art too early to have other flames. Perhaps, with fatuity common to mothers, she reasoned that with such a home as his he was not likely to be tempted by visions of domestic bliss under a vine and fig tree yet to be planted. It is a grievous problem to the maternal intellect why men who have the best mothers and sisters living and eager to spoil them with much serving, should be the earliest to marry out of certainty into hazardous uncertainty.

When the judge had gone to a political meeting, and May to entertain visitors in the drawing room, Mrs. Gilchrist divined the purport of the impending communication. Her fair hand grew clammy in toying with the short chestnut curls; in the silence through which she could hear the tinkle of the fountain on the lawn, she wet her dry lips that they might not be unready with loving rejoinder to what her idol was preparing to say. She knew March too well to expect conventional preamble. He was always direct and genuine. She did not start when he spoke at length.

"Mamma, darling."

"Yes, my son."

"It has come to me at last, and in earnest."

"I surmised as much." It was plain to see where he got his dislike of circuitous methods. "Is it Mrs. Wayt's sister?"

"It is Hetty Alling. She is a true, noble woman. I shall try to win her love. Should I succeed, you will love her for my sake, will you not?"

"You know that I will. But this is sudden. You have known her less than a fortnight. And, dear, it is out of the fullness of my love that I speak—I am afraid that the family is a peculiar one. Be prudent, my son. You are young, and life is long. I cannot bear that you should make a mistake here. Should this young girl be all that you think—even all that I hope to find in her—it is best not to force her decision. Give her time to study you. Take time, and make opportunities to study *her*. I ask it because you bear the names of two honorable men—your father and mine—and because it would break your mother's heart to see her only boy unhappy."

He drew her hand to his lips—the high-bred hand that would always be beautiful—and held it there for a moment. She had his pledge.

Hetty had followed Hester into the house. It was half-past five, and there were strawberries to be capped for the half-past six dinner. A parishioner had left a generous supply of Southern berries at the door while the girls were out, and had taken Mrs. Wayt and her little daughters to drive. Aunt and niece sat down at a table drawn before the dining-room window and fell to work. Hester's high chair brought her tiny, dexterous fingers to a level with Hetty's. The task went forward with silent rapidity, and neither noted the direction of her companion's eyes. Hetty seemed to her dazed self to bear about with her the charmed atmosphere of the nook under the king apple tree.

The mingled hum of bees and sighing wind and bird-note sounded in her ears like the confused song of a seashell. Now and then, a ray from hazel eyes flashed athwart her sight. Brain and heart were in a tumult that terrified her into questioning her identity. The "winged boat" of fancy was a novel craft to our woman of affairs. As novel was the self-absorption that made her unobservant of Hester's brilliant eyes and musing smile. As the dainty fingers, just reddened on the tips by the fruit, picked off and cast aside the green "caps," Hester's regards were fixed upon the Anak of the orchard, and Hetty's strayed continually to the same point. Both looked over and beyond a figure creeping on all-fours down the central alley of the broad, shallow garden, occasionally crouching low, as if to crop the grass of the borders.

Perry, studying his Latin grammar in his mother's chamber above, awoke the taciturn dreamers by a shout:

"Hello, Tony! what *are* you doing there?"

He turned his head, not his body, to reply:

"Now—jes' lookin' for somethin' I dropped."

"You'll drop yourself some day if you don't watch out!"

Hester's unmusical cackle broke forth.

"Does he look more like a praying mantis—or Nebuchadnezzar?" she said to her co-worker. "He reminds me of a funny thing I heard a man say when I was a child of a picture in my catechism of Nebuchadnezzar feeding in the pasture with a herd of cows. He said it was 'a fine study of comparative anatomy.' The advantage would be on the side of the cows if Tony were to take the field."

Hetty could not but laugh with her in looking at the grotesque object.

"A short sight is a real affliction—poor fellow! It is to be hoped that he has 'dropped' nothing valuable. I will take the bowl and 'caps' into the kitchen when I have laid you down upon the lounge. Your poor back must ache by this time."

She lingered a few minutes in the kitchen to make sure that everything was in train for dinner. Her practical knowledge of all departments of housewifery had already gained for her Mary Ann's profound respect. The cook recommended by Mrs. Gilchrist was a tidy body, a capital worker, and, as she vaunted herself, "one as took an *intrust* in any family she lived in."

"I ast that pore innocent feller if there was any parsley in the gairdin," she chuckled to Hetty, "an' he said he'd fetch me a bunch to gairnish me dishes. But I've niver laid eyes onto him since. I mistrust he don't know one yarb from another. Is he 'all there,' d'ye think, mem?"

"He is not quick, but he is not an idiot, by any means," returned his patroness. "He is a faithful, honest fellow, always thankful for a kind word, very industrious, and perfectly truthful. We think a great deal of Homer. I saw him in the garden just now, looking for the parsley. I will find him and send him in with it. Don't sugar the berries; we do that on the table. Keep them in a cool place until they are wanted for dessert."

She strolled down the garden walk, singing low to herself the catching tune to which she had set the words the Gilchrists had overheard the Sunday night of their first call:

O Life and Love! O happy throng

Of thoughts whose only speech is song.

O heart of man! canst thou not be

Blithe as the air is, and as free?

Homer had vanished from the main alley that led directly to the orchard, yet she walked on down the whole length of it. Blazing tulips had supplanted faded hyacinths; the faint green globes of snowball bushes were bleaching hourly in May sunshine and breeze; the lilac hedge, lining the post-and-board fence at the bottom of the parsonage lot, was set thick with purple and mauve and white spikes.

"Such a dear, old-fashioned garden!" Hetty said, half aloud. "It reminds me of the one we had at home!" Leaning upon the orchard gate she abandoned herself to reverie. The robins' whistle in the apple tree was low and tender; fleecy clouds, drifting toward the west, began to blush on the sunward side, the blending odors of a thousand flowers hung in the air. The word "home" took thought back—thoughts of the only one she had ever had, and the mother whose death lost it to her. Since then she had stood alone, and helped weaker people to stand. A great longing for rest in a love she could claim as all hers drove tears to her eyes. The longing was not new, but the hope that softened it was. Hitherto, it had been linked with her mother's image only. She wanted her now, as much, and more than ever before, but that she might sympathize with what she began to comprehend tremblingly. Her mother would enter into her trembling and her joy. Especially if she had seen what Hetty never could describe—a look the memory of which renewed the shy, delicious shame expressed in the blush March had pitied, while rejoicing in the sight of it.

Such a boundless, beautiful world opened to her while she stood there, looking down the blossoming vistas of the orchard—solitary, yet comforted! She would give rein to imagination for that little while. It could harm no one, even if it were all a chimera that would not outlast blossom-time. And must it be *that*? What had glorified other desolate women's lives might bless hers. Spring comes to every year, however long and cruel may have been the winter. Recalling March's prophecy of future association, she dared dwell upon visions of his visits, of the pleasant familiar talks that would make them better acquainted; of the books they would read and discuss; of the pictures he would paint, with her looking on.

"I am not beautiful or accomplished," she said humbly. "But I would make myself more worthy of him. I am young and apt. I would make no mistakes that could mortify him. He should never be ashamed of me, and, oh!" she stretched her arms involuntarily, as if to draw the unseen nearer to her heart—"how faithfully I would serve him, forever and forever."

The flight of fancy had indeed been fast and far!

The tinkle of the dinner bell in Mary Ann's vigorous hand ended the fond foolishness abruptly. It was the careful housewife who asked herself with a guilty start: "What has become of Homer and the parsley?"

Her first step in returning was upon something hard. She picked it up.

Homer met his young mistress at the back door. His weak, furtive eyes were uneasy before she accosted him. At her incisive tone the red rims closed entirely over them, his hands, grimy with groping in gravel and turf, fumbled with one another, and his loose jaw dangled.

"Homer, you said this afternoon that you had been out to do an errand. Do not leave the place again without letting me know where you are going, and for what."

"Now," he began wretchedly, "you wasn't at home, 'n I thought——"

"I forbid you to think! I will do the thinking for this family. You knew where to find me. If you had not, you ought to have waited until I got back. I mean what I say!"

He shifted miserably from one foot to the other, and, as she passed him, cleared his dry throat.

"Now, 'spose Mrs. Wayt was to send me out in a hurry?"

"Tell her that you have my orders."

"Now——"

She looked over her shoulder at him, impatient and contemptuous. He had never seen her so angry with him before. He plucked at the battered brim of an old military cap clutched in one hand. He had found it in the garret, and believed that it became him rarely.

"I was 'bout to say as I hed los' what I hed——"

"I found it. Not another word! There is no excuse for you!"

CHAPTER V.

MR. WAYT availed himself of an early opportunity to make known his intention to take no vacation that year. He "doubted the expediency of midsummer absences on the part of suburban pastors." While many residents of Fairhill went abroad and to fashionable resorts in America in July and August, a respectable minority was content to remain at home, and some of the vacated cottages and villas were taken by city people, to whom the breezy heights and shaded lawns were a blessed relief from miles of scorching stone and brick. He "foresaw both foreign and domestic missionary work in his own parish," he said to his session in explaining his plans for the summer campaign.

The resolution was politic and strengthened his hold upon his new charge. Not to be outdone in generosity, the people redoubled their affectionate attentions to their spiritual leader. Fruits, flowers, and all manner of table dainties poured into the parsonage; carriages came daily to offer airings to Mrs. Wayt and the children, and on the Fourth of July a pretty phaëton and gentle horse were sent as "a gift to the mistress of the manse," from a dozen prominent parishioners.

"Verily, my cup runneth over."

A real tear dropped upon Mr. Wayt's shirt front as he uttered it falteringly on the afternoon of the holiday. Yet he had been repeating the words at seasonable intervals, and more or less moistly, since the hour of the presentation.

The Gilchrists were upon the eastern veranda, the embowering vines of which were beginning to rustle in the sea breeze. All had arisen at the pastor's appearance, and March set a chair for him.

"I have thought, sometimes, that I had some command of language," he continued unctuously. "To-day I have no words save those laid to my use by the Book of books—'My cup runneth over.' It is not one of my foibles to expatiate upon the better 'days that are no more.' The trick is common and cheap. But to you, my best friends, I may venture to confide that my dear wife and I were brought up in what I have since been disposed to characterize as 'mistaken luxury.' Since the unselfish saint joined her blameless lot with mine she has never had a carriage of her own until to-day. I can receive favors done to myself with a manly show of gratitude. Appreciation of my wife makes a baby of me."

"By this time he should be in his second childhood, then, for everybody likes mamma," piped a familiar voice from within the French window of the library. Glancing around with a start that was *not* theatrical, he espied his eldest born established at her ease in a low chair. Her feet were on a stool; she wore a white gown, and May's white Chudda shawl covered her from the waist downward; her hair was a mesh of gold thread that drew to it all the light of the dying day. May sat on a cushion in the window and linked Hester in her comparative retirement with the veranda group.

"Ah, little one, are you there?" said the fond parent playfully. "I missed you from the dinner table and might have guessed that you could be nowhere but here."

Profound silence ensued, and lasted for a minute. Hester shrank into herself with a blush visible even in the shadowy interior.

March and May had gone through orchard and gardens to fetch her an hour ago. Her father had eaten his evening meal at the same table with her. In the circumstances there was nothing to say, a fact comprehended by all except the unconscious offender.

"I think Mrs. Wayt will find her horse gentle," said Judge Gilchrist, in formal civility too palpable to his wife.

With intelligent apprehension of the truth, too often overlooked, that confidence in the truth bearer must precede obedience to his message, she desired that her husband and son should like Mr. Wayt. To March she had confessed her fear that some of the family were "peculiar," and he might infer the inclusion of the nominal head in the category. Further than this she would not go. With pious haste she picked the fly out of the ointment, and with holy duplicity beguiled others into approval of the article that bore the trade mark of "The Church."

Ah, the Church!—in every age and, despite lapses and shortcomings and stains, the custodian of the Ark of God—her debt to such devout and loyal souls as this woman's will never be estimated until the Master shall make acknowledgment of it in the great day of reckoning.

When the judge's turn of the subject and the "horsey" talk that followed granted his wife leisure to reconsider the matter, she discovered that there was no cause for discomfiture. Mr. Wayt was absent-minded, as were all students of deep things. Only, her husband was quick of sight and wit, and neither March nor May had much to say, of late, of the new preacher who was doing such excellent work in the congregation. March went regularly to church and sat beside his mother through prayer and hymn and sermon, and afterward refrained from adverse criticism. This may have been out of respect to the girl he hoped to make his wife. Yet she had dared fancy that the graver tenderness of his behavior to herself and the unusual periods of thoughtfulness that occurred in their conversations had to do with the dawning of spiritual life in his soul. However much certain of Mr. Wayt's mannerisms might offend her taste, there was no question of his ability and eloquence. That these might be the divinely appointed nets for the ingathering into the Church of her best beloved was a burden that weighted every petition.

March had not spoken openly of his love for Hetty Alling since the evening on which he first avowed it to his mother, but, in her opinion, there was nothing significant in this reserve. The Gilchrists were delicate in their dealings with one another, never asking inconvenient questions, or pushing communication beyond the voluntary stage. If May divined the drift of her brother's affections, she did not intimate it by word or look. When the fruit of confidence was ripe it would be dropped into her lap. She *did* note what Mrs. Gilchrist had not the opportunity of seeing—how seldom Hetty had leisure to receive March or his sister. She was getting ready the wardrobe of the twin boys, who were to go to boarding school the 1st of October. Through Hester's talk May had learned incidentally that the Wayts employed neither dressmaker nor seamstress.

"Hetty is miraculously skillful with her needle," was Hester's way of putting it, "and so swift that it would drive her wild to see her work done by the 'young lady who goes out by the day.' I work buttonholes and hem ruffles and such like, and mamma gives her all the time she can spare from baby— and other things. But our Hetty is the motor of the household machine. I don't believe there is another like her in the world. The mold in which she was cast was broken."

She had said this in a chat held with her favorite this evening while the others were engaged with other themes outside of the window. May encouraged her to go on by remarking:

"You love her as dearly as if she were really your sister, don't you?"

"'As well!' The love I have for mother, sisters, and brothers is a drop in the ocean compared with what I feel for Hetty! See here, Miss May!" showing her perfectly formed hands. "These were as helpless as my feet. Hetty rubbed me, bathed me, flexed the muscles for an hour every morning and an hour every night. She tempted me to eat; obliged me to take exercise; carried me up and down stairs, and sat with me in her arms out of doors until she had saved fifty dollars out of her allowance to have my chair built. Hetty educated me—made me over! She is my brain, the blood of my heart—I don't believe I should have a soul but for Hetty!"

The warm water stood in May's eyes. But the weak voice, thrilling with excitement, reminded her of the danger of an excess of feeling upon the disjointed system. She spoke lightly:

"Oh, your father would have looked out for your soul!"

"Would he?"

The accent of intensest acrimony shocked the listener, corroborated as it was by the bitterness of scorn that wrung the small face.

In a second Hester caught herself up.

"They say that cobblers' wives go barefoot. Ministers have so little time to spare for the souls of their families that their children are paganed. If it wasn't for their wives and their wives' sisters, the forlorn creatures would not know who made them."

It was a plausible evasion, but it did not efface from May's mind the disdainful outburst and the black look that went with it. Both seemed so unnatural, even revolting, to a girl whose father stood with her as the synonym for nobility of manhood, that she could not get away from the recollection for the rest of the evening. This was before Mr. Wayt's arrival, and sharpened May's appreciation of the little by-play between Hester and her parent.

His departure at nine o'clock was succeeded by Hester's at ten, and, as was their habit, March and his sister took her home by the path across the orchard. The night was sultry; the moon lay languid under swathes of gray mist. She looked warm, and the stars near her faint and tired. Low down upon the horizon were flashes of purple sheet lightning. The town had kept the Fourth patriotically, and the odor of burned paper and gunpowder tainted the stirless air.

"The grass is perfectly dry," said May, stopping to lay her hand upon the mown sward. "That should be a sign of a shower."

"There is always rain on the night of the Fourth of July," returned March abstractedly.

Hester said not a word. As she looked up at the sick moon her eyes showed large and dark; her face was corpselike in the wan radiance. She was weary, and she had been indiscreet. She could not sleep without confessing to Hetty her lapse of temper and tongue, and Hetty had enough to bear already. She had not been so strong and bright as was her wont for a month past. It might be only excessive drudgery over sewing machine and household duties, but she looked fagged and sad at times. The phaëton and horse would benefit mamma and the children—when the vacant place beside the mistress of the Manse was not occupied by their lord and master. *He* got the lion's share of every luxury. Poor Hester's conscience and heart were raw, and the heat of the wounds inflamed her imagination. The evening at the judge's had not rested her. That was strange, or would have been had not the long, black shadow of her father lain across the memory of it.

The back door of the parsonage stood wide open, and the house was so still that, as March stooped to lift Hester from her carriage at the foot of the steps, he caught the sound of what was scarcely louder than an intermittent sigh in the upper story, but continuous as a violent fit of weeping. The arm that lay over his shoulder twitched convulsively; Hester shuddered sharply, then laughed aloud:

"Oh, Mr. Gilchrist! I thought I was falling! It is too bad to put you to all this trouble. I hope Tony hasn't blown himself up. He ought to have come for me."

"Didn't I promise your mother to bring you home safely?" said March reassuringly. And, as they reached the hall—"May I carry you upstairs?"

The offer seemed to terrify her.

"Oh, no, no! Just lay me on the settee there! Somebody will be down directly. Don't trouble yourself to bring the chair in. Tony will attend to that. Thank you! Good-night, Mr. Gilchrist! Good-night, Miss May!"

While she hurried all this out, a stumble on the back stairs was the precursor of Homer's appearance in the dim recesses of the hall. He alighted at the bottom of the flight on all-fours, picked himself up and shambled forward, one hand on his head, the other on his elbow, an imbecile grin spreading his jaws.

"*Now*, I a'most broke me *nake* on them stairs!"

March had deposited Hester upon the hall lounge, and although perceiving her anxiety to get rid of him, hesitated to commit her to the keeping of a man who was, apparently, but half awake.

"Let me carry you up!" he insisted to Hester. "He may fall again."

"Oh, Tony is all right!" in the same strained key as before. "He never lets anything but himself drop."

A rustle and swift step sounded above stairs. Someone ran down. It was Hetty. Her white wrapper was begirt with a ribbon loosely knotted; her rust-brown hair was breaking from constraint and tumbling upon her shoulders.

March's first pained thought was: "She knew I would be in, yet did not mean to see me again to-night!"

A second glance at the colorless face and wild eyes awakened unselfish concern.

"What is the matter? Who is hurt?" she queried anxiously. Hester's reply was a shriek of laughter.

"Nothing! Nobody! Only Tony has broken his neck again, and Mr. Gilchrist did not know that it is an hourly occurrence in our family life, so he insisted upon taking me upstairs himself."

"Mr. Gilchrist is very kind!" Hetty's tone was deadly mechanical; in speaking she looked at nobody. "I sent Homer down when I heard you coming. I am sorry he was not in time."

May had joined the group.

"I hope," she said in her cheery way, "that none of the rest of your household have come to grief to-day?"

Hetty turned to her with eyes that questioned silently—almost defiantly.

"I mean, of course, did the boys bring home the proper quantum of eyes and fingers?"

"Yes! oh, yes! thank you! they went to bed tired, but whole, I believe."

"That is fortunate, but remarkable for a Fourth of July report," said March. "Come, May! Good-night!"

He had seen, without comprehending, the intense relief that flooded the girl's visage at his sister's second sentence, also that she was feverishly anxious to have them go. And the sound above stairs, hushed by Hester's shrill tones—was it low, anguished weeping? The mourner was not Hetty, yet her dry eyes were full of misery. His big, soft heart ached with futile sympathy. By what undiscovered track could he fare near enough to her to make her conscious of this and of a love the greatness of which ought to help her bear her load of trouble?

"Hetty looks *dreadfully!*" broke out May at the garden gate. "She is worked and worried to death! I am amazed that Mrs. Wayt allows it. To reduce a girl like that to the level of a household drudge is barbarous. She has no time for society or recreation of any kind. It is toil, toil, toil, from morning until night. Mary Ann—the cook mamma got for them—says she 'never saw such another young lady for sweetness and kindness to servants as Miss Hetty,' but that she 'carries all the house on them straight little shoulders of hern.' Hester tells the same story in better English."

She repeated what she had heard that evening.

March stopped to listen under the king apple tree, where he had begun to love the subject of the eulogy. While May declaimed he reached up for a cluster of green apples and leaves and pulled it to pieces, his face grave, his fingers lingering.

"Heaven knows, May"—she was not prepared for the emotion with which it was uttered—"that I would risk my life to make hers happy. I hoped once—but you see for yourself how she avoids me. I could fancy sometimes that she is afraid of me!"

"Perhaps she is afraid of herself."

He looked up eagerly.

"Is that a chance remark? You women understand one another. Have you seen anything——"

"Nothing I could or would repeat, my dear boy! But there is a mystery somewhere, and I can't believe it is the phenomenon of such a sensible girl's failure to appreciate my brother. May I say something, March, dear?"

"Whatever you like—after what has gone before!"

"Maybe it ought not to have gone before—or after, either. For, brother, this is not just the sort of connection that you should form. To speak plainly, you might look higher. 'Strike—but hear!' Hetty is all that I have said, and more. But there is a Bohemian flavor about the household. We will whisper it— even at half-past ten o'clock at night, in the orchard—and never hint it to 'the people,' or to mamma! They are nomads from first to last—why, I cannot say. They have lived everywhere, and nowhere long. Mrs. Wayt is a refined gentlewoman, but her eyes are sad and anxious. You know how fond I am of Hester, poor child! Still a nameless something clings to them as a whole—not quite a taint, but a tang! Especially to Mr. Wayt. There! it is out! Let us hope the apple trees are discreet! I distrust him, March! He doesn't ring true. He is always on pose. He is a sanctimonious (which doesn't mean sanctified) self-lover. Such men ought to remain celibate."

March tried to laugh, but not successfully.

"I dissent from and agree to nothing you say. But——" He waited so long that May finished the sentence for him.

"But you love Hetty?"

"Yes! She *suits* me, May! As no other woman ever did. As no other woman ever will. I have tried to reason myself out of the persuasion, but get deeper in. She *suits* me—every fiber and every impulse of my nature. I seem to have known her forever and always to have missed her."

With all her pride in her family and ambition for her brother May had a romantic side to her character. Had she liked Hetty less, she would yet have pledged her support to the lover. She told him this while they strolled homeward, and then around and around the graveled drive in front of the Gilchrist portico, and had, in return, the full story of his passion.

"When I marry, my wife will have all there is of me," he had said, long ago, to his sister.

He reminded her of it to-night.

"She is not a brilliant society woman. Not beautiful, perhaps. I am not a competent judge of that at this date. She has not the prestige of wealth or station. But she is my counterpart."

He always returned to that.

When his sister had gone into the house he tarried on the lawn with his cigar. What freshness the fierce sun had left to the air was all to be found out of doors. As the gray swathes continued to smother the light out of the moon the heat became more oppressive. The gravel walks were hot to his feet; the bricks of the house radiated caloric. With a half-laugh at the whim, he entered the now silent and darkened dwelling, sought and procured a carriage rug, and pulling the door shut after him, whistled for Thor, and retraced his steps to the orchard. He spread the rug upon the grass kept cool by the down-leaning branches of the arbor and cast himself upon it. He meant to make a night of it.

"I have camped out, many a July night, in far less luxurious quarters," he muttered. "And this place is sacred."

When the mosquitoes began to hum in his ears, he lighted another cigar. He was the more glad to do it, as he fancied, once in a while, that the young apples or the wilting leaves had a peculiar and not pleasant odor, as of some gum or essence, that hung long in the atmosphere. He had noticed it when he pulled down a branch to get the spray he had torn apart, while May talked. The air was full of foreign scents to-night, and this might be an olfactory imagination.

As twelve o'clock struck from the nearest church spire, he was staring into the formless shadows overhead and living over the apple-blossom week, the symphony in pink and white. The young robins were full fledged and had flitted from the parent nest. The young hope, born of what stood with him for all the poetry of his six-and-twenty years of life, spread strong wings toward a future he was not to enjoy alone.

Thor was uneasy. He should have found his share of the rug laid upon elastic turf as comfortable as the mat on the piazza floor, which was his usual bed, yet he arose to his haunches, once and again, and, although at his master's touch or word, he lay down obediently, the outline of his big head, as March could make it out in the gloom, was alert.

"What is it, old boy?" said he presently. "What is going on?"

Thor whined and beat the ground with his tail, both tentatively, as asking information in return.

In raising his own head from the yielding and soft rustling grasses, March became aware of a sound, iterative and teasing, that vexed the languid night. It was like the ticking of a clock, or of an uncommonly strenuous deathwatch. While he listened it seemed to gather force and become rhythmic.

"Click! click! clack! click! click! *clack!* clicketty click! clicketty, clicketty *clack!* click! click! click! clicketty *clack!* ting!"

Somebody was working a typewriter on this stifling night, presumably by artificial light, in the most aristocratic quarter of Fairhill.

Thor knew the incident to be unprecedented. The rhythmic iteration made his master nervous; the sharp warning of the bell at the end of each line pierced his ear like the touch of a fine wire.

He sat up and looked about him.

An aperture in the foliage let through a single ray of light. It came from the direction of the parsonage.

"Tony's pet hallucination is of a wandering light in the garden and orchard, a sort of 'Will o' the Wisp' affair, which it is his duty to look after," Hester had said that evening. "He rushes downstairs at all hours of the evening to see who is carrying it. I told him last night that burglars were too clever to care to enter a clergyman's house, but he cannot be convinced that somebody, bent upon mischief, doesn't prowl about the premises. He is half blind, you know, and has but three-fourths of his wits within call."

Recollecting this, March arose cautiously, whispered to Thor to "trail," and stole noiselessly up the easy grade.

The light was in the wing of the parsonage and shone from the wide window of the pastor's study on the first floor. The shutters were open; a wire screen excluded insects, and just within this sat a woman at a typewriter—Hetty!

Across the shallow garden he could see that her hair was combed to the crown of her head for coolness, and coiled loosely there. Now that he was nearer to the house, he distinguished another voice, also a woman's, dictating, or reading, as the flying fingers manipulated the keys. Drawing out his repeater, he struck it. Half-past twelve!

"I have been sorely interrupted in my pulpit preparation this week," Mr. Wayt had informed Mrs. Gilchrist, on taking leave that night. "I fear the sunlight will extinguish my midnight argand burner. 'The labor we delight in physics pain,' and, with me, takes the place of slumber, meat, and drink."

Impressed by an undefined sense of trouble, March stood, his hand upon the gate, almost decided to go up to the house and inquire if aught were amiss. While he cast about in his mind for some form of words that might account for his intrusion, Mrs. Wayt's figure came forward, and offered, with one hand, a glass of water to her sister. In the other she held a paper. Without taking her fingers from the typewriter Hetty raised her head, Mrs. Wayt put the glass to her lips, and, while she drank, dictated a sentence from the sheet in her hand. In the breezeless hush of the July night a clause was audible to the spectator.

"Who has not heard the story of the drummer boy of Gettysburg?"

"Click-click-clack! Click-click-clack!" recommenced the noisy rattle.

While Hetty's fingers flew her sister fanned her gently, but the eyes of one were riveted to the machine, those of the other never left the paper in her hand.

March went back to his orchard camp, Thor at his heels.

It was close cloudy; the purple play of lightning was whitening and concentrating in less frequent lines and lances. When these came, it could be seen that thunderheads were lifting themselves in the west. But the night remained windless, and the iterative click still teased the ears of the watcher. It was an odd vigil, even for an anxious lover, to lie there, gazing into the black abysses of shade, seeing naught except by livid flashes that left deeper blackness, and knowing whose vital forces were expended in the unseasonable toil.

What could it mean? Did the overladen girl add copying for pay to the list of her labors? And could the sister who seemed to love her, aid and abet the suicidal work? Where was Mr. Wayt? The play of questions took the measure and beat of the type keys, until he was wild with speculation and hearkening.

At half-past two the rattle ceased suddenly. Almost beside himself with nervous restlessness, he sprang up and looked through the gap in the boughs. The light went out, and, at the same instant, the delayed storm burst in roar and rain.

CHAPTER VI.

SUNDAY, July 5, dawned gloriously, clear and fresh after the thunder-storm, to which Fairhill people still refer pridefully, as the most violent known in thirty years. The gunpowder and Chinese paper taint was swept and washed out of the world.

Mrs. Wayt, holding Fanny by the hand, and followed decorously by the twin boys in their Sunday clothes and churchward-bound behavior, emerged from her gate as the Gilchrists gained it. In the white light of the forenoon, the eyes of the pastor's wife showed faded; groups of fine wrinkles were at the corners, and bistre shadows under them. Yet she announced vivaciously that all were in their usual health at home, except for Mr. Wayt's headache, and nobody had been hurt yesterday.

"For which we should return special thanks, public and private," she went on to say, walking, with her little girl, abreast with Judge and Mrs. Gilchrist, the boys falling back with the young people. "At least, those of us who are the mothers of American boys. I can breathe with tolerable freedom now until the next Fourth of July. What a fearful storm we had last night! My baby was awakened by it and wanted to know if it was 'torpetoes or firetrackers?' Yet, since we owe our beautiful Sabbath to the thunder and rain, we may be thankful for it; as for many other things that seem grievous in the endurance."

"I hope Mr. Wayt's headache is not in consequence of having sat up until daybreak, as he threatened to do," the judge said, in a genial voice that reached his son's ears.

March listened breathlessly for the reply.

"I think not. I did not ask him this morning at what time he left his study. He is not inclined to be communicative with regard to his sins of commission in that respect, but I suspect he is an incorrigible offender. He attributes his headache—verbally—to the extraordinary heat of yesterday. We all suffered from it, more or less, and it increased rather than diminished, after sunset."

"Is Mr. Wayt well enough to take the service this morning?"

"Oh, yes!" quickly emphatical. "It would be a severe indisposition indeed that would keep him out of the pulpit. Both his parents suffered intensely from nervous and sick headaches, so he could hardly hope to escape. I have observed that people who are subject to constitutional attacks of this kind, are seldom ill in any other way, particularly if the headaches are hereditary. How do you account for this, Judge Gilchrist? Or, perhaps, you doubt the statement itself."

March did not trouble his brains with his father's reply. The volubility of one whose discourse was generally distinctively refined and moderate in tone and terms would of itself have challenged attention. But what was her object in saying that she had not inquired at what hour her husband left his study last night? Since she and her sister were in occupation of the room from midnight—probably before that hour—until two in the morning, she certainly knew that he was not there and almost as surely where he was and how engaged during those hours. Where was the need of duplicity in the circumstances? Was she committed to uphold the professional fiction, which her husband circulated vauntingly, that his best pulpit preparation must be done when honest people are asleep in their beds—that the beaten oil of the sanctuary must flow through lamp-wick or gas-burners? What end was subserved by supererogatory diplomacy and subterfuge?

"How are the two Hesters to-day, Mrs. Wayt?" asked May, from the side of her puzzled brother.

"Hester is rather languid. The heat again!"

She looked over her shoulder to say it, and they could see how entirely the freshness had gone from eyes and complexion. Her very hair looked bleached and dry. "The weather will excuse every mishap and misdemeanor until the dog days are over. Hetty stayed at home to watch over her. It is a source of regret to Mr. Wayt and myself"—comprehensively to the four Gilchrists—"that my sister is so often debarred the privileges of the sanctuary in consequence of Hester's dependence upon her."

"I have remarked that she is frequently absent from church," Mrs. Gilchrist answered.

Her dry tone annoyed her son. Yet how could she, bred in luxury and living in affluence, enter into the exigencies of a position which combined the offices of nurse, companion, housewife, seamstress, mother, and bread-winner?

Mrs. Wayt took alarm.

"Poor child! she hardly calls herself a church-goer at all. But it is not her fault. She thinks, and with reason, that it is more important for me to attend service regularly—for the sake of the example, you understand—and we cannot leave our dear, helpless child with the children or servants. She gets no Sabbath except as my sister gives it to her. I am anxious that the true state of the case should be understood by the church people. Hetty would grieve to think that her enforced absences are a stumbling block."

Her solicitude was genuine and obvious. Judge Gilchrist offered an assuasive:

"We must have a telephone wire run from the pulpit to Miss Hester's room. I have known of such things."

"I don't believe that Hester would care to keep her room Sunday mornings then!" whispered Perry, *l'enfant terrible* of the Wayt family. "She says family prayers are all she can stand."

March, the recipient of the saucy "aside," cast a warning look at the telltale. Inwardly he was amused by the unlucky revelation. Spoiled child as Hester was, she had marvelously keen perceptions and shrewd judgment. She saw through the jugglery that deceived the mass of Mr. Wayt's followers, and rated correctly the worth of his capital.

He juggled rarely to-day. Even his voice partook of the spread-eagle element which interfused Divine services as conducted by the popular preacher. The church was full to the doors, many of the audience being strangers and sightseers. The number of "transients" increased weekly.

"He is like fly-paper," Hester had said, this very Sunday, as the skirts of his well-fitting coat, clerically cut and closely buttoned, cleared the front door. "Out of the many that swarm and buzz about him, some are sure to stick— that is, take pews! That is the test of spiritual husbandry, Hetty! I believe I'll be an infidel!"

"Don't be utterly absurd!" answered her aunt in a spiritless way. "I haven't the energy to argue, or even scold. 'Let God be true, and every man a liar.' God forgive me, but I am ready, sometimes, to say that all men *are!* But I can't let Him go, dear!"

Mr. Wayt gave out the opening hymn in tones that would have been clarion, but for an occasional break into falsetto that brought to March's irreverent mind the wheezing drone of a bagpipe.

We are living, we are dwelling,

In a grand and awful time;

In an age on ages telling,

To be living is sublime.

Hark! the waking up of nations,

Gog and Magog to the fray!

Hark! what soundeth? 'Tis creation

Groaning for its latter day!

His text was, as was his custom, startlingly peculiar:

"Only the stump of Dagon was left to him."

It was a political discourse, after the manner of a majority of discourses which are miscalled "National." Government jobbery, nepotism, and chicanery; close corporations, railway monopolies, municipal contracts—each had its castigation; at each was hurled the prophecy of the day of doom when head and palms would be sundered from the fishy trunk, and evil in every form be dominated by God's truth marching on.

March listened for a while, then reverted to matters of more nearly personal interest. Last night's incident had left a most disagreeable impression on his mind, which was confirmed by Mrs. Wayt's demeanor. May's assertion of the Bohemian flavor recurred to him more than once. No! the specious advocate of public reforms and private probity did not "ring true." And protest as Hester might, with all the passion of a forceful nature, against her father's double ways, he *was* her father, and the ruler of his household. His wife, it was plain, believed in and imitated him.

Gazing at the pale, large-featured face of the orator, now alive with his theme, and glancing from this to the refined, faded lineaments of her whose meek eyes were raised to it from the pastor's pew, he was distrustful of both. He wished Hetty were not Mr. Wayt's wife's sister, or that he could marry her out of hand, and get his brother-in-law, once removed, a call to—Alaska! Her, he never doubted. Their acquaintance had been brief, and scanty opportunities of improving it had been vouchsafed to him of late; yet she had fastened herself too firmly upon affection and esteem to admit of the approach of disparaging suspicion. She might be a slave to her sister and her sister's children. She could never be made a tool for the furtherance of unworthy ends. *She* would not have said: "I did not inquire at what hour Mr. Wayt left his study last night!" If she spoke, it would be to tell the truth.

At this point an idea entered his brain, carrying a flood of light with it. Mrs. Wayt was an author—one of the many ministers' wives who eke out insufficient salaries by writing for Sunday-school and church papers! It was a matter of moment—perhaps of ten dollars—to get off a MS. by a given time, and Hetty had taken it down in typewriting from her dictation and the rough draught. Of a certainty, here was the solution of the mysterious vigil, and of Mrs. Wayt's equivocation! She looked like a woman who would write over the signature of "Aunt Huldah" in the Children's Column, or "Theresa Trefoil" in the Woman's Work-table, and dread lest her identity with these worthies should be suspected by her husband's people, or by even "dear Percy" himself.

March experienced a blessed letting-down of the whole system—a surcease from worrying thought, so sudden that a deep sigh escaped him that made his mother glance askance at him. Instead of admiring the brave industry of the true wife he had suffered a whimsical prejudice to poison his mind against her. He despised himself as a midnight spy and gossip hunter, in the recollection of the orchard vigil. The patient, unseasonable toil of the sisters became sublime.

"*Who has not heard the story of the drummer boy of Gettysburg?*" thundered the preacher, raising eagle eyes from the manuscript laid between the Bible leaves.

March jumped as if the fulmination were chain-shot. Mrs. Gilchrist, looking full at him, saw his color flicker violently, his fingers clinch hard upon the palms. Then he became so ghastly that she whispered:

"Are you ill?"

"A sharp pain in my side! It will be gone in a moment," he whispered back, his lips contracting into a smile. Rather a sword in his heart. The light within him was darkness. How foolish not to have solved the mean riddle at a glance! Mr. Wayt's sensational sermons were composed by his clever wife, and transcribed by her as clever sister! Here was the secret of the sense of unreality and distrust that had haunted him in this man's presence from the beginning of their acquaintanceship. The specious divine was a fraud out and out, and through and through a cheap cheat. No wonder now, at the swift itinerancy of his ministry! His talk of midnight study was a lie, his pretense of scholarship a trick so flimsy that a child should have seen through it. He had gone to bed the evening before, and taken his rest in sleep, while his accomplices got up to order the patriotic pyrotechnics for the next day.

No wonder that Mrs. Wayt's eyes were furtive and anxious, that there were crow's feet in the corners, and bistre rings about them after that July night's work!

No wonder that the less hardened and less culpable sister-in-law shunned church services!

The sword was double-edged, and dug and turned in his heart. For the girl who lent aid, willing or reluctant, to the deliberate deception practiced in the Name which is above all other names, had a face as clear as the sun, and eyes honest as Heaven, and he loved her!

The main body of the audience could not withdraw their eyes from the narrator of the telling anecdote of the drummer-boy of Gettysburg. The story was new to all there, although he had assumed their familiarity with it. It was graphic; it was pathetic to heart-break; it thrilled and glowed and coruscated with self-devotion and patriotism; it was an inimitable illustration of the point just made by the orator, who was carried clear out of himself by the theme. And not one person there—not even March Gilchrist, fiercely distrustful of the man and all his works—suspected that it was an original incident, home-grown, homespun, and home-woven. Write it not down as a sin against the popular pastor of the Fairhill First Church that the Gettysburg hero was a twenty-four-year-old child of the speaker's brain. If the Mill of the Press, and the Foundry of Tradition cannot turn out illustrations numerous and pat enough to suit every subject and time, private enterprise must supply personal demand.

"I think young Gilchrist was ill in church to-day," observed Mr. Wayt to his wife that afternoon, as she fed him with the dainty repast he could not go to the table to eat.

He lay on the settee in the wide, cool hall, supported by linen-covered cushions. She had brought him, as a persuasive first course, a cup of delicious bouillon, ice-cold, and administered it to him, spoonful by spoonful.

"He changed color, and seemed to be in great pain for an instant," he continued, after another sip. "His mother looked very uneasy, and apparently advised him to go out. I judged from his fluctuations of color that it was vertigo—or a severe pain in the head. He would not leave until the services were over. I have few more attentive hearers than March." Another sip. "If I should be the means of bringing him into the Church, it would be a happy day for his pious mother. Should my headache abate in the course of an hour or so, I will look in and inquire how he is. It would only be courteous and neighborly."

In the adjoining dining room, the door of which the draught had opened a few inches, the family circle of the solicitous pastor heard every word of the communication, although his accents were subdued by pain.

Sharp-eared-and-eyed Perry winked at Hetty.

"He won't find Mr. March Gilchrist," he mouthed in a fashion invented by himself, to convey pert speeches only to the person for whom they were invented. "He went to New York on the five o'clock train. I saw him. He said he was going to dine with a friend. I heard him. A man asked him. Another slice of beef, please, Hetty! Rare, and a bit of fat! Some gravy on my potatoes, too!"

Hetty had shunned the orchard since the day of the last sitting. Seated behind the shutters of her chamber-window, she had seen, almost every day, Thor bound across the grass in pursuit of a figure partially hidden by the lower branches. Since March frequented the spot, it was no resort for her. She had no time for play, she told Hester, gently, when she pleaded for a return to the pleasant lounging and talk "under green-apple boughs." Homer could draw the carriage down the garden-walk and through the gate and leave the cripple there with books and color box, whenever she wanted to go. Hester often brought back stories of chats and readings and painting lessons with the brother or sister—sometimes with both. Occasionally, March came to the parsonage with a message from his sister to the effect that she had taken Hester home with her for the day or evening, and would return her in good order. He was apt to insist upon leaving the message with Hetty, if Mary Ann or one of the children answered his ring. Mr. Wayt's wife's sister would obey the summons in person, but she did not invite the bearer in.

She ran down in her simple morning gown, or almost as plain afternoon dress, without waiting to remove her sewing apron, heard what he had to say gravely, and replied civilly, as might a servant or governess. And day by day, he marked the lessening round of cheek and chin, and the deepening of the plait between the brows. She could not know that he went away, each time pitying and loving her the more, and furious at the cruelty of the demands upon her time and strength. She could not have altered her behavior, unless to grow more formal, had she divined all.

But for the orchard outings Hester would have had but a dull summer of it. As it was, it was the happiest of her life. She actually gained flesh, and her cheeks had the delicate flush of a sweet-pea blossom. She mellowed and mollified in the intercourse with the sound, bright natures of her new friends. Prosperity was teaching her unselfishness.

Hetty had a proof of this after the Sunday dinner was eaten, and there still remained a long hour of sunful daylight.

"I have a charming book which Miss May lent me yesterday," she said, as her custodian inquired what she should do for her entertainment. "And now that mamma has set the children to studying their Sunday-school lessons for next week, you ought to have a breathing spell, my poor dear. You are bleaching too fast to please me. You can't plead 'work to do' for once."

Hetty yielded—the more, it would seem, because she had not the strength to resist love pleadings than from any desire for the "outing" recommended by Hester. Taking shawl and cushion with her, she passed down the garden alley to the gate. There was a broad track through the orchard, worn by the wheeled chair and Hester's attendants. It led straight to the king apple tree. From this bourne another track, not so distinctly marked, diverged to the white picket fence shutting in the Gilchrist garden. Hetty's feet had never trodden this, she reflected with a pang, after she had settled herself against the brown trunk. It was most probable that she never would.

Her one little dream was dead, and she was too practical a business woman to resuscitate it. Her consistent plan of avoiding March Gilchrist and abjuring the painful sweet of association with his sister was adopted before she returned to the house from her ineffectual quest for Homer and the parsley.

She was filled with wonder, in looking back to the time—was it three minutes, or thirty?—she had wasted, leaning on the gate, enveloped in lilac perfume as in a viewless mantle, and daring to feel as other and unexceptional girls feel—that she could have forgotten herself so utterly. *She* said—"so shamelessly."

"The worm on the earth may look up to the star," if it fancies that method of spending an ignoble life, but star-gazing and presumptuous longing for a million centuries would bring planets and worms no nearer together. Hetty was very humble in imagining the figure. Some people must live on the shady side of the street, where rents are low, and green mold gathers upon stones, and snails crawl in areas. If the wretches who pune and pale in the malaria-breeding damps would not go mad, they must not look too often across the way where flowers and people bloom. If they do, they must support the consequences.

This misguided girl had looked. She was now suffering. That she merited what she had to bear did not make the pain less.

Unwittingly she had spread her shawl where March had laid his rug last night. The rough bark of the tree-bole hurt her presently. Her gown was thin, and her flesh less firm than it had been six weeks ago. She slid down upon the shawl, her head on the cushion, and reached out, in idle misery, to pick up some withered leaves and small, unripe apples scattered on the grass. March had dropped them while hearkening to his sister's criticism of the Bohemian household. She was as idly—and as miserably—tearing apart the leaves toughened by the heat of the day, when she heard a joyous rush behind her and felt the panting of hot breath upon her neck, and Thor was kissing her face and licking her hands. She sprang to her feet and cast a wild glance along the path and under the trees. There was no one in sight. The grounds were peremptorily posted, and no vagrant foot ever crossed them. She took in the situation at once. March had gone to New York in the five o'clock train; the dog, wandering aimlessly about and missing his master, had espied her, and accepted her as a substitute. She knelt down and clasped her arms about his head, laid her cheek to his burly muzzle.

"O Thor! Thor! you would help me if you could." Just as she had fondled him in those far-away, blissful days. Her hand was tangled in his coat when, looking across his huge bulk, she had met March Gilchrist's eyes. True eyes—and bonny and true, which must never read her soul again.

"Thor! dear Thor!" She cried it out in a passion of tears.

The faithful fellow moaned a little in sympathy. The more eloquent than human longing to comfort the sorrowing, never seen except in a dog's eyes, filled and rounded his.

"I wouldn't cry if I could help it, dear," said Hetty, her arch smile striking through the rain. "And nobody else should see me shed a tear. You are my only confidant; and I do believe you understand—a little."

He was not an indifferent consoler, it appeared, for in fifteen minutes both of them were asleep, their heads upon the same pillow.

The sunset sea breeze rustled the stooping boughs. Arrows of greenish gold, tipped with fire, were shot at random between the leaves at the sleeping pair. Hetty was very pale, but the grieving droop of the facial lines, the slight fullness of the lower lip, and the slow curve of the arm thrown above her head made her seem like a child. She looked what she was, fairly tired out— weariness so intense that it would have chased slumber from the eyelids of an older sufferer. She had cried herself to sleep, Thor's presence giving the sense of protecting companionship the child feels in his mother's nearness. The cool breath of the approaching twilight, the grateful shade, and Sabbath stillness did the rest.

Now and then a long, broken sigh heaved her chest, and ran through her body. There was the glisten of tiny crystals upon her eyelashes. Once she sobbed aloud, and Thor moved uneasily and sighed sympathetically. By and by he began to beat his tail gently against the turf, his beautiful eyes gleamed glad and wistful, but he did not offer to lift his head. Hetty patted it in her sleep, and left her hand there.

She and Thor were walking over a wilderness prairie. The coarse grass flaunted up to her chin, and she would have lost the dog had she not wound her fingers in his hair. Such a long, tiresome, toilsome way it was, and the grass so stiff and strong! Sometimes it knotted about her ankles; sometimes the beards struck like whips across her face. A bitter wind was blowing, and stung her eyes to watering. In passing it lashed the grass into surges that boomed like the sea.

Miles and miles away an orange sunset burned luridly upon the horizon, and right between her and it was a floating figure, moving majestically onward. A mantle blew back in the bitter wind until she could almost touch the hem; a confusing flutter of drapery masked the head and shoulders; the face was set steadfastly westward and kept away from her. At long intervals a hand was tossed clear of the white foldings and beckoned her to follow.

"And follow I will!" she said, between her set teeth, to herself and to Thor, "I will follow until I overtake him or die!"

And all the while the blasting wind hissed in her hair and howled in the pampas grasses, and her feet were sore and bleeding; her limbs failed under her; her tongue clave to the roof of her mouth with dryness; her heart beat faint——

Hark! At the upward fling of her leader's arm music rained down from heaven, and the earth made joyous response; strong, exultant strains, like an organ peal, and such vibrant melodious chimes as Bunyan heard when all the bells of the holy city rang together for joy. The majestic, floating figure turned to lean toward her with outstretched arms, and eyes that gazed into hers as she had vowed they should never look again.

"Oh! I knew it must be you!" She said it aloud, in her rapturous dream. "It could be nobody else! Thank God! Thank God!"

Thor bounded from under her hand....

March Gilchrist's New York friend was a bachelor cousin, who was always delighted to have "a good fellow" drop in upon him on Sunday evening. March, in the uneasy wretchedness that beset him, honestly intended to visit him when he took the five o'clock train. He wanted to get away from the place for a few hours, he said; away from tormenting associations and possible catechists, and think calmly of the next step to be taken. By the time he reached Jersey City he had discovered that he was trying to get away from himself and not from his home; moreover, that he wanted neither dinner nor the society of the genial celibate. He stepped from the train, turned into the station restaurant, sat down at the table he had occupied on the day he landed from the *City of Rome* and missed the noon train, and ordered at random something to eat.

The long table built in the middle of the room was surrounded by a party of men and women. The men wore full black beards and a great deal of waistcoat, crossed by gold ropes. The women had round, black eyes, high-bridged noses and pronounced complexions. March tried not to see them, and tried to eat what was set before him. It made him sick to observe that Hetty's place was filled by an overblown young lady whose bang made a definite downward peak between her black brows, and who had ten rings on the left hand and five on the right.

He caught the 6.30 train back to Fairhill. He had made up his sensible mind to talk over his family to a project marvelously well developed when one remembers that the inception was not an hour old when he swung himself off upon the platform of the Fairhill station. He would set out next week for the Adirondacks, set up a forest studio, and begin "serious work." The phrase jumped with his mood. Nothing else would draw the inflammation out of the wound. He meant to bear up like a man under the blow he had received, to forget disappointment in labor for a worthy end; love, in ambition.

He took the orchard in his walk home from the station. It was quite out of his way, and he was not guilty of the weakness of denying this. He went there deliberately and with purpose, vaulting the fence from the quiet street at the foot of the hill, as he had done on that memorable Sunday when the orchards were "all a-flutter with pink." One more look at the nook under green apple-boughs would be a sad satisfaction, and the contrast between what he had hoped and what he knew to be rock-bottomed reality, would be a salutary tonic. One look he must have—a look that should be farewell to folly and regret.

While still twenty yards away from the arbor he espied something that looked like a mass of white drapery lying upon the turf. He stood just without the drooping boughs fencing the sleeper about, his face framed in an opening of the foliage, as Hetty, aroused by Thor's bound from her side, raised her eyelids and closed them again with a smile of dreamy delight upon eyes swimming in luminous tears.

"I thought it was you!" she repeated in a thrilling whisper, and again, and more drowsily—"Thank God!"

The church bells, chiming the half-hour notice of evening service, went on with the music of her dream.

Thor, enacting a second time the role of *Deus ex machina*, thought this an auspicious moment for thrusting his cold nose against her cheek.

With a stifled scream she attempted to rise, and catching her foot in the shawl, would have fallen had not March rushed forward to her help. Having taken her hands to restore her to her balance, he continued to hold them.

She struggled to free them—but feebly. Surprise and confusion had robbed her of strength and self-possession.

"I thought—they said—that is, Perry saw you take the train for New York," she managed to articulate.

"Hetty!"—imploringly, while the eyes she had seen in her vision overflowed hers with loving light—"why do you shun me so persistently? Are you determined never to hear how dear you are to me?"

CHAPTER VII.

THIS, then, was the outcome of March Gilchrist's iron-clad resolve to forget in serious work one who could never make him or his family happy!

Verily, the ways and variations of a man in love are past finding out by ordinary means and everyday reasoning. Our sensible swain could only plead with his sister in defense of his fast grown passion, that the girl "suited him." Having decided within eight hours that no alliance could be more unsuitable than one with Mr. Wayt's wife's sister, he had cast himself headforemost into the thick of impassioned declaration of a devotion the many waters of doubt could not drown, or the fires of opposition destroy.

Dizzied and overwhelmed as she was by his vehemence, Hetty was the first to regain the firm ground of reason. He had seated her, with gentle respect, upon the cushion that had pillowed her head, and dropping on one knee, the "true, bonny eyes" alight with eagerness, poured out the story whose outlines we know. Earnestness took the tinge of happiness as he was suffered to proceed; the deep tones shook under the weight of emotion. Not until she made a resolute effort to disengage her hands, and he saw the burning blushes fade into dusky pallor and her eyes grow set and troubled, did his heart begin to sink. Then the gallant, knightly soul forbore importunity that might be persecution. If his suit distressed her for any cause whatsoever, he would await her disposition to hearken to the rest.

Releasing her, he arose and stood a little space away, respectfully attending upon her pleasure.

"I did not mean to impose all this upon reluctant ears," he said, when she did not speak. Her face was averted, her hands pressed hard together. The rust-brown bandeaux, ruffled by the pressure of her head upon the pillow, gleamed in the dying sunlight like a nimbus. The slight, girlish figure was not a Madonna's. It might be a Mary at the tomb in Bethany before the "Come forth!" was spoken.

"A word from you will send me away," continued March, with manly dignity, "if you wish to dismiss me and the subject forever. I cannot stop loving you, but I can promise not to annoy you by telling you of a love you cannot receive."

"Annoy me!" repeated the poor, stiff lips. "*Annoy* me! You must surely know, Mr. Gilchrist, that *that* is not a word to be used by you to me!"

"No?" coming a step nearer, eye kindling and voice softening. "You will let me try to overcome *indifference*, then—will you not?"

In the depth of her distress she appreciated the adroit twist he gave her answer. The corners of the pale mouth stirred. Her strength was slipping from her. She must be brief and decisive.

"If that were all"—looking courageously into the glowing eyes—"I would give a very different answer from the one you must accept without questioning. I know that I can never give any other, unprepared though I was for what you have said. There are reasons not immediately connected with myself why I ought not to think for a moment of—the matter you were speaking of. You have paid me the greatest compliment a man can offer a woman. But while my sister and the children need me as they do now I must not think of leaving them, and I see no prospect of their needing me less for years and years to come. My sister opened her house to me when I was orphaned and homeless. I owe her more than I could make you understand. She is peculiarly dependent upon me. Hester could not do without me. You have seen that. I cannot bear to think how she would suffer if I were to go away."

In her desire to deal gently and fairly with him she had made a concession fatal to the integrity of her cause. He laid hold of it at once.

"Mrs. Wayt has a husband; the children have a father. He is a man in the prime of life, whose talents are approved by the Church. He is popular, and in the receipt of a good salary. Fairhill will probably remain Hester's home for many years to come. If this is all that separates us—why, my darling——"

The strangest expression flashed over her face—a wild ecstasy of joy that gave place, the next second, to anguish as wild. She put her hands over the tell-tale face, and bent her forehead upon her knees.

"Don't! oh, don't!" she moaned. "This is too hard! too cruel! If you could only know all, you would not urge me! I did not think you could be so unkind!"

"Unkind? To *you*, Hetty?"

"No! no!" moved to tears by the hurt tone, and hurrying over the words. "You could never be *that* to anybody—much less—I cannot say what I would!"

March knelt down by her, and raised her head with tender authority she could not resist. He wiped the tears from her face with his own handkerchief; smiled down into the wet eyes. Loving intimacy with his mother and sister had taught him wondrously winsome ways.

"Listen to me, dear!" as he would address a grieving child. "Sometime, when you are quite willing to talk freely to me of this awful 'all,' I will prove to you how chimerical it is. Until then, nothing you can say or do can shake my purpose of making you my wife, in God's own good time. We were *made* for one another, Hetty! I have known that this great while. I am positive I could convince you of it, if you would give me a chance."

She arose nervously, her hands chafing one another in an action that was like wringing them in impatience or anguish.

"I must go, Mr. Gilchrist! It is wrong to allow you to say all this. Then, too, Hester will be uneasy and need me."

"Let me go with you and explain why you have outstayed your time," March suggested, demurely. "We could not have a more sympathetic confidante than Hester. And I must tell somebody."

She looked frightened.

"There is nothing to tell! There never can be. Cannot you see? haven't I convinced you of this?"

"Not in the least. Until you can lay your hand upon your heart—the heart you and I know to be so true to itself and to others—and say, with the lips that cannot frame a lie—'March Gilchrist, I can never love you in *any* circumstances!' I shall not see this other 'never' *you* articulate so fiercely. If you want to get rid of me instantly, and for all time, look at me and say it now—*Hetty!*"

His lingering enunciation of the name she had never thought beautiful before, would of itself have deprived her of the power to obey. She stood dumb, with drooping head and cheeks burning red as the sunset, her figure half turned away, a lovely study of maiden confusion, had the spectator been cool enough to note artistic effects.

Chivalric compassion restrained all indication of the triumph a lover must feel in such a position.

"I will not detain you, if you must go in," he said, in a voice that was gentlest music to her ear. "Forgive me for keeping you so long. I know how conscientious you are, and how necessary you are to Hester. We understand one another. I will be very patient, dear, and considerate of those whose claims are older than mine. But there is one relation that outranks all others in the sight of God and man. That relation you hold to me. Don't interrupt me, love! Nothing can alter the fact. Give me those!" as she stooped blindly for shawl and cushion. "It is my duty to relieve you of all burdens which you will permit me to carry for you. You would rather not have me go to the house with you?" interpreting her gesture and look. "Only to the gate, then? You see how reasonable I can be when possibilities are demanded."

He made a remark upon the agreeable change in the weather within the last twenty-four hours, and upon the sweet repose of the Sabbath after the tumult of the National holiday, as they walked on, side by side. At the gate he stayed her with his frank, pleasant laugh.

"I have a confession I don't mind making now. At half-past twelve o'clock last night I stood on this spot watching you. Thor and I were camping out in the orchard. It was too hot to go into the house. I heard a queer clicking, and saw a light in this direction, and came to look after Homer's Jack-o'-lantern. Instead, I saw you at the study window, busy—oh! how wickedly busy—with the typewriter!"

He stopped abruptly, for the face into which he smiled was bloodless, the eyes aghast. She made a movement as if to grasp the shawl and pillow and rush away—then her forehead fell upon the hand that clutched at the pickets for steadiness.

"Are you angry?" pleaded March, amazed and humble. "If I had not loved you, I should not have been here. Was it an impertinent intrusion?"

"No! And I am not angry—only startled." Her complexion was still ashy, and her tongue formed the syllables carefully. "I can understand that you must have thought strange of what you saw. But I am used to typewriting. I earned fifty dollars"—with mingled pride and defiance March thought engaging—"last winter by copying law papers. And I told you—everybody must know how poor we are."

"I know more than that, dearest!" laying his hand over her cold fingers. "I surmised when I saw Mrs. Wayt dictating to you, what it meant."

She was all herself again. In defense of her sister's secret, as he imagined when she began to speak, she rallied her best forces. Her speech was grave, dignified, and direct.

"I do not know what you surmised. The truth is that Mr. Wayt was taken suddenly ill last night. His sermon must be ready by this morning. There was not time to get a substitute. So my sister found his notes. They were very full. She read them aloud to me. Nobody else can make them out. I copied the sermon with the machine from her dictation. You will understand that we would not like to have this spoken of. Good-evening!"

She was beyond reach in a moment, in another beyond call.

March went back to the sylvan retreat that may be regarded as the stage set for the principal scenes of our story. Step and heart were light, and the same might be said of a brain that whirled like a feather in a gale. While he had been loath to admit the gravity of the misgivings that had embittered the slow hours between 11:30 A. M. and 7 o'clock P. M. of that eventful Sunday, he was keenly alive to the rapture of their removal. What a boorish bat he had been to suffer a suspicion of the lofty rectitude of the noblest woman upon earth to enter his mind! How altogether simple and convincing was her explanation of what should have been no mystery to any honorable man! Yet he could not be ashamed, in the fullness of his happiness. He called himself all the hard names in his vocabulary with cheerful volubility, and gloried in the lesson he had thus learned of implicit trust in the girl he loved. No accumulation of circumstantial evidence or even the witness of the eye should ever call up another shadow of a shade of doubt. Among other occasions for thankfulness was the recollection that he had not let a lisp of what he had seen last night and suspected this morning, escape him in conversation with his mother and sister. He found himself tracing, with a fine sense of the drollery of the conceit, the analogy between prostrate Dagon, *sans* arms, legs, and head, and the suspicion which had menaced the destruction of his happiness. Mutilated, prone, and harmless, it lay on the threshold of the temple of love and truth, ugly rubbish to be thrust forever out of sight.

He had hardly noticed, in the ecstasy of relief, Hetty's haste to be gone after she had explained her nocturnal industry. He passed as lightly over the incoherence that had replied to his question when he could see her again.

"Give me time to think! Not for a day or two! Not until you hear from me!" she had said just before reaching the gate.

He was shrewd enough to see how well taken was his vantage ground. She had not demurred at his stipulation. He was positive, in the audacity of youth and passion, that she would never utter the words he had dictated. The turf under the tree was flattened by her reclining form. He lay down upon it, his arms doubled under his head for a pillow, Thor taking his place beside him. The golden green changed into dull ruddy light, this into purple ash, and this into gray that was at first warm, then cold. The second vesper bell had set the air to quivering and sobbed musically into silence that embalmed the memory of the music. Rapt in dreams, in summer fragrance, and in tender dusks, the lover lay until the stars twinkled through rifts in the massed leaves. Now and then, the far-off roll of an organ and the sweet hymning of accompanying voices were borne across his reverie, as the wanderer through the twilight of an August day meets waves of warm, perfumed air, or currents of balsamic odors floating from evergreen heights.

At nine o'clock the moon showed the edge of a coy cheek above the horizon hills, and shortly thereafter March heard the click of the garden gate. Instinctively he put out his hand to keep Thor quiet, an unwarrantable idea that Hetty might revisit the spot darting through his mind. The shuffling of feet over the sward quieted his leaping heart. In another minute he distinguished the outlines of a figure stealing across the moonlit spaces separating black blotches of shade. As it neared the covert he spoke quietly, not to alarm the intruder.

"Good-evening, Homer."

"O Lord!" The three-quarter-witted wight bounded a foot from the ground, then collapsed into a shaking huddle.

"It is I—Mr. Gilchrist," March hastened to add. "I am sorry I frightened you."

"Now—I was jes a-lookin' fer a light I see from the back porch down this 'ere way," uttered Homer, in an agitated drawl.

March could see the coarse fingers rubbing against the backs of his hands, and a ray of light touched the pendulous jaw.

"It was the match I struck to light a cigar I smoked a while ago," he said. "I dare say that may account for the light you have seen at other times."

"Ye-es, sir"—dubiously. "I been saw the light lots o' nights, when I aint spoke of it. 'Tain't like er sergar. It's like a lantern a-swinging this er way"— swaying one hand—"I clumb this tree one night, an' sot thar till nigh mornin', a-waitin' an' a-watchin' fer it ter come again. There's a man what tole me 'twas the devil a-watchin' out for *me.*"

"I am surprised you try to catch him. From what I have heard, he is a slippery chap."

"*No-ow*—I aint a-feerd on him fer myself. *Now*, I'd be loath fer him to worry Miss Hetty."

"You are a good fellow, Homer! A brave fellow!" responded the listener, with sudden energy. "When you do get on the track of the light, let me know, and I'll lend a hand to nab the devil."

"Ye-es, sir! *Now*, I've been a-turnin' over in my mind what that man say to me. He's a man as ought to know what he's talkin' about. He t'reatened me orful a couple o' times, since we come to Fairhill. Sometimes I can't sleep fer thinkin' 'bout it. 'You stay outen that orchard!' he say. 'Ther' war a man murdered thar onct,' he tell me, 'an' the devil is a-lookin' fer him. Ef he come acrost you he'll ketch you by a mistake,' he say. But then, there's Miss Hetty, you know, Mr. Gilchris'!"

"What under heaven has she to do with your man, or his devil, or the light? Who is the man who threatened you? Does he live in Fairhill?"

Homer plucked at his lower lip and glanced apprehensively around.

"I dunno!" he answered, in sullen evasion. "I met him on the street one day. Two times I come acrost him in the orchard. Onct he come to the garding gate. That was the time he tell me 'bout the murder an' the devil."

"He is a cruel, rascally liar!" cried March indignantly. "And you don't know his name? What is he like? Did you ever speak of this to Miss Hetty?"

"No, sir. She got 'nough to fret her a'ready, Miss Hetty has. I'm 'fraid for her 'bout the man. *She* aint 'fraid o' nothin'. 'You do what I tell you, Homer,' sez she, 'an' I'll stan' between you an' harm,' she say. But she aint know 'bout the devil. Nor I aint heerd o' the murder when she tell me *that*. That mought make a dif'rence."

"She is all right, all the same. She is always right. Mind her, and you're sure to be safe. When did you last see this man who is so well acquainted with the devil?"

An uneasy pause, during which Homer cracked each one of the knuckle-joints in his left hand.

"I dunno! I don' jis reklec'! You won't mention him to Miss Hetty—nor to nobody—will you please not, Mr. Gilchris'? He's an orful man! He'd get even with Miss Hetty, some way, sure's you born, Mr. Gilchris'? 'Nurver you let on a word to *her!* sez he to me—'or 'twill be the wustest day she ever see,' he sez."

"Why, this is outrageous!" ejaculated the aroused listener. "Do you suppose I will allow this sort of thing to go on? I insist upon knowing who the wretch is! He'll find himself behind bars before he is a day older, if I get hold of him."

"*Now*"—resumed Homer, dazed and dull—"you'd better not meddle nor make with him. Me'n' Miss Hetty, we could manage 'bout him, but when he sot 'bout fetchin' the devil in—that aint a fa'r shake—*that* aint! I'll say that much, ef I die fer it—'taint by no means 'fa'r nor squar'!"

"Pshaw!" March laughed in vexed amusement. "Did you ever know the devil to do the fair and square thing? Or any of the devil's men? Why didn't you set Mr. Wayt after your friend? It's his trade to fight Old Nick, you know."

"Yes, sir. So I been heerd tell. What's *that?*"

It was the sound of the gate-latch falling into the socket, and firm quick footsteps.

"O Lord!" whispered Homer again. "Don't let on as I've been here!"

In a twinkling, he had gone up the tree like a cat.

By the time March recognized the latest comer, the rustling boughs were still. Thor growled fiercely. His master advanced a step into the moonlight.

"Be quiet!" to the dog. "Good-evening, Mr. Wayt! The beauty of the night has tempted you out, as well as myself."

"Ah, Mr. Gilchrist!"—suave and stately as usual. "As you say, it is a glorious night. I have been sitting for half an hour with your respected parents. Seeing you change color suddenly during the morning service, and missing you from church this afternoon, I feared lest you had been taken ill, and so went over to inquire.

"Mrs. Gilchrist appeased my anxiety by saying that yours was a passing indisposition. I was the more solicitous because I have suffered all day from the onslaught of my constitutional enemy, 'the rash' and crucial headache which my mother gave me. It is more than malady. It is *affliction!* requiring pagan fortitude and Christian resignation. There is some occult connection between it and the course of the natural sun in the heavens. It seized me this morning with the rising of the god of day and left me at the going down of the same. Mrs. Wayt will have it that it is the penalty for much study which, if not weariness to the flesh, occasionally revenges itself in neuralgic pangs. I know no fatigue while the oracular rage of composition is upon me. Last night it *possessed* me! I wrote the entire sermon to which you listened this morning between the hours of half-past nine Saturday night and four o'clock this morning. In all that time I did not leave my desk. The thunder-storm wrought strange, glorious excitement in my brain. It was as if seven thunders uttered their voices to the ears of my spirit."

The Rev. Mr. Wayt prodded holes in the turf with his cane while speaking, holding it in his right hand almost at arm's length, in a straight line from his body. His face showed chalky-white in the moon rays, his brows and hair very black; his eyes glittered, the smile upon his thin, wide-lipped mouth was apparent in the clearing radiance. He was disposed to be affably loquacious to the heir of a rich parishioner, and the pastor's "influence with young men" was one of his specialties. This important member of an important class did not interrupt him, and the intent expression of his figure—his back was to the moon—was pleasantly provocative to continued eloquence.

"The Sabbath has been superb—truly superb!" resumed the orator, pulling out the cane after an unusual artesian feat in jabbing it into the earth. "I could think of nothing as I looked out at daybreak upon the brightening face of nature but Mrs. Barbauld's 'rose that's newly washed by the shower.' My spirit put on wings to meet the new morning. I said, aloud, in a sort of divine transport: 'This is the day the Lord hath made. Let us rejoice and be glad in it!'"

"Do you ever preach extemporaneously, Mr. Wayt?" asked March.

The sentence passed his lips almost unawares. In his perplexity and disdain, he spoke at random. He could not stand here all night, the victim of the modern Coleridge. He recollected, while the flowing periods went over him, that the Rev. Percy's admirers likened him to the long-winded poet. The girl of his heart *in esse* and of his home *in posse* might be Mr. Wayt's wife's sister, but Mr. Wayt himself was an imposing liar and hypocrite, who disgraced the coat on his back. The sooner she was removed from his house the better. He credited poor Tony with more sense than he was reputed to possess, in that he doubted, inferentially, his employer's powers as an exorcist.

"Now and then, my dear sir, now and then! But I long ago arrived at the conclusion that natural fluency is a lure to indolence. Whatever is worth the hearing should be worth careful preparation. The *vice versa* occurs to you, of course. I would give my audience ripe matter, the slow accretion of amber-clear thought, not the fervid exudation of momentary excitement. Every line of this morning's sermon was written out in full. The reporter of a New York paper took it from my hand as I descended from the pulpit. 'Mr. Wayt!' he said, 'that discourse can be printed without the alteration of a word. It is perfect!'"

The man's supreme egotism pushed March into indiscretion, which he afterward considered dishonorable.

"You never use the typewriter, then?"

"Occasionally," carelessly. "I might say, semi-occasionally. But not when I am in the Spirit—as I reverently believe I was last night. Mrs. Wayt is a deft operator on it. She learned expressly to copy my sermons and lectures for the press. What will not a good wife do for her husband?"

"What, indeed?" assented March fervently.

He was thinking of the wifely equivocations to which he had hearkened on the way to church, and, with genuine satisfaction, how straightforward was Hetty's simple tale of the sermon-writing episode. Again he resolved to tear her out of this web of needless deceits at the earliest possible moment.

He left the vicinity of the apple tree, partly to shake off his companion, partly to allow Homer opportunity to escape. Once he had his lips open to intimate his presence in the orchard at midnight, and that he had seen the light in the study. The reverend humbug should be warned of the danger of gratuitous and wholesale lying. He withheld the caution. It was not his province to reprove a man so much his senior, and—he added mentally—such an old offender.

Mr. Wayt sauntered on with him to the gate opening into the Gilchrist shrubbery, bade him "good-night," and marched back. March leaned upon the fence, seeming to stare at the moon, and enjoying a nightcap cigar, until the long, black figure entered the parsonage garden. While the young man lingered he saw Homer drop, monkeylike, to the earth and skulk homeward, keeping in the shadow when he could.

"I would sooner take the fool's chances of evading the devil than his pompous and pious master's!" soliloquized Mrs. Gilchrist's son.

Hetty was dusting the big parlors next morning, and making ineffectual attempts to evolve coziness out of carpeted space, when a cough at the door attracted her notice.

Homer stood there, military cap in hand, and wet up to the knees with dew. His love for flowers was a passion, only surpassed by his exquisite tenderness for dumb animals and children. Hetty had said of her *protégé* that he had the soul of a painter-poet, but that the wires were cut between spirit and speech. He had been on his knees since there was light enough to show the difference between weeds and precious plants, cleaning out the garden borders.

"*Now*" (fumbling with his shabby headgear), "I was wishful fer to speak with ye before ennybody else came down. Leastways, Mary Ann, she's in the kitchen, but don't count, bein' busy an' out of the way."

Hetty smiled languidly. Her eyes were heavy-lidded; her motions slow for her. She had lain all night, staring into the blackness above her, now crying to a deaf heaven to show her a plain path for her feet, now trembling with ecstatic anguish in the recollection of the interview that opened a vista of Eden she yet dared not enter.

"Come what may, he has called me darling!" she was thinking for the hundredth time, as the interruption came.

"What is it, Homer? Are your flowers all right?"

He ventured, after a glance at his feet, to step upon the unbroken breadths of Brussels.

"*Now*—I was up a tree in the orchard las' night. An' Mr. Gilchris'—the *young* one—and Mr. Wayt, they were a-talkin' on the groun' under the tree——"

Hetty wheeled upon him with blazing eyes and cheeks.

"You were in the orchard! In what tree? When? But no!" Her excitement subsided as quickly as it had arisen. "You were in the house when I came in. Go on!" She drew a long breath.

Homer twiddled his thumbs in the crown of his cap. His speech could never be hurried. If urged to talk fast, he was dumb.

"Now, I was up in that big tree where the picter was painted. Mr. Gilchris'— the young Mr. Gilchris'—he war a-lyin' onto the grass when I came along. 'Twar after you had gone upstairs—nigh onto ten o'clock, I guess, or may be nine—I aint certain. I'd saw the same light, an', for all them boys ken say, I've been saw it many a time——"

"Never mind the light." Hetty said it patiently. "Tell me how you happened to climb the tree."

"Now, Mr. Gilchris'—the young gentleman—he spoke very civil an' kind to me, an' we war talkin' quite a spell, when I heerd Mr. Wayt a-comin', an' I clumb the tree so's he wouldn't see me, an' may be go fur me, you know. An' while I war in the tree I heerd him a-tellin' Mr. Gilchris'—I meantersay the young Mr. Gilchris'—how he'd sot up 'tell daybreak, four o'clock Sat'day night, a figurin' onto his sermon what he preached on Sunday——"

"Homer!"

"Yes, ma'am! He war talkin' very high Scotch, mos'ly like he does all times, 'specially to comp'ny-folks, but I got the sense of that much. He said as how he an' the thunder-storm they figured up the sermon together, near's I could make out. An' Mr. Gilchris'—the young gentleman—he said precious little— an' Mr. Wayt, he splurged out considerable 'bout seein' the sun rise an' so forth, an' 'bout his headache comin' on an' a-goin off with the sun. An' then the two of 'em walked off quite frien'ly, an' soon's as they was out o' sight, I lighted out and come home."

Hetty was sitting upon the sofa, too sick and weak to stand.

"Are you sure that you heard all this? Did Mr. Gilchrist know you were in the tree?"

"Now—he see me go up. I ast him not to let on to *him*. But what I come to say war, 'taint noways nor nurver safe to say what aint jes' true, jes' for the sake of talkin' big, an' Mr. Wayt, bein' a edicated man, he'd ought to be tole that. T'ould a' been better not to say nuthin' 'bout Sat'day night 'thout somebody ast h'm."

"There!" His young mistress put out her hand imperatively. "That will do. Don't speak of this to anybody else. Go back to your work."

On their way to school, the twins left a thin envelope at Judge Gilchrist's door. It was addressed to March.

"I have heard what was the substance of Mr. Wayt's conversation with you last night. Knowing you as I do, I am sure, that in mercy to the innocent, you will not let it go further. I recognize in the incident one more added to the many reasons why I can never be more than

"Your friend,
H. ALLING."

CHAPTER VIII.

MARCH GILCHRIST'S name was brought up to the sewing room at eleven o'clock Monday morning. Hetty was cutting out shirts for the twins at a table of Homer's contrivance and manufacture. Her face was flushed, perhaps with stooping over the board, when she looked up.

"Please say that I am particularly engaged this morning, Mary Ann, and beg to be excused."

"My dear!" expostulated Mrs. Wayt. "He has probably called with a message from his mother or sister."

"In that case ask him to leave it with you, Mary Ann, unless you care to go down, Frances?"

"He said 'Miss Alling' most particular," ventured Mary Ann.

"Then take my message just as I gave it, if you please."

"Did you know," pursued Miss Alling, when the girl had gone, "that Perry is an inch taller than his brother? His arms are longer, too. They were exactly the same size until this summer."

Mrs. Wayt eyed her sister with a helpless, distraught air, while the scissors flashed and slipped through the muslin, and the worker appeared to have no interest in life beyond the manipulation of both.

"Dear," she said timidly at length, without noticing the other's query. "I never blame you for any action, however singular it may seem to me. I know you always have some excellent reason for what you do or say. But the Gilchrists are our best neighbors, and are leading people in the church. It would be unwise to offend them. Do you object to telling me why you would not see Mr. March Gilchrist?"

Hetty shifted the pattern to a corner of the stuff, turned it upside down and regarded it solemnly, her head on one side. Then she pinned it fast and fell again to cutting.

"I do object—decidedly!" she said composedly. "But it is perhaps best that you should know the truth. It may prevent unpleasant complications. Mr. Gilchrist did me the honor last evening to offer to marry me, and I refused him."

"Hetty Alling!"

"That is likely to remain my name. I supposed that you would be surprised. *I* was!" as coolly as before. "I trust to your honor to keep Mr. Gilchrist's secret, even from Mr. Wayt. It is not a matter that concerns anybody but ourselves. And we will not allude to it again."

Struck by something unnatural in the girl's perfect composure, the tender-hearted matron leaned forward to stroke the head bowed over the work.

"There is something behind all this, Hetty, dear. I am sure of it. It would make me very happy to see you married to such a man as March Gilchrist. What objection can you have to him as a suitor?"

"The very question which he asked and I answered. Excuse me for reminding you that nobody else has the right to press it."

The rebuff did not end the discussion. The matter was, in Mrs. Wayt's mind, too grave to be lightly dismissed.

"Don't be angry with me!" staying the progress of the clicking shears, that her sister might be compelled to hear what she said, "I love you too dearly to let you make a blunder you may regret for a lifetime. March is a noble young fellow, of unexceptionable family and character. His disposition is excellent; his manners are charming; he has talent, energy——"

"Spare me the rest of the catalogue, please!" retorted Hetty curtly. "It is not like you, Francis, to force a disagreeable subject upon me. And this is one of the least agreeable you could select. Discussion of it is indelicate and a breach of confidence on my part—and altogether useless on yours."

Yet she was especially gentle and affectionate with her sister for the rest of the day. On bidding her "good-night" she embraced her fervently.

"I love you dearly; better this minute than ever before, if I was so savage this morning," she said, with shining eyes, to March's champion.

Upstairs she read "Locksley Hall" through to Hester, who was sleepless, until twelve o'clock. Not until the clock had struck the half-hour after midnight was Hetty free to take from her pocket and look at a letter the afternoon mail had brought. The superscription was in a hand she had seen in notes to Hester and upon the fly-leaves of books, and it was still sealed. She sat looking at it, as it lay within the open palm of a lax hand for a good (or bad) quarter of an hour.

Hester's regurgitate breathing—worse to-night than usual—was the only sound in the chamber. Now and then she raised her hands strugglingly, as if dreaming, but she slept on.

To open that letter and take the contents into her empty heart would be to the lonely orphan Heaven on earth. It was long, for the envelope held several sheets. It was eloquent, for she had heard him talk upon the theme set forth in every line. She had will-force sufficient to conceal from the sister, whose heart would be broken by the truth, her reasons for refusing to link hers with the unsmirched name of the man she loved. She was not strong enough to put her finger under the flap of that envelope and read a single line, and then persist in doing right. Perhaps, in spite of the repulse of the morning, he had again called her "darling!"

She durst not risk the seeing; she had strength given her to keep the resolution, but she did no more that night. The answer must wait until morning. The letter was hidden under the pillow, and her hand touched it while she slept and while she lay awake. In the still, purple dawn, she arose quietly, not to disturb Hester, dressed herself and knelt for a brief prayer, such as the busiest member of the household had time to offer. While she prayed she held the unopened letter to her heart. Arising, she kissed it lingeringly.

"God bless my love!" she whispered.

With steady fingers she wrote upon the reverse of the envelope: "*I cannot read this. Do not write again,*" slipped it into a larger cover, addressed it, and, before the family was astir, sent Homer with it to the nearest letter box.

She had acted bravely, and, she believed, decisively, but she had blundered withal. An unopened letter, unaccompanied by a word of extenuation of the flagrant discourtesy, might damp the ardor of the most adoring lover. Yet March's eyes were lit by a ray of affectionate amusement in receiving back this, the first love letter he had ever penned. He kissed the one-line sentence before putting the envelope away.

"Perhaps she is afraid of herself!" May had suggested sagely, *à propos* of Hetty's avoidance of his visits.

The bright-natured suitor's conclusion, after reading what was meant as a quietus to his addresses, was not dissimilar. If the case were hopeless she would have written nothing. Nevertheless, he bowed to the laconic: "Do not write again." He did more than she had commanded. Without attempting to see Hetty again, he escorted his sister in the second week of July to Long Branch, and stayed there a fortnight, then went with her to Mt. Desert for ten days more.

The malign influence of a dog-day drought was upon Fairhill when the pair returned. The streets were deep in dust, the sun, a red and rayless ball, had rolled from east to west, and taken his own time in doing it, and was staining to a dingy crimson horizon-vapors that looked as dry as the dust, as brother and sister paused upon the piazza for a look over the familiar landscape.

"It is stifling after the seashore!" breathed May. "But it is home! I am *glad* to be back!"

"And I—always!"

March said it, in stooping, hat in hand, to kiss his mother. There was the ring of sincerity in his voice; his eyes were placid. He had come home to her cured of an ill-starred fancy for an ineligible girl. There was no sign of anything more than neighborly interest in his face when May asked at dinner-time how the Wayts were.

"Well, I believe," replied Mrs. Gilchrist. "I have seen comparatively little of them while you were away, except at church. It has been too hot for visiting. Yesterday I took Hester out to drive. She misses you sadly, May. She is thinner and has less color than when you went away."

"Dear little Queen Mab!" said Hester's friend. "I must have her over to-morrow to spend the day. I have some books and sketches for her. And Hetty?"

"Is as busy as usual, Hester tells me. She goes out very little, I believe. The young people hereabouts call her a recluse."

The unconscious judge came to the relief of all parties.

"Mr. Wayt's congregation continues large," he remarked. "He preached a truly remarkable sermon last Sunday. At this rate we will have to pull down our church and build a larger by next year."

The wife looked gratified. It was much to have her husband speak of "our church."

May was content to wait for the morrow's meeting with her pet. Hester was wild with impatience to be again with her worshiped friend. Hetty might remonstrate, and her mother entreat her not to intrude upon the family on the evening of the travelers' arrival. The spoiled child was unmanageable. She could not sleep a wink, she protested, until she had kissed Miss May, and exchanged reports of the weeks separating them from the dear everyday intercourse. She would take with her the portfolio she had almost worked herself ill to fill with what May must think showed diligent endeavor to improve.

"Then, there is the great news to tell!"

"Wouldn't it be well to wait a while before speaking of that?" dissuaded the mother.

"It is a week old, already!" Hester pouted, "and I said never a word to Mrs. Gilchrist yesterday. 'The Seasons'"—the *mot de famille* at the Gilchrists' for brother and sister—"are our only *own* friends, mamma. You can trust them to hold their tongues!"

"What seems a great event to us will be small to them," cautioned Mrs. Wayt—then gave Hester her way.

Nine o'clock saw her in Homer's charge on the orchard road, the shortest, as it was the most secluded, to the Gilchrist place.

"Where *are* you taking me, Tony?" she aroused from a happy, expectant reverie to ask, midway.

The aftermath of the June mowing was tall by now, and the chair was almost hidden in it.

"Now—I don' keer fur to take ye near that big tree. 'Taint wholesome nor proper!" grunted the charioteer. He was slightly afraid of the testy little damsel, and took on doughty airs at times to disprove the fact. "We'll soon git inter the path agi'n."

"But I won't stand this!" cried Hester, irate. "Go back to the path! Not wholesome! not proper! What do you mean!"

"Now—I seen the light there oftener'n anywheres else"—Homer was beginning, when they were hailed by a well-known voice.

"What are you doing over there?" called March.

"Swimming for our lives," returned Hester. "Won't you dive, and drag me out by the hair of my head?"

Her tone was tremulous with delight. As he took her hand, it quivered like a poplar leaf in his large, cordial grasp. He was fond of Hester on her own account, fonder of her because he linked her with Hetty. He had strolled down the street with his cigar after giving his mother a detailed account of the pleasure making of the last three weeks. He felt the heat inland to be oppressive after the surf breeze. His mother was glad that his saunter was not in the direction of the parsonage. She knew nothing of the short cut from the back street, or with what ease an athlete of six-and-twenty could vault a five-barred fence. Besides, was not her boy a cured and discharged patient!

The meeting with Hester, if not the best thing he had hoped for, was so much better than a solitary ramble in dream-haunted grounds that he greeted her joyously. It was not the first time the idea had come to him of making a confidante of the keen-witted, deep-hearted child, but it suddenly took the shape of determination.

"Going to see May!" He echoed her reply to his next question. "She is tired out, and has gone to her room by this. She means to claim you for the whole of to-morrow. Give me a little chat in our arbor instead, and I will take you home. I have not seen you for an age, and I have something very interesting to me and important to you, to say to you."

She laughed up in his face in sheer pleasure.

"And I have something particularly interesting to me, and not important to you, to tell in return. We have an event in our family—an agreeable happening as to results, although it comes by a dark and crooked road—or so mamma persists in saying."

March had propelled her into the open track and stopped as she said this to lean forward and peer into the saucy face. A disagreeable—an absurd—thrill passed over him. Had he lost Hetty?

"An event! Accomplished or prospective?"

"Both!" chuckled Hester.

"Is it an engagement?" bringing out the word courageously.

The question was never answered. A vigorous onward push had brought them into the moonlit area surrounding the king apple tree. Thor rushed forward, bellowing ferociously at a long black body that lay half under, half beyond the dipping outward branches, now weighted almost to the ground with growing fruit.

"Homer!" shouted March to the figure retreating toward the garden. "Come back! hurry!" And, hastily, to Hester: "I will send you home with him and go for the police. Don't be frightened. It is only a drunken tramp, or may be a sleeper. In either case he cannot stay here. These are my father's grounds."

Hester had not uttered a sound, but the slight figure, bent toward the recumbent man, had a strained intensity of expression words could not have conveyed. Her eyes were fixed, as by the fascination of horrified dread—one small hand plucked oddly at her throat.

"Take her home, Homer!" March ordered, "and say nothing to alarm the ladies. I'll attend to *him!*"

"No! *no!* NO!" shrilled Hester in an unearthly tone that made him start. "You must go home! you! *you!* and say nothing! tell nobody! O God of mercy, it has come at last! Don't touch him!" her voice rising into a husky shriek. For, parting the boughs, March passed to the head of the prostrate man, and stooped to raise him. His quick eye had perceived that he was well dressed and no common tramp in figure, also that he had lain, not fallen, where he was found. In bending to take hold of him, he detected, even in the intensity of his excitement, the peculiar, heavy, close odor of drugs that had hung in the air on the Fourth of July night. In company with a policeman, our young artist had once visited a Chinese "opium dive" in New York, and he recognized the smell now.

Homer was beside him, and lent intelligent aid.

"*Now*," he drawled, without the slightest evidence of alarm, "*I* mos'ly lif's him up *so*-fashion!"

The action brought the features into a rift of moonlight.

"Great Heavens!" broke from March in a low tone of horror and dismay. "It is Mr. Wayt!"

Laying him on the turf he went back to Hester and seized the bar of her chair.

"You must go home! You must not see him, my poor child! It is your father, and he is very ill—unconscious. Not a moment is to be lost. I must go for a doctor immediately!"

"*Let go!*"

Beside herself with fury, she actually struck at the hand grasping the propeller; her eyes flashed fire; her accents, hardly louder than a wheezing whisper, were jerky gasps, painful to hear.

"Let go, I say! and do you go to your safe, decent home, as I told you! Tony and I are used to this sort of thing!"

"Hester! you do not know what you are saying!" March came around and faced her, trying to quiet her by cold, stern authority.

It was thrown away. She raved on—still tearing away with her tiny fierce hands at her heaving throat as if to give speech freer vent.

"I do know—oh, we are graduates in these frolicsome escapades! It is inconsiderate in him—" with a horrid laugh—"to give his wife, his wife's sister, and the family factotum such a job as carrying him all this way. To do him justice, he seldom forgets the decencies so entirely. If I had my way, he should lie here all night. Only his wife would come out and stay with him. What are you staring at me for, Mr. Gilchrist? Here is our family skeleton! Does it frighten you out of your wits?"

Her croaks of laughter threatened dissolution to the fragile frame. It was an awful, a repulsive exhibition.

"It is you who have lost yours!" rejoined March gravely. "Your father may be dying, for aught you know. A hundred men fell in the streets of New York to-day, overcome by the heat—and we are wasting precious minutes in wild, nonsensical talk. If you will let Homer take you to the house, and compose yourself sufficiently to prepare your mother for the shock of seeing her husband brought in insensible, we may save him yet. Go! and send Homer back at once."

The wild eyes surveyed him piercingly; with a low, meaning laugh, she sank back among her cushions.

"I think"—she said distinctly and deliberately—"that you are the best man God ever made! Go on, Tony!"

Left alone with the unconscious man, March stooped and rolled him entirely over. He had been lying, face downward, his cheek to the sward; one arm was by his side, the other was thrown in a natural position above his head. His pulse was almost normal, although somewhat sluggish; his respiration heavy, but not stertorous: his complexion was not sanguine. His breath and, March fancied, his whole body reeked of opium. March shook him gently. He slept on. With a disgustful shiver, he forced himself to pass an arm under his head and lift it to his knee. There was no change in the limp lethargy. The young man laid him down, and, rising, stood off and looked at the pitiable wreck. Hester's frenzied tirade had disabused the listener's mind of the suspicion of suicide. He could no longer doubt that here was the unraveling of the complex design that had vexed his heart and head. The popular preacher was not the first of brilliant parts and high position who had fallen a victim to a debasing and insidious habit, but his skill and effrontery in concealing the truth were remarkable. Yet—might not March have divined the nature of the mystery before this revelation? The peculiar brilliancy of the deep-set eyes; his variable spirits; his fluent and, at times, erratic speech; the very character of his pulpit eloquence—might have betrayed him to an expert. His wife's nervous vigilance and eager assiduity of devotion—above all, the episode of the midnight toilers, and the conflicting stories of the need of that toil—finally—and he recalled it with a bursting heart—Hetty's declaration to her lover that there were insurmountable obstacles to their union—were as clear as daylight now. The sudden illness of that memorable Saturday night was stupor like that which now chained the slave of appetite to the earth.

How often and with what excess of anguish the revolting scene had been enacted only the two unhappy sisters knew, unless the still more hapless daughter were in the secret. Her wail, "Oh, God of mercy! it has come at last!" was a key to depths of suspenseful endurance and labyrinths of unavailing deception.

Unavailing, for the instant of detection was the beginning of the end. The man was ruined beyond redemption. A whisper of his infirmity would be the loss of place, reputation, and livelihood, and his innocent family would go down quick into the pit with him. This was the vision of impending gloom that had disturbed what should be sunny deeps in the sweetest eyes in the world to him. This was the almost certain prospect that made her write, "I can never be more than your friend!"

The Gilchrist was clean, honest blood. Hetty testified her appreciation of this truth by refusing to marry him. He could think how his mother would look when she had heard the story and how Fairhill gossip would gloat over the "newest thing in clerical scandals!"

Why should it be made public? Why should he not help to keep it quiet instead of pulling down ruin upon the helpless and unoffending? Hetty had written, "In mercy to the innocent." He seemed to hear her say it now, in his ear.

A faint melodious chime just vibrated through the sultry air. The fine bell of the "Old First" had struck the half hour. The church in which he was baptized; the church of his mother's love and prayers! At thought of the pulpit desecrated by this fellow's feet, a rush of indignant contempt surged up to his lips.

"Sacrilegious dog!" he muttered, touching the motionless heap with his foot.

Homer shambled back out of breath. He had brought a lantern.

"*Now*—it's powerful shady under the trees!" he replied to March's remark that the moon gave all the light they required. "An' ther's somethin' come ter me, as I want ter see!"

He set down the lantern, hugged the tree bole, and went up a foot or two. Then were heard a scratching and a rattling overhead.

"*Now*—would ye a mind holdin' this 'tell I git 'em all?"

The "all" were four bottles and a tin box. Two phials were long and empty. A name was blown in the glass. March held one down to the light.

"*Elixir of Opium!*"

The others were larger and of stout blue glass. A printed label said "*Phosphate.*" March pulled out a cork and smelled the contents. Opium again!

The box held the same drug as a dark paste.

"I mistrusted them horsephates a coople o' times!" said Homer, imperturbably sagacious. "He wor too everlastin' fond of 'em. He skeered me with the devil inter goin' ter the drug store with a paper ter tell 'em for ter give me that ar' one," designating an empty phial. "Leastways, one like it. An' Miss Hetty, she foun' it in the garding, where I drapped it. Then, 'twas she tole me nivver to go nowhar 'thout 'twas she sent me. An' I aint sence! An' he's t'reatened me orful a many a time 'cause what she said to me that time. I guess he bought 'em in New York, mos' likely. He's a sharp un—Mr. Wayt is!"

March eyed him suspiciously.

"How did you know where these things were, if you had nothing to do with hiding them!"

"*Now*"—stolid under the implied doubt, or not noticing it—"you reklec' the Sunday night me 'n you was talkin' here, 'n' *he* come along, an' I shinned up the tree? I bet"—with more animation than March had ever seen him display before—"he was a-comin' for a drink then! 'Twas the very night before, when Miss Hetty, she come all the way up to my room, an' sez she, 'Homer,' sez she, 'Mr. Wayt has done it agin,' she say. An' so he had, an' him a lyin' on the study floor jes' as you see him now—an' Mrs. Wayt a-cryin' over him. You see she'd b'lieved, sure an' certain, he'd nuvver do so no more. But *I* mistrusted them horsephates. *Now*, that very night—Sunday night 'twas, 'n' me an' you was a-talkin' here—as I was a-slidin' down the tree I kotched inter a hole, an' somethin' sort o' jingled, like glass. I nuvver t'ought no more 'bout it tell jes' ez I come up to-night an' see him a-sprawlin' thar, an' I smelled the stuff. I'll jes' hide 'em in the grass, an' to-morrow early I'll bury 'em in the garding. But it's a quare cupboard, that is."

While talking, he was busy spreading upon the turf a heavy shawl, such as were worn by men, forty years ago. "*Now*—ef you'll lend a lift to him!" to the wondering observer.

The plan was ingenious, but Homer's dexterity in carrying it out, and the *sangfroid* he maintained throughout, betokened an amount of practice at which March's soul recoiled. It was frightfully realistic. Mr. Wayt was laid in the middle of the big plaid; the two ends were knotted tightly upon his chest, inclosing his arms, the other two about his ankles.

"I'll hitch on to the heavy eend," quoth the bunch of muscle and bone March had begun to admire. "Me bein' useter to it nor what you be. You take holt on his feet."

In such style the stately saint was borne up the back steps and laid upon the settee in the parsonage hall.

Mrs. Wayt was upon the porch. Her first words gave one of the bearers his cue.

"Oh, Mr. Gilchrist! This is dreadful! And he seemed so well at dinner time! The heat often affects him seriously. He had a sunstroke some years ago, and every summer he feels the effects of it. Lay him down here and rest before taking him upstairs. There. Thank you."

While she undid and removed the clerical cravat and collar from his throat, March straightened his spine and looked around for Hetty. The house was as still as a grave. The front door was closed; the rooms on both sides of the hall were dark and silent. It was Thursday night, the universal "evening out" for Fairhill servants. March recollected it in the mechanical way in which one thinks of trifles at important junctures. He was glad—mechanically—that Mary Ann was not there to carry the tale of Mr. Wayt's fainting fit, or semi-sunstroke, or whatever name his wife chose to put to it, to Mrs. Gilchrist. He was beginning to ask himself what he should say at home of what he had done with himself between nine and ten o'clock that evening.

The transportation up to the second story was slow and difficult. Mrs. Wayt supported her husband's head, and, like a flash, recurred to March Hester's sneer of the task laid upon "his wife, his wife's sister, and the family factotum." It must have been barely accomplished on the July night when he and May brought Hester home, and Hetty ran down out of breath, her hair disheveled and eyes scared! That *her* hands should be fouled by such a burden!

His face was set whitely, as, having deposited the load upon the bed, he accosted the wife:

"Would you like to have a physician?"

His tone was hard and constrained. She did not look up.

"You are very good but it is not necessary—thank you! I have seen him as ill before from the same cause and know what to do for him. And he is morbidly sensitive with regard to these attacks. He thinks it would injure him in his profession if the impression were to get abroad that his health is unsound or his constitution breaking up. I shall not even dare tell him that you have seen him to-night."

She was putting extraordinary force upon herself, but she could not meet his eye.

"I cannot thank you just now as I would, Mr. Gilchrist. I am all unnerved, and although I know this seizure is not dangerous, it is a terrible ordeal to me to witness it. May I ask that you will not mention it, even to Judge and Mrs. Gilchrist? My husband would be mortified and distressed beyond measure were his illness the subject of even friendly remark."

March hesitated, and she turned upon him quickly. Her face was that of an old woman—gray, withered, and scored with lines, each one of which meant an agony.

His resolution dissolved like the frost before fire.

"You may depend upon my discretion and friendship," he said impulsively.

She burst into tears, the low, convulsive sobbing he had heard above stairs on that other night.

Unable to bear more he ran down the staircase, and recognized before he reached the foot that he had committed himself to a lie.

"Mr. Gilchrist!"

His hand was upon the lock of the front door when he caught the low call.

Hetty stood upon the threshold of the library, a shadowy figure in white that seemed to waver in the uncertain light.

"I should like to speak to you, if you can spare a few minutes," she pursued, leading the way into the room.

With a bow of acquiescence he sat down and waited for her to begin. His mind was in a tumult; dumb pain devoured him. He felt as any honorable man might feel who condones a felony.

CHAPTER IX

"MY sister has begged you to keep secret what you have seen to-night—has she not?" was Hetty's first inquiry, spoken without haste and without excitement.

A mute bow replied.

"And you have promised to do it?"

"I told Mrs. Wayt that she might depend upon my discretion."

"Which she construes into a pledge to connive at a wrong done to a church and a community," in precisely the same tone and manner as before.

March stared at her perplexedly. What did the girl mean? And was this resolute, impassive woman of business the blushing trembler who, a month ago, could not deny her love for him? She was very serious now, but apparently very tranquil.

"You would say, if you were not too kind-hearted, that this is what I am doing—what I have been doing for nearly ten years—and you would be right. It would not exculpate me in your opinion if I were to represent that Mr. Wayt's profession is all that stands between his family and the poorhouse; that I do not habitually attend the church in which he officiates, and that my name has never appeared upon the record of any one of the parishes of which he has had charge since I became a member of his family. Mr. Wayt and I have not exchanged a syllable directly for over five years. I neither respect nor like him. He can never forgive my knowledge of his character, and my interference with his habits. These were confirmed before I came to my sister."

"Let me beg," interposed March, "that you will not go on with what cannot but be distressing to you. You need no justification in my sight. If you will permit me to call to-morrow morning we can talk matters over calmly and at leisure. It is late, and you have had a severe nervous strain."

"Unless you insist upon the postponement I would rather speak now, while my mind is steady in the purpose to make an end of subterfuge and concealment. I *am* weary, but it is of falsehoods, acted and spoken. Hester has told me of your generous pretense of misunderstanding the nature of Mr. Wayt's attack. There it is again!"—relapsing into her usual tone, and with whimsical vexation that made March smile. "I am afraid I have forgotten how to be frank! My poor sister's eager talk of 'attacks' and 'seizures' and 'turns' and 'sunstroke' and 'constitutional headaches' has unbalanced my perceptions of right and wrong."

"You cannot expect me to agree with you there?" the suppressed smile becoming visible.

She was not to be turned aside from the straight track.

"Nothing so perverts conscience as a systematic course of concealment, even when it is practiced for what seem to be noble ends. I have felt this for a long time. Lately the sense of guilt has been insupportable. It may be relief—if not expiation—to tell the truth in the plainest terms I can use. It may leave me more wretched than I am now. But right is right."

Her chin trembled and she raised her hand to cover it. Her admirable composure was smoldering excitement, kept under by will and the conscience whose rectitude she undervalued. With a sub-pang, March perceived that this disclosure was not a confidence, but a duty.

"Mr. Wayt was a confirmed opium eater and drinker, twelve years ago," she resumed in a cold monotone. "He would drink intoxicating liquors, too, when narcotics were not to be had. I believe the appetite for the two is a common symptom of the habit. His wife shielded him, then, as she does now, and so successfully that he kept a church in Cincinnati for four years. Hester was a beautiful, active child, eight years old, and a great pet with her father. He does not care for children, as a rule, but she was pretty and clever and amused him. One day she begged her mother to let her take 'dear papa's' lunch up to him. It was always 'dear papa' with her. He had a way of locking himself in his study from morning until night Saturday. Even his wife did not suspect that he wrote his Sunday sermon with a glass of laudanum and brandy at his side. He was busy upon a set of popular discourses on 'Crying Sins of the Day.' They drew immense crowds."

A sarcastic gleam passed over her face, and for the first time the listener saw a likeness to the witty and wise cripple.

"Hester knocked again and again without getting answered. Then her father called out that he was busy and did not want any lunch. She was always willful, and he had indulged her unreasonably. So she declared that she would not go away until he opened the door and took the tray—not if she had to stand there and knock all day. He tore open the door in a fury, threw the tray and the lunch downstairs, and flung the child after it. The drugged drink had made him crazy."

March shuddered.

"And that was the cause——"

"It left her what you see, now. The effect upon her character and feelings was, if possible, more deplorable. From that hour she has never spoken to her father at all, or of him as 'papa.' It is always 'he' and 'him' to the family,

'Mr. Wayt' to strangers. It seems horribly unnatural, but she loathes and despises him. While she lay crushed and suffering for the months that passed before she left her bed, she would go into convulsions at sight of him. Her mother begged her, on her knees, to 'forgive poor papa, who had a delirious headache when he pushed her away from the door.' Hester refused passionately. She is no more forgiving now. Yet she was so proud and shrewd, even then, that she never betrayed to the doctors how she was hurt. She let everybody believe that it was an accident. I had been her nurse for six months before she told me the fearful story.

"The truth never got abroad in Cincinnati, but flying rumors of Mr. Wayt's growing eccentricities and the possible cause gathered an opposition party in the church. It was headed by a prominent druggist, who had talked with others in the trade from whom Mr. Wayt had bought opium, laudanum, and brandy. He has been more cunning in his purchases since then. He was obliged to resign his charge, and became what poor Hester calls 'an ecclesiastical tramp.' He controls his appetite within tolerably safe bounds for a while, sometimes for months, then gives way, and we live on the verge of discovery and disgrace until the crisis comes. The end is always the same. We break camp and 'move on.'"

"Yet he brought clean papers to the Fairhill church."

A dreary smile went with the answer.

"Clerical charity suffereth long and is kind! Out of curiosity I attended once a meeting of a presbytery that dismissed him from his church and commended him to another presbytery. We had narrowly escaped public exposure at that time. The sexton found Mr. Wayt in the condition you have seen this evening upon the floor of the lecture room and called in a physician, who boldly proclaimed that the man was 'dead drunk.' The accused put in a plea of indisposition and an overdose of brandy, inadvertently swallowed. His brethren, assembled in solemn session, spoke of his faithful work in the vineyard and the leadings of Divine Providence, and said that their prayers went with him to his new field of labor.

"I don't want to be unjust or cynical, Mr. Gilchrist, and I can see that there is a pleasanter side to the case. There *is* such a thing as Christian charity, and more of it in the world than we are willing to admit. However church people may gossip about an unpopular pastor, and maneuver to get rid of him, when the parting comes they will not brand him in the eyes of others. And clergymen are very faithful to one another. It is really beautiful to see how they try to hide faults and foibles. It is a literal fulfillment of the command, 'Bear ye one another's burdens.' In some—in most of Mr. Wayt's charges— the secret of his frequent change of pastorate was not told. He was 'odd,' and 'had nomadic tastes.' Sometimes the climate did not agree with his health.

The air was too strong or too weak. Twice poor Hester's condition demanded an immediate change. We went to Chicago to be near an eminent surgeon, who, after all, never saw her.

"I will not weary you with the details of a life such as I pray God few families know. After a few years Hester and I became hopeless of anything better. Wherever we might go, change, and the probability of disgrace, were a mere question of time. My sister never loses faith in her husband and in an overruling Power that will not forsake the righteous. For, strange as it may seem, she believes in the piety of a man whose sacred profession is a continual lie.

"Oh, Mr. Gilchrist!" the enforced monotony of her tone wavering into a cry of pain—"I think *that* is the worst of all! When I recollect my mother's pure religion—when I see your mother's beneficent life and firm faith in goodness and in God—when I know that, in spite of the seeming untruthfulness which is, she thinks, necessary to protect her husband—my sister holds fast to her love and trust in an Almighty Friend, and walks humbly with her God, I feel such indignation against a man who is the slave of passion, selfish, vain, and conscienceless, and yet assumes to show such souls the way to heaven, that I dare not enter the church where he is allowed to preach, lest I should cry out in the face of his hearers against the monstrous cheat!"

Her eyes flamed clear; the torrent of feeling swept away reserve and coldness.

"I understand!" March said, with sympathetic warmth. "You never disappoint me. Tell me what I can do to help you. I cannot let you endure all this alone any longer."

"Nobody can take my share of the burden. I would hardly know myself without it. It will be the heavier for my sister's distress and Hester's anger when they hear what I have decided to do. Hester was on her way over to your house when you met her, full of news she could not wait until to-morrow to tell. My mother's only brother went to Japan thirty years ago and became rich. He died last March, leaving most of his fortune to benevolent institutions in America. To each of us, his sister's children, he bequeathed ten thousand dollars. It is not a fortune, but with our modest tastes, and when joined to the little I already have, it will support us decently. My first thought, when the news reached us, a week ago, was 'Now, Mr. Wayt need never take another charge! We need not live upon tainted food!'"

"You are a noble woman, Hetty——"

She interrupted him.

"I am not! This is not self-sacrifice, but self-preservation. If the money had not been given to us, I must have found some way out of a false position. I want you to tell your father all you know. Keep back nothing I have told you. He is a good and a merciful man. Let him speak openly to Mr. Wayt and forbid him ever to enter the pulpit again upon penalty of public exposure and suspension from the ministry. What Judge Gilchrist says will have weight. With all his high looks and sounding talk, Mr. Wayt is a coward. He would not venture to resist the decision. Then we will go away quietly. I have thought of the little town in which my sister and I were born. Living is cheap there and there are excellent schools for the children. Twenty-five thousand dollars will go very far in that region, and we can be honest people once more."

"You have arranged it all, have you?" said March, not at all in the tone she had expected to hear. "Give them the cheap town, and the good schools, and the twenty-five thousand dollars by all means. They can have everything but *you!*"

CHAPTER X.

THE long storm in August set in next day. A fine, close drizzle veiled the world by 7 o'clock. At 8.30, the twins and Fanny needed their waterproof cloaks for the walk to school. By noon the patter on the piazza roof and falling floods upon lawn and garden and streets were slow, but abundant. It was scrubbing day and closet day, and, as Hester fretted sometimes to methodical Mary Ann on Friday, "all the rest of the week," below stairs. Hetty had to prepare a dessert and to set the lunch table. Before going down she made up a little fire in the sewing room, and put out Hester's color-box, glass of water, stretching board, paper, and easel within easy reach, should she decide to use them. Silently, and not too suggestively, she set upon the table near by a vase containing some fine specimens of the moccasin flower sent in by May Gilchrist, with a note addressed to "Queen Mab." Hester hated hints, but if she lacked a study she would not have to look far for it.

It was "a bad day" with her. Her mother attributed it partly to her disappointment at not seeing her crony teacher.

Hetty, who had put the excited child to bed as soon as she got into the house the night before, held her peace. Mrs. Wayt, hovering from the nursery and her husband's chamber to the sewing room, saw that in her taciturn daughter's countenance that warned and kept her aloof. Another of Hester's biting sayings was that her mother, on the day succeeding one of her spouse's "seizures" was "betwixt the devil and the deep sea." She never admitted, even to her sister, that "dear Percy" was more than "unfortunate," yet read Hetty's disapprobation in averted looks and studiously commonplace talk.

Wan and limp the cripple reclined among the cushions Hetty packed about her in her wheeled chair. Blue shadows ringed mouth and eyes, and stretched themselves in the hollowed temples; the deft fingers were nerveless. Most of the time she seemed to watch the rain under drooping eyelids, so transparent as to show the dark irides beneath.

At half past eleven her mother stole in like a bit of drifted down.

"Dear, I have promised papa to go up to your room and lie down for half an hour. Annie is with him. She amuses him, and will be very good, she says. I told her to let you know if she wanted anything. May I leave the door open? She cannot turn this stiff bolt."

Annie was one of Hester's weak points. "Baby" never made her nervous or impatient, and much of the little one's precocity was due to intimate companionship with the disabled sister, whose plaything she was.

"Yes. All right!" murmured Hester, closing her eyes entirely.

She was deathly pallid in the uncolored gloom of a rainy noon.

"Or—if you feel like taking a nap, yourself?" hesitated Mrs. Wayt.

Tactful with her husband, and tender with all her household, she yet had the misfortune often to rub Hester's fur the wrong way. The delicately pencilled brows met over frowning eyes.

"No! no! you know I never sleep in the day! If you would never bother yourself with my peace and comfort, mamma, we should be on better terms. I am not a baby, or a—husband!"

She was not sorry for her ill humor or for the long gap between the last article and noun, when left to herself.

She lay upon a bed of thorns, each of which was endued with intelligent vitality. Earth was a waste. Heaven had never been. Hate herself for it as she might she had never, in all her rueful existence, known suffering comparable to that condensed into the three little minutes she had lived twelve hours ago.

When Hetty had come up to bed her face was beautiful with a strange white peace, at sight of which Hester held her breath. Coming swiftly, but without bustle, across the room, she kneeled by the bed and gathered the frail form in the dear, strong arms that had cradled it a thousand times. Her eyes sparkled, her lips were parted by quick breaths, but she tried to speak quietly.

"Precious child! you should be asleep. But I am glad you are not, for I have a message for you. We—you and I—are to take no anxious thought for to-morrow, or for any more of the to-morrows we are to spend together. March told me to say that and to give you this!" laying a kiss upon her lips. "For he loves me, Hester, darling, and you are to live with us! Just as we planned, ever and ever so long ago! But what day dream was ever so beautiful as this?"

For one of the three awful minutes Hester thought and hoped she was dying. The frightened blood ebbed back with turbulence that threw her into a spasm of trembling and weeping. She recollected pushing Hetty away, then clutching her frantically to pull her down for a storm of passionate kisses given between tearless sobs. Then she gave way to wheezing shrieks of laughter, which Hetty tried to check. She would not let her move or speak after that.

"How thoughtless in me not to know that you were too much unnerved to bear another shock—even of happiness!" said the loving nurse. "No! don't try to offer so much as a word of congratulation. It will keep! All we have to do to-night is to obey the order of our superior officer, and not think—only trust!"

In the morning there was no opportunity for speech-making. A night of suffering had beaten Hester dumb.

"Nobody could be surprised at that!" cooed Hetty, as she rubbed and bathed the throbbing spine. "If I could but pour down this aching column some of my redundant vitality!"

Hester detested herself in acknowledging the fervent sincerity of the wish. Hetty would willingly divide her life with her, as she had said yesterday that she meant to divide her fortune.

"Half for you while I live! All for you when I am gone!"

The sad sweetness of the smile accompanying the words was as little like the wonderful white shining of last night as the lot cast for Hetty was like that of the deformed dwarf whose height of grotesque folly was attained when she loved—first, in dreams and in "drifting"—then, all unconsciously, in actual scenes and waking moments—one whose whole heart belonged to the woman who had "made her over," to whom she owed life, brain, and soul!

She was to live with them! Hetty must make her partaker of her every good. By force of long habit, Hester fell to planning the house the three would inhabit. She was herself—always helpless, never less a burden than now—a piece of rubbish in the pretty rooms, a clog upon domestic machinery—a barrier to social pleasure—the inadmissible third in the married *tête-à-tête*.

She writhed impotently. More useless than a toy; more troublesome than a baby—uglier than the meanest insect that crawls—she must yet submit to the fate that fastened her upon the young lives of her custodians.

"I doubt if I could even take my own life!" she meditated darkly. "In my fits of rage and despair, I used to threaten to roll my chair down the stairs and break my neck to 'finish the job.' I said it once to mamma. I wonder sometimes if that is the reason Tony puts up gates across the top of the stairs wherever we go? He says it is to keep baby Annie from tumbling down. I haven't cared to die lately, but to-day I wish my soul had floated clean out of my body in that five minute make-believe under the pink tent of the apple tree, three months ago.

"I suppose he will be coming here constantly, now. Hetty won't belong to me anymore. I am very wicked! I am jealous of her with him, and of him with her! I am a spiteful, malicious, broken-backed toad! Oh, how I despise Hester Wayt! And I owe it all to *him!*"

She glowered revengefully at the door her mother had left unclosed.

Baby Annie was having a lovely hour with "dee papa." He had not left his bed, but the nausea and sense of goneness with which he had awakened, were yielding to the administration of minute potions of opium by his wife, at stated intervals. A fit of delirium tremens, induced by the failure to "cool him off" *secundum artem*, had brought about Homer's introduction to his nominal employer. Routed from his secret lodgings under the roof-tree at one o'clock of a winter morning, Hetty's waif had first run for a doctor, and, pending his arrival, pinioned the raving patient with his sinewy arms until the man of intelligent measures took charge of the case. Mrs. Wayt had run no such risks since.

Her lord never confessed that he took opium or ardent spirits. Indeed, he made capital of his total abstinence even from tobacco. There was always a cause, natural or violent, for his attacks. The Chicago seizure followed upon his rashness in swallowing, "mistaking it for mineral water," a pint of spirits of wine, bought for cleaning his Sunday suit. Other turns he attributed, severally, to dyspepsia, to vertigo, to over-study, and to extreme heat. A sunstroke, suffered when he was in college, rendered him peculiarly sensitive to hot weather. His wife never gainsaid his elaborate explanations. He was her Percy, her conscience, her king. She not only went backward with the cloak of love to conceal his shame, but she affected to forget the degradation when he became sober.

Many women in a thousand, and about one man in twenty millions, are "built so." The policy—or principle—may be humane. It is not Godlike. The All-Merciful calls sinners to repentance before offering pardon. The Church insists upon conviction as a preliminary to conversion. Mrs. Wayt was a Christian and a churchwoman, but she clung pathetically to belief in the efficacy of her plan for the reclamation of her husband. In life, or in death, she would not have upon her soul the weight of a reproach addressed to him whom she had sworn to "honor." Love was omnipotent. In time he would learn the depth of hers and be lured back to the right way.

He was plaintive this forenoon, but not peevish. His eyes were bloodshot; his tongue was furry; there was a gnawing in the pit of his stomach and an unaccountable ache at the base of the brain.

"I have missed another sunstroke by a hair's breadth," he informed his wife. "I almost regret that we did not go to the seashore. My summer labors are exhausting the reserves of vital energy."

"Why not run down to the beach for a day or two next week?" suggested Mrs. Wayt. "Now that your wife is an heiress, you can afford a change of air, now and then."

A dull red arose in the sallow cheek. He pulled her down to kiss her.

"The best, sweetest wife ever given to man!" he said.

After that he bade her get a little rest. She must have slept little the night before. Annie would keep him company. While his head was so light and his tongue so thick Annie's was the best society for him. She made no demand upon intellectual forces. He sent the best wife ever given to man off lightened in spirit, and grateful for the effort he made to appease her anxiety and to affect the gayety he could not be supposed to feel. She looked back at the door to exchange affectionate smiles with the dear, unselfish fellow.

He watched the baby's pretty, quaint pretense of "being mamma," and hearkened to the drip and plash of the rain until the gnawing in his stomach re-asserted itself importunately. He knew what it meant. It was the demand of the devil-appetite he had created long ago—his Frankenstein, his Old Man of the Sea, his body of death, lashed fast to him, lying down when he lay down, rising up at his awakening, keeping step with him, however he might try to flee. The lust he had courted rashly—now become flesh of his flesh and bone of his bone.

His wife had carried off the phial of opium. But he had secreted a supply of the drug for such emergencies since she had found out the phosphate device and privately confiscated the stout blue bottle. He always carried a small Greek Testament in his hip pocket. Mrs. Wayt's furtive search of his clothes every night, after making sure that he was asleep, had not extended to the removal of the sacred volume.

He arose stealthily, steadied his reeling head by holding hard to the back of his neck with one hand, while the other caught at the chairs and bed-foot; tiptoed to the closet, found his black cloth pantaloons, drew out the Testament, and extracted from the depths beneath a wad of silken, rustleless paper. Within was a lump of dark brown paste.

"Tan'y! tan'y!" twittered Annie's sweet, small pipe. "Give baby a piece! p'ease, dee papa!"

He hurried back into bed. If the child were overheard Hetty might look in. And Hester's sharp ears were across the hall.

"No, baby; papa has no candy." He was so startled and unmanned that he had to wet his lips with a tongue almost as parched before he could articulate. "Papa's head aches badly. Will Annie sing him to sleep?"

Hester heard, through her stupor of misery, the weak little voice and the thump of the low rocking chair as baby crooned to the dolly cuddled in her arms and to "dee papa," the song learned from Hester's self:

"S'eep, baby, s'eep.

The angels watch 'y s'eep.

The fairies s'ake 'e d'eamland t'ee,

An' all'e d'eams 'ey fall ow'ee.

S'eep, baby, s'eep!"

The rain fell straight and strong. The heavy pour had beaten all motion out of the air, but the gurgling of water pipes and the resonance of the tinned roof gave the impression of a tumultuous storm. Through the register and chimney arose a far-off humming from the cellar, where Homer was "redding up." Hester's acute ears divided the sound into notes and words:

"An' we buried her deep, yes! deep among the rocks.

On the banks of the Oma-ha!"

Annie stopped singing. "Dolly mus' lie down in her twadle, an' mamma mate her some tea!" Hester heard her say. At another time she would have speculated, perhaps anxiously, as to the processes going on when the clatter of metal and the tinkle of china arose, accompanied by the fitful bursts of song and a monologue of exclamations.

"Oh! oh! *tate tare*, dee papa!" came presently in a frightened tone. Then louder: "Papa! dee papa! wate up! you'll det afire!"

Wee feet raced across the hall, a round face, red and scared, appeared in the doorway.

"Hetter! Hetter! tum, wate up dee papa! 'E bed is on fire!"

Through the doors left open behind her Hester saw a lurid glare, a column of smoke.

Shrieking for help at the top of her feeble lungs she plied the levers of her chair and rolled rapidly into the burning room. Upon the table at the foot of the bed had stood the spirit lamp and copper teakettle used by Mrs. Wayt in heating her husband's phosphate draughts at night. Annie had lighted the lamp and contrived to knock it over upon the bed. The alcohol had ignited and poured over the counterpane.

Mr. Wayt lay, unstirring, amid the running flames. Hester made straight for him, leaned far out of her chair, to pull off the blazing covers, "Papa! papa! papa!"

He had not heard the word from her in ten years. He was not to hear it now.

Mrs. Wayt, Hetty, March Gilchrist, and the servants, rushing to the spot, found father and child enwrapped in the same scorching pall.

"Mr. Wayt died at midnight," reported the Fairhill papers. "He never regained consciousness. The heroic daughter who lost her life in attempting to rescue a beloved parent lived until daybreak.

"'They were lovely and pleasant in their lives, and in their deaths they were not divided.'"

"I must be going, dear heart!" whispered Hetty's namechild, as the August dawn, made faint by showers, glimmered through the windows. "I cannot see you. Would Mr. March mind kissing me 'good-by'?"

"Mind?" He could not restrain the great sob. A tear fell with the kiss.

"Dear little friend! my sweet sister!"

The glorious eyes, darkened by death and almost sightless, widened in turning toward him. She smiled radiantly.

"Thank you for calling me *that*. Now, Miss May! And poor mamma! I wish I had been a better child to you! Hetty, dearest! hold me fast and kiss me last of all! You will be very happy, darling! But you won't forget me—will you? I heard the doctors say"—a gleam of the old fantastic humor playing about her mouth—"that I had swallowed the flame. I think they were right—for the—*bitterness is all—burned—out—of my heart!*"

A SOCIAL SUCCESS.

PART I.

"I KNOW it is *horrid* to swoop down upon you at this barbarously early hour, but I couldn't help coming the minute I received your card. We get our mail at the breakfast table, and I fairly screamed with joy when I opened the envelope. 'Jack!' I said, '*who* do you think has come to New York to live?'

"'The Picaninnies and the Joblillies and the Garyulies, and probably the grand Panjandrum himself,' said my gentleman.

"You know what a tease he is. Oh, no, you don't! for you never met him. But you will before long! 'Better than all of them put together, with the little round button on top,' said I. (You see I am used to his chaff!) 'My very dearest school friend, of whom you have heard me talk ten thousand times— Susie Barnes, now Mrs. Cornell. She has been living five years in Brooklyn (and I've always declared I'd rather go to Canada than to Brooklyn) and here's her card telling me that she has returned to civilization. Mrs. Arthur Hayward Cornell, No. — West Sixty-seventh St.' At that he pricked up his ears.

"'That's the new cashier in the Pin and Needle Bank,' says he. 'Somebody was talking of him at the Club last night.' And nothing would do but I must tell him all about you. In going over the story and thinking of the dear old times, my heart got so warm and full that I rushed off by the time he was out of the house."

Mrs. John Hitt, a well-dressed, prettyish woman, whom the cold morning light showed to be also a trifle society-worn, embraced her hostess anew, and then held her off at arm's length for inspection.

"You *sweet* old girl! what sort of life have you led that you have kept your roses, your dimples, and the sparkle in your eyes all these years? Do you know that you are absolutely bewitching?"

The lately recovered friend smiled, coloring as a woman of Mrs. Hitt's world could not have done.

"You are the same impulsive Kitty!" she said affectionately. "I have had a quiet, busy, happy life with Arthur and the children. Three babies in five years do not give a housekeeper much time for anything but domestic duties."

"I should think not, indeed!" The shiver of shoulders was well-executed, the heavenward cast of eyes and hands dramatic. "I wonder you live to tell it! One child in six years has been enough to unsettle *my* wits. Now that you are once more within my reach (Oh, you *darling!*) we must make up for lost time and see a great deal of each other! Do you ever sing nowadays? Or have you let your music go to the dogs? I suppose so, if Providence *has* interfered to save your wild-rose complexion. I was *raving* to Jack this morning over the voice you used to have, and your genius for theatricals and all that. 'Indeed,' said I, 'there was nothing that girl *couldn't* do.' To think of wasting such an organ, or wearing it thin in crooning nursery ditties."

Mrs. Cornell laughed a soft, merry burst of amusement, at which the other eyed her curiously.

"You behave less like an exhumed corpse than anybody could imagine who knew of your five years in Brooklyn, and the three younglings. What amuses you?"

"Nothing, except your determination to regard me as dead, buried, and resurrected. So far from giving up my music, I have practiced more steadily than if I had spent more evenings abroad. You know I studied vocal and instrumental music with the intention of making it my profession. Arthur agrees with me that what is once learned should never be lost. Then, when my little girls are ready to be taught, I can instruct them myself. We had a number of musical friends in Brooklyn, and a pleasant circle of acquaintances. We have not lived in—*Hoboken*," cried the hostess in whimsical vexation. "I don't see why New Yorkers always talk of Brooklyn as if it were as far off and as much a *terra incognita* as the moon. We are inhabitants of the same planet as yourselves."

The visitor patted the back of her companion's hand, soothingly. "You are a New Yorker *now*—one of us!" she purred. "In six months you would as soon cross the Styx as the East River, even on that overgrown, preposterous Bridge the Brooklynites give themselves such airs over. How prettily settled you are!" staring, rather than glancing about the apartment. "These are nice drawing rooms and furnished in excellent taste."

Mrs. Cornell had regarded them as "parlors," but her first concession to Mrs. Hitt's better knowledge was to look accustomed to the new term. She fought down with equal success the impulse to classify Kitty's open admiration with the amiable patronage of which Brooklyn people are inclined to suspect New Yorkers. She plumed herself modestly upon her taste in house-furnishing and upon the ability to make cheap things look as if they had cost a good deal. She had withheld the fact of the change of residence from metropolitan acquaintances until her house was in order that might defy unfavorable criticism. It was kind in Kitty to run in so unceremoniously and to be glad of the chance to renew their early intimacy. In spite of Arthur and the children, she had begun to be somewhat homesick in the great whirling world about her.

"Like a chip in the Atlantic Ocean!" Thus she had described her sensations to her husband that very morning. "I suppose I shall get used to it after a while, especially as Brooklyn and New York are, to all intents and purposes, one and the same city."

She asserted it stoutly, knowing all the while that Moscow and New Orleans were as nearly homogeneous.

Yes! Kitty was heartily welcome to the stranger in an unknown territory. Mrs. Hitt was not intellectual, and judged by standards Arthur Cornell's wife had come to revere sincerely, she was not especially refined in speech and bearing. Or were Susie's tastes too quiet and her ideas old-fashioned, that her interlocutor's crisp sayings sounded pert, and the bright brown eyes and fixed flush upon the cheekbones were artificially aggressive? Her former chum had always been warm-hearted, if inconveniently outspoken. And she was a New Yorker, and fashionable. Susie's cherished ambition, unavowed even to Arthur while it was expedient for them to live simply, was to be fashionable, brilliant, and courted—a member in good and regular standing in the Society of which Mrs. Sherwood lectured, and Ellen Olney Kirk wrote, and to which Jenkyns Knickerbocker was *au fait*. A certain something that was not air or tone, deportment or attire, and yet partook of all these as pot-pourri of rose-breath, spices, and perfumed oils—marked Kitty Hitt as an *habituée* of the charmed Reserve. She was not, perhaps, one of the Four Hundred selected from the Upper Ten Thousand by processes as arbitrary, to human judgment, as those by which Gideon's three hundred were picked out from the hosts of Israel. Susie was no simpleton, albeit ambitious. Mr. Hitt was a stockbroker; hence manifestly in the line of promotion, but there were degrees of elevation upon even Olympus. Her imagination durst not lift eyes to the cloud-wreathed summit where chief gods held revel, guarded from vulgar intrusion by Gabriel Macallister. The climate and manner of life a few leagues lower down would, as she felt, suit her better than the rarified atmosphere of the extremest heights. She had always meant to climb, and successfully, when time and opportunity should serve. From the moment the passage of the river was determined upon as a business necessity, she felt intuitively that both of these were near.

"We think them cozy!" she assented quietly to the visitor's praise of her rooms.

"Cozy! they are *lovely!*"

While she talked she raised her eye-glasses to make note of some fine etchings upon the walls and a choice water-color upon an easel, and took in, in passing, the circumstance that the rugs laid upon the polished floor were of prime quality, although neither large nor numerous.

"I do hope you don't mean to shut yourself up in your pretty cage as so many pattern wives and mothers—particularly Brooklyn women" (roguishly) "do?

That's the reason American society is so crude and colorless. With your face and figure and accomplishments (I haven't forgotten how divinely you recite) you ought to become a Social Success—a star in the world of Society. You ought indeed!" drowning the feeble murmur of dissent. "There's many a so-named leader of the gay world who doesn't hold, and who never did hold such a card. Just trust yourself to me, and I will prove all I promise."

"But, my dear Kitty, I lack the Open Sesame to the Gotham Innermost— Money! Only the repeatedly-millionaired can pass the outer courts."

"There it is! Epigrams and bon-mots drop from your lips as pearls and diamonds used to tumble out whenever the good little girl in the Fairy-tale opened her mouth. As to millions of money—bah!" with a gesture of royal disdain. "Our best people are not the richest. The true New Yorker knows that. Of course one must live and dress well, but your husband's means amply warrant *that*. Jack says cashiers get from ten to fifteen thousand dollars a year. Your face, your manner, and your talents are all the passport you require when once you are introduced. I claim the privilege of doing it. And, as an initial step, I want you and Mr. Cornell to dine with us to-morrow evening. I'll ask six or eight of the nicest people I know to meet you. They'll excuse the shortness of the notice when they see what a reason I have for calling them together. Put on a pretty gown and look your loveliest and bring along some music. I mean that you shall capture all hearts. I shall be grieved to the quick if you don't. The hour will be seven—*sharp*. Punctuality is the soul of good humor in a dinner company. I must run away. I have an appointment with a tyrannical dressmaker at half-past ten; Mr. Lincoln's Literature Class at eleven; a luncheon at half-past one; and afternoon tea, anywhere from four to six; a dinner party, and after that the opera. Such a whirl! Yet, as I say to Jack when he grumbles that we never have a quiet home evening—it is the only life worth living, as you'll own when you've had a taste of it! (You *dear* thing! it rests my tired eyes just to look at you!) Here's Jack's card for Mr. Cornell. I'm just dying to see him and if he is good enough for you."

"A great deal too good!" ejaculated Susie, earnestly, through this accidental gap in the monologue. "The dearest, most generous fellow!"

"*Cela va sans dire*—with the Brooklyn model! I'm so happy that you are one of us, and no longer a pattern article. Good-by!"

"There! I let her go without showing her the children," reflected Mrs. Cornell, when she got back her breath. "But we had so much to talk of it is no wonder we forgot them. There are no friends like the old friends. How unjust we are sometimes! I came near not sending her my card because she had never been over to Brooklyn to see me all the while I was there. And Arthur advised me against doing it. He would have it that it is no further from New York to Brooklyn than from Brooklyn to New York. He predicted, too, that she would never come to see me here. He says there's no other memory so short as that of a woman who has risen fast upon the social ladder. This ought to be a lesson in Christian charity to us both. Kitty's heart is always in the right place."

With a becoming mantling of rose-pink in her cheeks, she went singing about her "drawing" rooms, altering the angle of chairs and sofas, and the arrangement of bric-a-brac, already viewing her appointments through Kitty's eye-glasses. Her thoughts were running upon the projected dinner party. She was the proud owner of a black velvet gown with a trained skirt, and a V-shaped front, and of dainty laces wherewith to fill the triangle. She had a diamond pin and earrings—wedding gifts from the wealthy aunt for whom she was named. The same generous relative had bestowed upon her, at different holiday seasons, the rugs and pictures that adorned her house. Aunt Susan might always be depended upon to do the handsome thing, and she was fond of this niece and her "steady" husband. The home of Susie's girlhood had been more plainly furnished, as Kitty had known and must recollect. It was natural that the elegant grace characterizing Mrs. Cornell's abode should mislead the shrewd observer in the estimate of the cashier's income. Without surmising what had suggested the remark, or that it was a "feeler," Mrs. Cornell smiled, yet a little uneasily, in recalling it.

"Kitty is so used to hearing of big sums that her ideas are vague on the subject of salaries," meditated the better informed wife. "She doesn't dream how handsomely people can live on six thousand dollars. Or that we got along on one-half that much in Brooklyn and laid aside something yearly. It is none of my business to set her right. Arthur doesn't care to have his money affairs discussed."

It did not occur to her as a possibility that from the pardonable disingenuousness any serious trouble could ever arise, yet she knew what Arthur would say. She heard, in imagination, his warning:

"Never sail under false colors, Susie!"

Therefore, in her animated description of call and conversation, she omitted all mention of Kitty's tentative allusion to their income. Not knowing his wife's old comrade, he might think her prying and impertinent in touching upon such a subject at all. Poor, dear Kitty! there were disadvantages in being so impetuously frank. A clear-headed cool reasoner like Arthur, for instance, was almost sure to misread her.

As our heroine had told Kitty, her married life had been quiet. Her vivacious friend would have called it "stupid." The circle of congenial friends had been circumscribed and most of them were people of moderate means and desires. Brooklyn might be called a segregation of neighborhoods, each district having manners, customs, and social code peculiar to the village that was its germ. As one settlement ran into another, a city grew that claims the respect of the mightier sister across the river. The Cornells had lived in a pleasant house in a pleasant street, and Susie had spoken truly in saying that they lived well. With no pretense of entertaining, they were cordially hospitable, "having" friends to supper, or to pass the evening, whenever fair occasion offered. For the children's sake the mother took her principal meal with them at one o'clock, but the hearty tea prepared for the father who had lunched frugally in town was invariably appetizing, being well cooked and daintily served. He had the privilege not always accorded to richer men who sit down daily to late "course dinners"—that of bringing a crony home with him whenever he pleased. It was like Arthur Cornell to choose as chance guests men who had not such homes as his—bank clerks from the country, Bohemian artists of good character and light purses, and the like. Such were the honored recipients of the hostess' smile and warm handshake. She had won the admiring reverence of more than one homeless bachelor by her skill in delicate and savory cookery and the gracious friendliness of her welcome, and these, oftener than any other class, composed the delighted audience of the music Arthur called for every evening.

Once or twice a month husband and wife went to the theater or a concert, and twice or at the most three times a year to the opera. They were pretty sure to have complimentary tickets to the water-color exhibition and other displays of paintings in Brooklyn or New York. Of receptions, they knew comparatively little except such as followed weddings among their acquaintances. Neither had ever attended a regular dinner party gotten up by a professional caterer, and the ladies' luncheon of eight, ten, or a dozen courses was unknown by the seeing of the eyes and the tasting of the palate to the bright woman whose social successes in a new arena were foretold by the sanguine admirer who craved the pleasure of bringing her out. There are still in fast growing American cities tens of thousands of such people who live honestly, comfortably, and beneficently, and whose homes are refined centers of happiness and goodness.

There was, then, cause for the wife's pleasurable flutter of spirits and the doubtful satisfaction expressed, against his intention, in the husband's visage at the close prospect of a state banquet given in honor of their undistinguished selves, at which anonymous edibles would be washed down with foreign wines, and spicy *entrées* be punctuated by spicy hors *d'œuvres*. Arthur's predominant quality was sound sense, and as his spouse had anticipated, his first emotion after hearing her tale was wonder at the sudden and violent increase of friendship consequent upon their change of residence, in one who had apparently forgotten the unimportant fact of her favorite schoolfellow's existence for more than five years.

"I can't imagine why she should care to take us up now," he demurred.

Susie's ready flush testified to the hurt he had dealt her pride or affections. She thought to the latter.

"If you would only not let your prejudice master your reason!" she sighed. "All New York women hate and dread ferries."

"There is the Bridge!" put in the Brooklyn-born literalist.

"Which would have taken visitors *miles* away from us. I was afraid you would wet-blanket the whole affair. I really dreaded to tell you of what I was silly enough to look forward to with pleasure. You see you don't know what a fine, genuine creature Kitty is. But we won't dispute over her or her dinner party. I can write to her and say that we regret our inability to accept the invitation."

Arthur closed his teeth upon another struggling sentence. Although even less of a society man than she was of a society woman, he had a definite impression that invitations to dinner were usually sent out some days in advance of the "occasion." Less distinct, because intuitive, was the idea that gay young women, already laden with social obligations, did not press attentions upon everyday folk from Brooklyn, E. D., unless they hoped to gain something by it, or were addicted to patronage. The former hypothesis being, as he conceived, untenable, it followed that Mrs. Hitt, a good-natured rattle, must have said more than she meant of her intentions toward the strangers, or that she had a native fondness for playing the lady patroness.

Loving and admiring his wife from the full depths of a quiet heart, he held all this back. Susie was vivacious, ready of wit and speech, and he was not. She dearly enjoyed excitement and new acquaintances. Give him dressing jacket, slippers, and an interesting book, or his wife's music and his own fireside, and he would not have exchanged places with Ward Macallister at his complacent best. Susie would shine anywhere; she was born to it! He was not even a first-class reflector of her rays. Yet this noblest of women had stood by him with cheerful gallantry in their less prosperous days. He had told her over and over that she had hidden her light under a bushel in becoming the mistress of such a home as he had to give her, but she had loyally denied this, and borne her part bravely in the struggle to lap the non-elastic ends of their common income. To her capital management he owed much of their present comfort.

Arthur Cornell reasoned slowly, but always in a straight line.

"I am a selfish, brutal fellow, darling," he said at this point of his cogitations. "I am afraid I am a little tired to-night. We have had a busy day at the Bank.

You mustn't mind my growls. When we have had sup—dinner, I would say!—you'll find me more than willing to listen and sympathize."

Her satisfactory answer was to come over and kiss him silently, taking his head between her hands and laying her cheek upon it. The hair was getting thin on the top, and the gaslight brought into gleaming conspicuousness a few gray hairs. He was older than she by nine years. It would not be surprising if, for a long time yet, he continued to say "supper" instead of "dinner." She was certain he would never learn to talk of the "drawing room." But he was her very own, and dearly beloved, and the kindest, noblest fellow in the world. Whatever he might do or say, she could never be angry with or ashamed of him.

PART II.

THE evening meal—an excellent one, to which Mr. Cornell did ample justice—was over. Father and mother, as was their custom, had visited the nursery in company, heard the children's prayers, and kissed them "good-night." The orderly household had settled down into cheerful quiet that fell like dew upon weary nerves. Susie went to the piano presently and played a pensive *nocturne*, then sang softly a couple of Arthur's favorite ballads. The night was blustering, and in the silence succeeding the music, the wedded pair, seated before the soft-coal fire in the back parlor, heard the hurrying tread of passers-by echoing sharply from the frozen stones.

Arthur ended the restful pause. His choice of a theme and the lightness of his tone were heroic.

"Low neck and short sleeves for me to-morrow night, I suppose, old lady? That is to say, claw-hammer, and low-cut vest. It's lucky I had them made for Lou Wilson's wedding last winter. There wouldn't be time to get up the proper rig, and regrets based upon 'No dress-coat' would be rather awkward."

"Decidedly! No man of whatever age should be without one," rejoined the nascent fashionist. "Some men never sit down to dinner except in evening dress. It must be very nice to live in that way. I like such graceful ceremony in everyday customs."

Arthur cast about for something neater to say than the dismayed ejaculation bitten off just in time.

"It must help a fellow to feel altogether at his ease in his company accouterments"—inspiration coming in the nick of time. "Most men look, and, judging by myself, feel like newly imported restaurant waiters when decked out in their swallow-tails."

The conventional "dress coat" is a shrewd test of innate gentlehood. A thoroughbred is never more truly one than when thus appareled. The best it can do for the plebeian, who would prefer to eat his dinner in his shirt-sleeves, is to bring him up to the level of a hotel waiter.

Arthur looked like an unassuming gentleman on the following evening, when he joined his wife below-stairs. If he had not an air of fashion, he had not a touch of the vulgarian. Susie's mien was, as he assured her, that of a queen. Her head was set well above a pair of graceful shoulders, she carried herself and managed her train cleverly. Arthur had brought her a cluster of pink roses, all of which she wore in her corsage except one bud which she pinned in his buttonhole. He put a careful finger under her chin, and lifted her face to let the full light of the chandelier rain upon it.

"It would have been a pity to keep you all to myself to-night," he said.

The weather was raw, with menace of rain or snow, but neither of them thought of the extravagance of a carriage. As she had done upon previous festal occasions, the wife looped up the trailing breadths of velvet, and secured them into a "walking length" of skirt with safety pins. Over her gala attire she cast a voluminous waterproof, buttoned all the way down the front. A bonnet would have deranged her *coiffure*, and she wore, instead, a black Spanish lace scarf knotted under her chin. Slippers and light gloves went in a reticule slung upon her arm.

It lacked five minutes of seven when they alighted from a street-car within a block of the Hitts' abode. Four carriages were in line before the door, and from these stepped men swathed in long, light ulsters, who assisted to alight and ascend the stone steps apparitions in furred and embroidered opera cloaks that ravished Susie's wits, in the swift transit of the gorgeous beings from curbstone to the hospitable entrance. A dizzying sensation of unreality, such as one experiences in finding himself unexpectedly upon a great height, seized upon her. Could these people be collected to meet *her?* Humbled, yet elated, she entered the house, and obeying the directions of the footman at the foot of the stairs, mounted to the dressing room.

Four women in such elaborate toilets that our heroine felt forthwith like a crow among birds-of-paradise, glanced carelessly over their shoulders at her without suspending their chatter to one another, and went on talking and shaking out their draperies. Each, in resigning her wraps to the maids in waiting, stepped forth ready for drawing-room parade. Susie retreated to a corner and began hurriedly to disembarrass herself of her waterproof and to let down her skirt. A maid followed her presently.

"Can I help you?" professionally supercilious.

"Thank you. If you would be so good as to take off my boots, I should be obliged."

The formula was ill-advised and justified the heightened hauteur of the smart Abigail. With pursed mouth and disdainful finger-tips, she removed the evidences that the wearer had trudged over muddy streets to get here, and as gingerly fitted on the dry slippers. The heat in Susie's cheeks scorched the delicate skin when she found that the time consumed in her preparations had detained her above-stairs after everybody else had gone down. And Kitty had enjoined punctuality! She met her husband in the upper hall with a distressed look.

"We are *horribly* late," she whispered.

"I don't suppose it makes any difference," responded he to comfort her. "It's fashionable to be late, isn't it?"

"Not at dinners," she had barely time to admonish him when they crossed the threshold of the drawing room.

Kitty advanced with *empressement* to meet them, but that they were behind time was manifest from the celerity with which she introduced her husband, and without the interval of a second, the man who was to take Mrs. Cornell in to dinner. Then she whisked Mr. Cornell up to a dried-up little woman in pearl-colored velvet, presented him, asked him to take charge of her into the dining room, herself laid hold of another man's arm, and signaled her husband to lead the way.

Arthur seldom lost his perceptive and reasoning faculties, and having read descriptions of state dinners and breakfasts, bethought himself that had his wife and himself been in truth chief guests, they would have been paired off with host and hostess. Moreover, although there was a vast deal of talking at table and he did his conscientious best to make conversation with the velvet-clad mummy consigned to him, he had all the time the feeling of being left out in the cold. Nobody addressed him directly in word, or indirectly by glance, and at length, in gentlemanly despair of diverting the attention of his fair companion from her plate to himself, he let her eat in peace and pleased himself by comparing the rosy, piquant face of his wife with the bismuth-and-rouge-powdered visages to the right, left, and front of her. Susie seemed to be getting on swimmingly. The man next to her was chatting gayly, and evidently recognized a responsive spirit in his fair companion. How easily and naturally she met his advances, and how gracefully she fitted into her novel position! What were pomps and vanities to him accorded with her tastes. Again he thought how niggardly would have been the refusal to allow her to take the place she so adorned.

Not even love's eye penetrated the doughty visor she kept jealously closed throughout the meal. To begin with, she *took the wrong fork for the raw oysters!* As course succeeded course, the dreadful implement, in style so unlike those left beside other plates, actually *grinned* at her with every prong. Everybody must be aware of the solecism and deduce the truth that this was her first dinner party. She was sure that she caught the waiters exchanging winks over the fork, and that out of sheer malice, they allowed the tell-tale to lie in full sight. The apprehension that she would eventually be compelled to use the frail absurdity or leave untouched something—meat or game, perhaps—assailed her. While she hearkened to the flippant nothings her escort mistook for elegant small-talk, and plucked up heart for repartee, hot and cold sweats broke out all over her. Had she obeyed inclination that approximated frenzy at times, she would have crept under the table and rolled over on the floor in anguished mortification. If her sleight-of-hand had been equal to the rash adventure, she would have pocketed the wretched bugbear in desperation akin to that which makes the murderer fling far from him the weapon with which the deed was done.

When the ghastly petty torture was ended by the removal of the obnoxious article, and the substitution of one larger, plainer, and less obvious, the poor woman could have kissed the perfunctory hand that lifted the incubus from her soul.

She made other blunders, but none that were so glaring as this. Each was a lesson and a stimulus to perfect herself in the *minutiæ* of social etiquette. Before long, she would need no schooling; would lead, instead of following. She would know better another time, too, how to dress herself. Kitty's gown of cream-colored *faille*, flounced with lace; the pale blue brocade of one woman, and the pink-and-silver bravery of a third, the maize velvet and black lace of the dowager across the table, and the mauve-and-white marvel of still another toilet, threw her apparel into blackest shade. She caught herself hoping people would think that she was in slight mourning. Besides her allotted attendant nobody at table spoke a word to her, but Kitty shot many a smile at her during the feast, and nodded several times in significance that might be approval or reassurance. Mr. Hitt, a rather handsome man with big, bold eyes, looked hard at her now and then, but did not accost her, even after he grew talkative under the faster flow of wine. His glasses were filled so often and emptied so quickly that Susie wondered to see his wife's smiling unconcern. Perhaps she had faith in the strength of his brain.

Arthur did not touch one of the five chalices of different shapes and colors flanking his plate, and Susie was weak enough, perceiving that his conduct in this respect was exceptional, to feel mortified by his eccentricity. It was in bad taste, she thought, to offer tacit censure of the practice of host and fellow-guests. To nullify the unfavorable impression of her husband's singularity, she sipped from each of her glasses, and dipped so deeply into the iced champagne which cooled thirst excited by highly seasoned viands, the heated room and agitation of spirits, that her bloom was more vivid when she arose from dinner than when she sat down. She was quite at ease now, and enjoying, with the zest of an artistic nature, the features of the novel scene.

The tempered light streaming over and repeated by silver, china, and cut-glass; the flower-borders that criss-crossed the lace table-cover laid over rose-colored satin, the superb costumes of the women and the faultless garments of the men; the rapid, noiseless exchange of one delicacy for another, some of the dishes being as new to her as would have been an *entrée* of peacocks' brains or a *salmi* of nightingales' tongues—were fascinating to one whose love of the picturesque and beautiful was a passion. This was the sort of thing she had read of in English novels and American newspapers, the enchanting mode of life for which she had yearned secretly, the atmosphere in which she should have been born.

The return in feminine file to the drawing room of part of the company was a stage of the pageant with which *Jane Eyre's* life at Thornhill, and Annie Edwards' and Ouida's stories of hospitality at English country houses had made her familiar. She hoped nobody else noticed Arthur's surprised stare, as the men arose and remained standing, with no movement in the direction of the escaping fair ones. With flutter and buzz and silken rustle, the dames swept through the hall back into the drawing room and disposed themselves upon couches and in easy-chairs, where tiny glasses of perfumed liqueur were handed to them.

"Exactly like a story of Oriental life," mused entranced Susie.

Now, for the first time, Kitty had the opportunity to show to her school-friend the pointed and peculiar attentions the rhapsodies of yesterday had authorized her to expect. Up to this moment nobody had been introduced to her except the man who took her to dinner.

"I must have you know all these friends of mine," she purred, taking Susie's hand in both of hers, and leading her with engaging "gush" up to the mauve-and-white marvel.

"Mrs. Vansittart, this is my *dear* old school-fellow, Mrs. Cornell, who is going to play something for us now, and after a while, to sing several somethings, and when our audience is enlarged by the return of the men to us lorn women, she will, if properly entreated, give us some of her charming recitations. Ah! you may well look surprised. It is granted to few women to combine so many talents, but when you have heard her, you will see that I do not promise too much.

"Mrs. Roberts!" to the symphony in pink-and-silver—"I bespeak your admiration for my friend and school-crony"—etc., etc., until the blushing *débutante* was the focus of six pairs of eyes, critical, indifferent, and amiable, and wished that dear Kitty were not so incorrigibly enthusiastic in praising those she loved.

Anyone but a refined novice would have divined at once that the act of passing her around, like a plate of hot cakes, argued one of two things— either that she was a "professional" of some sort, or that her hostess was lamentably ignorant of the law demanding that the one to be honored by an introduction should stand still and have the other party to the ceremony brought to her. Kitty, at least, was no novice, and everybody except her "school-crony" comprehended exactly what the scene meant. Although she did not suspect it, she was on trial when she sat down to the piano, the show-woman beside her, as the guileless guest supposed, to give her affectionate encouragement. The first flash of her fingers across the keys was the signal for general silence, and the clapping of gloved hands at the conclusion of the brilliant overture attested intelligent appreciation. She was not allowed to leave the music stool for half an hour, one piece after another being called for, and the choice of selections putting her on her mettle. Her auditors were used to good music, and the assumption that she would gratify them was a delicate compliment.

Kitty came to her elbow at length with a glass of clear liquid, sparkling with pounded ice.

"Only lime-juice and water," she whispered, "to clear your voice. I have praised your singing until everybody is *wild* to hear you."

Susie smiled happily, glancing over her shoulder with an unconscious and graceful gesture of gratitude; a bow, slight, but comprehensive, she might have but had not copied from a popular prima donna. Another rapid run of the nimble fingers over the responsive ivory, and she glided into the prelude to Gounod's never-trite song, *"Chantez! Riez! Dormez!"*

She had sung but a few bars when her ear caught the muffled tread of feet in the hall. A side-glance at the mirror showed her a picture that might have been clipped from her British *contes de société*, the grouping of manly faces and fashionable dress coats in the curtained arch, all intent upon herself as the enchantress who held them mute and eager. Electric fire streamed through her veins, her voice soared and swelled as never before; her enunciation, exquisitely pure and clear, carried each word up to the loftiest story of the stilled mansion:

"Ah! riez, ma belle! riez! riez, toujours!"

"Fine, by Jove, now!" cried a big mustached man at Arthur's side, as the last notes died upon ecstatic ears. "Patti couldn't have done it better!"

The husband repeated this with other encomiums to the songstress after they got home. He made the tired but animated little woman sit down in an armchair and pulled off her rubbers and unbuttoned her boots in far different fashion from that in which the sleepy Abigail had put them on the feet and helped truss up the train of "the woman who hadn't come in a carriage like decent folks."

He had had a stupid evening. He couldn't make the women talk to him. He was not "a ladies' man," and every mother's daughter of them took in the truth at a glance. The men gabbled over their wine of what did not interest him, of clubs and horse races, and the fluctuations of fancy stocks. He neither smoked nor drank, and was the only man there who did not do both. His wife's music was to him the only redeeming feature of the occasion, and he would have enjoyed that more in his own parlor. But she was enraptured with everything and full of delightful anticipations. "Everybody had been so nice and kind, and what did ill-natured people mean by saying there was no real sociability among fashionable people? For her part, she believed that the higher one mounted in the social scale the more genuine goodness and refined feeling she would find." Several of the ladies had promised to call upon her, and, as one said, "to take her in with them."

Arthur hearkened silently. He had never been able to give her such pleasures, a fact that smote him hard when he saw how zestfully she drank of the newly opened spring. He would not "wet-blanket" her enthusiasm, so did not hint at a discovery made to him by a chance remark of a guest to the host. Invitations for this particular dinner party had been out for ten days.

"Then Susie and I were second fiddles," inferred the sensible cashier. "I wonder why she asked us at all!"

PART III.

MR. CORNELL'S unspoken suspicion that Mrs. Hitt would drop her school-friend as suddenly as she had picked her up was in a way to be falsified, if the events of the next few months were to be taken as testimony.

The two matrons were nearly inseparable—shopping, driving, walking, and visiting together. For Susie had a New York visiting list speedily, and almost every name stood for an introduction by her indefatigable "trainer." The epithet was the taciturn husband's, and, as may be surmised, was never uttered audibly. Susie's wardrobe, furniture, table—her very modes of speech—sustained variations that amazed old friends and confounded him who knew her best. The cherished black velvet she had thought "handsome enough for any occasion" was pronounced "quaintly becoming, but too old for the wearer by twenty-five years." Slashed and dashed and lashed with gold-color, it did duty as a house evening gown. For small luncheons, she had a tailor-made costume of fawn-colored cloth embroidered and combined with silk; for "swell" luncheons, a rich silk—black ground relieved by narrow crimson stripes, and made en *demi-train*.

For at-home afternoons were two tea gowns; before she received her second dinner invitation, she had made by Mrs. Hitt's dressmaker—("a Frenchwoman who doesn't know enough yet to charge American prices, my dear, and I hold it to be a sin to *throw* money away!") a robe of white brocade and sea-green velvet, in which garb she showed like a moss-rose bud, according to her dear friend and trumpeter.

These strides into the realm of fashion, if at first startling to the *débutante*, were quickly acknowledged to be imperatively necessary if one would really live. Kitty's taste in dress approximated genius. Even she was hardly prepared for the ready following of her neophyte.

Had she needed corroborative evidence of the cashier's liberal income, his wife's command of considerable sums supplied it. With all her frankness, Mrs. Cornell did not confide to her bosom-friend where she obtained the ready money that gained her credit with new tradespeople.

Now and then an uneasy qualm stirred the would-be comfortable soul of the wife as to how much or how little Arthur speculated within his sober soul upon the probable cost of her new outfit. There were two thousand dollars deposited in her name, and drawing interest in a Brooklyn Savings Bank. The rich aunt had given her namechild three-quarters of it from time to time. The young couple had saved the rest, and it was tacitly understood that it should not be touched except of necessity. No landmark in her new career was more pronounced than Susie's resort to this fund for the equipment without which her dawning social success would, she felt, lapse into obscurity more ignominious than that from which she had emerged. She must have the things represented by the money, and intoxicated though she was, she had still too much sense and conscience to deplete her husband's purse to the extent demanded by the exigency. He would have opened an artery to gratify her, had heart's blood been coin, but she knew he would look grave and pained did he suspect her visits to the Bank and their result.

He was sober enough, nowadays, without additional cause of discomfort. When questioned, he averred that all was going right at the Bank, and that he was well. Nor would he confess to loneliness on the evenings when she was obliged to leave him in obedience to Kitty's summons to rehearsal or consultation in some of the countless schemes of amusement the two were all the while concocting.

"Don't trouble yourself to come for me or to sit up for me, dear," the pleasure-monger would entreat in bidding him "good-by." "I'll have one of the maids call for me," or "I have a carriage," or—and after a time this was most frequent of all—"Jack Hitt is always very obliging about bringing me home."

With a smile upon his lips and gravity she did not read in his eyes, he would hand her to the carriage, or commit her to the spruce maid, hoping that she would have a pleasant evening, and having stood upon the steps until she was no longer in sight, would go back—as she supposed—to sitting room or book. Whereas, it grew to be more and more a habit with him to turn into the nursery instead, and sit there in the dark until he heard the bustle of her return below-stairs. He invariably sat up for her—she never asked why or where. The fire burned cheerily to welcome her, and the offices of maid, assumed, in the beginning in loverly supererogation, half jest, half caress, were now duty and habit. Upon one point he was resolute. If she went to bed late, she must sleep late next morning. This was a matter of health, a concession she owed those to whom her health was all-important.

The two older children had breakfasted with their parents for a year, and he made much of their company when their mother was not the fourth of the party. Sometimes he sent for the baby as well, holding her on his knee with one hand, while the other managed coffee cup and toast.

Susie surprised him thus one morning, having awakened unsummoned, and dressed hastily that she might see him before he went out.

"Arthur Cornell!" The ejaculation was the first intimation he had of her presence. "You spoil the children and make a slave of yourself! Where is their nurse?"

"Don't blame Ellen, dear!" checking her motion toward the bell. "I sent for the children. They are very good, and I enjoy their company."

Mrs. Cornell flushed hotly; her lips were compressed.

"I understand! After this, I will make a point of giving you your breakfast. It was never *my* wish to lie in bed until this hour."

"It was—and is mine!" rejoined her husband, steadily, unmoved by her unwonted petulance. "As it is, you are pale and heavy-eyed. You have had but five hours of sleep."

"My head aches!" passing her hand over her forehead. "That will go off, by-and-by. Baby! come to mamma, and let dear papa get his breakfast in peace. Let me pour out a cup of hot coffee for you, first."

Her softened tone and fond smile cleared the atmosphere for them all. Arthur sunned himself in her presence as a half-torpid bird on an early spring day. The children prattled merrily in answer to the pretty mother's blandishments; the baby stood up in her lap to make her fat arms meet behind her neck. She looked pleadingly into the proud face bent over mother and child. He was startled to see that the sweet eyes were misty.

"Dear! can't you go with me to-night?"

He fairly staggered at the unexpected appeal.

"If I had known——" he began.

"Yes, I know! I ought to have spoken before you made your engagement. I was careless—forgetful—silly! I do nothing but silly things nowadays. But I *wish* you could go, darling!"

"I'm afraid it's impossible," said Arthur regretfully. "The president made a point of my attending the meeting. I am sorrier than you can be, little wife."

She shook her head and tried to laugh.

"That shows how little you know about it! Don't make any more engagements without consulting me. 'I'm ower young'—not 'to leave my mammy yet'—but to be running about the world without my dear, old, steady-going husband—and I'm not willing to do it any longer."

He carried the memory of words and glance with him all day. Coming home at evening, he found a note from her, stating that Kitty had sent for her.

"There is a dress rehearsal at seven," she wrote. "I wish you could be there and see how ravishing I can be! If your business meeting is over by ten o'clock, won't you slip into society toggery and come around in season to see 'the old lady' home?"

"The fever has run its course!" thought the husband, with kindling eyes. "I knew I should get her back some day."

His dinner was less carefully served than in the olden supper days, but he dined as with the gods, and ran briskly upstairs to send Ellen down to her meal while he undressed the children and put them to bed. He had done this often during the winter, pretending to make a joke of the disrobing, but knowing it to be duty and vicarious. According to his ideas the mother should see to it in person. No hireling, whose own the bairns are not, can care for them as those in whose veins runs answering kindred blood. Usually, the task was done in heaviness of spirit. To-night, no effort was required to bring laughter to his lips, lightness to his heart. To-morrow mamma would breakfast with them, and resume her place in the home, so poorly filled by him or anybody else. She had come back to them. He tried to sing one of her lullabies as he rocked the baby to sleep, but failed by reason of a "catch in his throat." Mamma would warble it like a nightingale to them to-morrow night.

The business meeting was unexpectedly brief—"Thanks," as the president was pleased to say, "to the admirable epitome of the matter in hand prepared and presented by Mr. Cornell."

At ten o'clock the husband was in his dressing room, hurrying the process of "slipping into society toggery." He repeated the phrase aloud while tying his cravat with fingers uncertain from nervous haste. He was thankful beyond expression that he had never cast the shadow of his disapproval over Susie's spirits, even when they threatened to carry her out of the bounds of reason. She was young and pretty; so affluent of vitality, so richly endowed with talents, that a humdrum fellow like himself could not comprehend the stress of the temptation to plunge into and riot in the mad vortex of social parade.

"If there were any one thing I could do as cleverly as she does everything, I should be doing it all the time," he confessed in contrite candor.

Yesterday he had thanked Heaven that Lent was close upon the panting racers over the pleasure grounds. Now, he was indifferent to the advance and duration of the penitential season. His darling had returned of her own right-headed, right-hearted self to the sanctuary of home, having detected, unaided by his pessimistic strictures, the miserable vanity and carking vexation of the hollow system. He sewed two buttons upon his shirt before he could put it on, and when he pushed the needle through a hole and the linen beneath into the ball of his thumb, he began to whistle "Annie Laurie."

Susie had practiced "Annie Laurie" for an hour before dinner yesterday. He wondered if she had sung it last night at the Hitts'. She had been overrun with business of late, getting ready for the chamber concert and private theatricals, and mercy knew what else of frolic and folly gotten up by Mrs. Hitt for the benefit of the "Industrial Home" which was the latest charitable fad in her set. He had paid ten dollars for a reserved seat last week at the behest of the volatile Lady Patroness. She had let him have it "at a bargain because he had the good luck to be Susie's husband."

"Mr. Vansittart and Mr. Peltry paid fifty apiece for theirs, and I made Jack give me thirty for his. My rooms will seat comfortably just one hundred and fifty people, and I won't sell a ticket over that number at any price. None will be for sale at the door, and none are transferable. Of course, the rush for them is *fearful!*"

Before going Arthur peeped into the nursery, dropping the most cautious of kisses upon the cheek and forehead of each sleeper. Three-year old Sue made up her lips into a tempting knot as he touched her velvety face.

"Dee' mamma!" she murmured in her sleep.

He kissed her again for that, the "catch in his throat" in full possession.

"I don't wonder they love her!" he said brokenly. "Who could help it?"

The block on which the Hitt mansion stood was lined with waiting carriages, and Mr. Cornell supposed that the entertainment, which he called to himself "a show," must be nearly over. For an instant, he meditated waiting without until the crowd began to pour out, then, making his way into the hall, to send word to his wife that he awaited her pleasure. Something in the immobility of the doors changed his plan. He did not care to lurk for an hour or more among the coachmen who stamped and swore upon the pavement, reminding him of some verses Susie had read to him in other days when she had time for books and the talk over them after they were read. He recalled the first and last verses, and smiled in going through the discontented ranks and up the flight of stone steps:

"My coachman in the moonlight there

Looks through the side light of the door;

I hear him with his brethren swear,

As I could do—but only more.

.   .   .   .   .

Oh, could he have my share of din,

And I his quiet!—past a doubt,

'Twould still be one man bored within,

And just another bored without."

A surge of hot and scented air enveloped him with the opening of the door. The crowd in the hall contradicted the hostess' declaration that no more people would be admitted than could be comfortably accommodated. Struggling up to the dressing room he got rid of hat and overcoat, and struggled down again and to the door of the rear drawing room. A curtain was rung up from a stage at the end of the apartment as he gained a view of it.

The scene was the interior of an old-fashioned barn. Wreaths of evergreen hung against the walls and depended from the rafters, and the floor was cleared for dancing. From a door at the side a figure tripped into the middle of the stage. Arthur looked twice before he recognized the wearer of the colonial gown of old-gold brocade, brief of waist, and allowing beneath the skirt glimpses of trim ankles in clocked stockings. Her hair was piled over a cushion and powdered; eyebrows and lashes were deftly darkened, and the carmine of cheek and mouth owed brilliancy to rouge-pot and hare's foot. She was the belle of the ball to be held in the barn, and while waiting for the rest of the revelers, she began to recite, in soliloquy, the old rhymes of *Money Musk*.

At the second line, from an unseen orchestra, issued low and faint, like the echo of a spent strain, the popular dance tune. It stole so insidiously upon the air as to suggest the musical thought of the soliloquist, and was rather a background than an accompaniment to the recitative. Gradually, as the story went on, the lithe figure began to sway in perfect time to the phantom music; the eyes, smilingly eager, seemed to look upon what the lips described; the feet stirred and twinkled rhythmically; form and face were embodied melody. Vivified by reverie, expectant and reminiscent, the radiant impersonation of the poet's picture floated airily through the enchanting measures. As a morning paper put it, "she seemed to respire the music to which she swayed and chanted."

The audience, "though *blasé* with much merrymaking and sight-seeing, hung entranced upon every motion, until, wafted by gentle degrees toward the side-scene opposite to that by which she had entered, she vanished on the last word of the poem."

Recalled by a tumult of applause, she courtesied in colonial fashion, and kissed her hand brightly to her admirers, but instead of vouchsafing a repetition of what had stirred the spectators out of their *nil admirari* mood, beckoned archly to the left and right. A troop of young men and girls obeyed the summons and fell into place in the country dance that went forward to the now ringing measures of *Money Musk*.

The comedietta to which this was the prelude had been composed by a well-known author, who was called out at the close of the second act, and led forward the prima donna of the clever piece.

The interlude showed a moonlighted dell. On the distant hilltop was the gleam of white tents; in the foreground stood a woman as colorless in robe and visage as the moonbeams. Her voice, silvery and plaintive, thrilled through the crowded rooms:

"Give us a song!" the soldiers cried,

The outer trenches guarding,

When the heated guns of the camps allied

Grew weary of bombarding.

And so, in distinct, unimpassioned narrative up to—

They sang of love and not of fame,

Forgot was Britain's glory;

Each heart recalled a different name,

But all sang "Annie Laurie."

Again the invisible orchestra bore up the uttered words; at first a single cornet bringing down the air from the tented hilltop; then deeper notes joining it, like men's voices of varying tone and strength, but all singing "Annie Laurie."

"Something upon the *women's* cheeks

Washed off the stains of powder."

said dissonant, derisive tones at Arthur Cornell's back, as the curtain fell. "Battered veterans of a dozen seasons are snivelling like *ingenues* of no season at all. What fools New Yorkers are to be humbugged with their eyes open!"

"The fair manager hath a way of whistling the tin out of our pockets," replied a thin falsetto. "A wonderful creature, that same manager."

A disagreeable, wheezing laugh finished the speech.

Arthur made an ineffectual effort to extricate himself from the packing crowd, a movement unnoticed or uncared-for by the speakers.

"I admire—and despise—that woman!" continued the harsh voice. "As an exhibition of colossal cheek she is unrivaled. For four years she has preyed upon the majority that is up to her little 'dodge,' and the minority that is *not*, pocketing her half of the profits of every 'charitable' show; borrowing from innocents that don't know that she pays not again, and actually—so I am told—receiving a commission for introducing wild Westerners and provincial Easterners into what she calls 'our best circles.' And we go on buying her tickets and accepting her specimens, like the arrant asses we are."

"Madame du Bois, upon a limited scale."

"Exactly! Madame is her model. Her aping is more like monkeying, but the resemblance is not lost. New Yorkers rather enjoy the sublime audacity of Madame's fleecing, and she *does* have the *entrée* of uppertendom, sham though she is, with her drawing-room readings, where geniuses are trotted out at big prices to ticket buyers, and no price at all to Madame, and ranchmen's daughters are provided with blue-blooded Knickerbocker husbands. Her schemes are on a large scale. She engineers benevolent pow-wows, clears her one thousand dollars a night, and nobody dare charge her with pocketing a penny. You can see where Kit learned her trade. To my certain knowledge she dresses herself and pays for all her hospitable entertainments by these tricks."

"Her latest investment isn't a bad notion, but Kit is working the scheme for all it's worth. Anybody but the newest of the new would see through the game."

The other laughed gratingly.

"'New' is a mild way of putting it. We call her 'Kit's windfall' at our Club. Madame's disciple had, as she fondly imagined, netted a couple of veritable musical lions, and ten people were invited to hear their after-dinner roar. The very day before the feast the male lion fell sick, and the lioness wouldn't or couldn't leave her mate. Kitty was tearing her false bang over the note apprising her of the disaster when a card was brought in, telling her that an old schoolmate who had been educated as a music-teacher, and had a niceish talent for recitation, had removed to the city. Kit caught at the straw; raced around to inspect her, judged her to be more than eligible, and roped her in. Delorme was at the dinner and told me the story, which his wife had from Kit's own lips. The new 'find' had beauty as well as a voice and a taste for theatricals, and a neat income, so Kit says—some thirty thousand a year. Moreover, she is tremendously grateful for the lift in the world, and so daft with enjoyment of her first glimpse of *le bon ton* that she would send Kit ten out of the thirty thousand sooner than lose her social standing. She doesn't guess that she will be tossed aside like a squeezed orange next year, poor thing!"

Arthur leaned against the door-frame, too giddy and sick to move, had action been practicable in such a press. One of the tedious "waits" inseparable from amateur performances gave every woman there a chance to outscream her neighbor. It might be dishonorable not to make himself known to the gossips who considered themselves absolved by the payment of an entrance fee from the obligation to speak well, or not at all, of their hosts. He did not put the question to himself whether or not he should continue to listen. In a judicial mood he would have weighed the *pros* and *cons* of fact or fiction in the tale he had heard. Every word had, to his consciousness, the stamp of authenticity. In the shock of the confirmation of his worst misgivings with regard to his wife's chosen intimate, his ruling thought was of the anguish the truth would cause her. How best to lessen the shock to her tender, loving heart, how to mitigate her mortification, began already to put his deliberate faculties upon the strain.

The wiry falsetto and wheezy laugh struck in from his very elbow.

"Kit's exemplary spouse may not share her pecuniary profits, but he has an eye to innings of another sort. I met him at the Club last night, and saw that he had about six champagnes and four cocktails more than his brain could balance. An hour later, I was passing the house of our pretty prima donna when a carriage drew up and out stepped Jack and turned to help out his wife's favorite. And, by Jove! the way he did it was to put his arm about her waist, swing her to the side-walk and try to kiss her! She espied me, I suppose, for she broke away from him with a little screech, and flew up her steps like a lapwing. She must have had her latchkey all ready, for she got the door open in a twinkling, and slammed it. I guffawed outright, and didn't Jack swear!"

"What a beastly cad he is!" said the deep voice disgustfully.

Few men in the circumstances would have kept so forcibly in mind the shame to wife and children that would follow a blow and quarrel then and there, as the commonplace husband upon whose ear and heart every vile word had fallen like liquid fire. He rent a path through the throng, got his hat and coat and went out of the abhorrent place. He had seen to it that Susie's hired carriage was always driven by the same man—a steady, middle-aged American—and recognizing him upon the box, signaled him to draw up to the sidewalk, stepped into the vehicle, and prepared to wait as patiently as might be until the man's number should be called by the attendant policeman.

The "show" was not over for an hour longer, and his carriage was the last called. The fair manager had detained her lieutenant to exchange felicitations over the triumph of the evening. Susie appeared, finally, running down the steps so fast that her attendant only overtook her at the curbstone. He had come out bareheaded, and without other protection against the bitter March wind than his evening dress and thin shoes. Mrs. Cornell's hand was on the handle of the carriage door, and he covered it with his own.

"Are you cruel or coquettish, sweet Annie Laurie?" he asked in accents thickened by liquor and laughter.

By the electric light Arthur saw the pale terror of her face, as she tried to wrest her fingers from the ruffianly grasp. Without a second's hesitation the husband leaped out through the other door, passed behind the carriage, lifted the man, taller and heavier than himself, by the nape of the neck, and laid him in the gutter.

"The fellow is drunk!" he remarked contemptuously to the policeman who hastened up, imagining that the gentleman had tripped and fallen. "It is lucky you are here to look after him."

He handed his trembling wife into the carriage, swung himself in after her, and bade the coachman drive home.

Then—for as I have expressly affirmed, this man was heroic in naught save his love for wife and children—he put strong tender arms about the sinking woman, who clung to his neck, convulsed by sobs, as one snatched from destruction might hang upon the saving hand.

"There, my darling! It is all over! I ought to have taken better care of you. The old account is closed. We'll begin another upon a clean page."

He was only a bank cashier, you see, and familiar with no figures except such as he used every day.

THE ARTICLES OF SEPARATION.

BEFORE and since the day when a certain man—idling while Israel and Syria warred—drew a bow at a venture (the margin has it, "in his simplicity,") that let a king's life out, the air has vibrated to the twang of other bowstrings, and millions of barbs, as idly sent, have been dyed with life-blood.

In every 50,000 cases of this sort of manslaughter, 49,999 fall by the tongue.

The Hon. Simeon Barton, radiating prosperity from every pore of his snug person, and clothed with complacency as with a garment, rolled about the soon-to-be-vacated bachelor quarters of his nephew-namesake, thumbs in armholes, and chin in air, while he discoursed:

"You're a pluckier fellow than your uncle, me boy! Of course, it is on the cards that your head may be level. There are literary women *and* literary women, no doubt, and this must be a favorable specimen of the tribe, or you wouldn't have been in your present fix, but none of the lot in mine, if you please. When my turn comes—and I aint sure that I shan't look out for a match some day, when I am too stiff to trot well in single harness, I shall hold the reins. No inside seat for me."

The nephew laughed in a hearty, whole-souled way. He was not touched yet.

"You mix your figures as you do your cobblers—after you get hold of the sherry bottle—with a swing. Wait until you see my 'match.' She is a glorious woman, Uncle Sim. The wonder is that she ever got her eyes down to my level."

The forty-year-old celibate continued to roll and harangue. His dress coat was new and a close fit to his rotund dapperness; with one lavender glove he smote the palm of his gloved left hand; the rose in his buttonhole was paler than the hard red spots on cheeks like underglazed pottery for smoothness and polish, his mustache curled upward and wriggled at animated periods.

"Quite the thing, me dear boy, altogether proper. For me part, I wouldn't care to be under obligations to a woman when she *had* worked down to my level, but tastes differ, and a man of twenty-six who has a living to make ought to cast an anchor to windward, in case of squalls. A woman who can chop a stick, at a pinch, to set the pot to boiling is a convenience. Literature's a better trade now than it used to be, I suppose. Jones of Illinois was telling me last night of the prices paid to good selling authors, and by George! I was surprised. All the same, I'd fight shy of the Guild if I were contemplating matrimony. If you could see some of the many objects that hang about the Capitol in wait for Tom, Dick, or Harry to pick up a 'personal,' or lobby a bill, or get subscriptions to a book or magazine, you wouldn't wonder at my 'prejudice,' as you are pleased to style it. Pah!"

To rid his mouth of the taste he caught up a tumbler of sherry cobbler, filmy without and icy amber within, and drained it.

The expectant bridegroom glanced at the clock. His best man was to call for him at a quarter-past seven. It was exactly seven now, and the minutes drove heavily.

"But Uncle Sim,"—still good-humoredly,—"Miss Welles is not a newspaper reporter, nor a lobbyist, nor yet a penny-a-liner. She wrote to please herself and her friends until her father's death, six years ago. He was considered fairly wealthy, but something went wrong somewhere, and his widow would have suffered for the want of much to which she had been accustomed but for the talents and courage of her young daughter. I am afraid the poor girl worked harder than her mother suspected for a while, although the public received her favorably from the outset. Mrs. Welles survived her husband three years. Agnes then went to live with her only sister, Mrs. Ryder, the wife of my partner. I first met her at his house. She has continued to write and has supported herself handsomely in this way. She is as heroic as she is sweet—a thorough woman."

"With a masculine intellect! I comprehend, me boy. Don't multiply epithets on my account. As I've said, I don't presume to question the wisdom of your choice in this particular case, and that your inamorata is the best of her kind, but personally, I don't take to the *kind*. By Jupiter! I was telling Jones of Illinois, last night, of an incident that gave me a 'scunner' against woman authors, twenty years ago. Mrs. Shenstone of New York was a literary light in her day. There's a fashion in writers, as in everything else, and she went out with balloon skirts and *chig-nongs*. But she was a star of the first magnitude in her own opinion, and, at any rate, something in the stellar line in others' eyes. Her husband had money and she was a poor girl when she married him. They say he made a show of holding his own while the shekels lasted. A more meek-spirited atomy I never beheld than when they called upon my friends, Mr. and Mrs. Lamar from Charleston, then staying at the Fifth Avenue Hotel, one evening, when I chanced to be sitting with the Lamars in their private parlor. And as sure as I am a sinner and you're another, the card brought in to Mrs. Lamar was 'Mrs. Cordelia Shenstone *and husband.*' The last two words were added in pencil. Fact, 'pon honor! Mrs. Lamar carried the card home and had it framed as a domestic and literary curiosity."

"You cite an extreme case"—another glance at the slow clock. "If that woman had been a shopkeeper, or a dressmaker, with the same arbitrary, selfish spirit, she would have been guilty of the same gross violation of taste and feeling."

"Maybe so! maybe so! But the writing woman is a prickly problem in modern society. She is leading the van in all revolutionary rot about women's wrongs and women's rights. The party can't do without her, for the rank and file couldn't draft a resolution or write a report to save their lives, and they've flattered up our blue-stocking until she steps out of all bounds. It makes a conservative patriot's blood run cold to think what the upshot of it all is to be. And I confess I don't like to anticipate seeing your cards engraved—'Mrs. Clytemnestra Ashe and husband.'"

A dark red torrent poured over the listener's face. Physically and morally, he was thin-skinned.

"There is nothing of the Clytemnestra in her make-up, sir. No woman ever made could rule me, were she my wife. Agnes is too gentle and too sensible to attempt it. As to the cards!" He went to a drawer and took out a bit of pasteboard which he tossed to his kinsman, with a derisive laugh. "That is all settled, you see. Come in!" to a knock at the door.

When the tardy best man appeared, the Hon. Simeon Barton, his head on one shoulder, and eyes half shut, after the manner of an impudent cock-sparrow, was scanning the engraved inscription,

---

MR. AND MRS. BARTON ASHE,

170 West —— St.

"Leave the 'Simeon' out, do you? Clytem—*Agnes* doesn't like it, maybe?" And without waiting for a reply—"Good-evening, Mr. White. I'm just advising Bart here to use up this batch of cards plaguey quick, to make room for 'Mrs. Ashe *and husband*.'"

Mr. White laughed a little and politely. The jest was in miserable taste, but much was pardonable in rich uncles who were self-made men, when they showed a disposition to help make their nephews. A glimmer of like reasoning may have entered Barton's mind, for he turned an unshadowed brow to the eccentric millionaire.

"When that time comes I shall employ you to draw up the articles of separation. White, here, is witness to the agreement."

An hour later, he would not have believed the words had passed his lips. Jest upon such a horror would have seemed profanation to the newly made husband. As the woman who would never again answer to the name of Agnes Welles stood beside him, his were not the only eyes that paid silent homage to her strange beauty—strange, because to the guests, and to the assembled relatives, this phase of one whom most people had hitherto thought only "interesting" and "pleasing," was new and unexpected. She was but a few inches shorter than her manly partner, and slender to fragility. Straight and supple as a willow-wand, she was ethereal in grace when clad in the misty robes and veil which were the wedding gift of her godmother. Her dark eyes were full of living light, illumining the colorless face into weird loveliness, that belonged neither to feature nor complexion. The short, tense bow of the upper lip, the fine spirited line of the nostrils, the perfect oval of cheek and chin, were always high-bred—some said, haughty. To-night they were chastened into lofty sweetness that was pure womanly.

"She might pass for *twenty*-two," said an audaciously young *débutante* to a crony just behind Mr. Barton.

And—"By George!" thought that astute individual—"the young dog never hinted that his divinity was six years his senior. I should have been surer than ever of receiving that card. Pity! pity! pity! *That's* a fault that won't mend with time."

Agnes knew better than he could have told her what risks the woman takes who consents to marry her junior in years. Early in their acquaintanceship she had contrived to apprise Barton of this disparity. When he declared his love she set it boldly in the foreground of hesitation and demur.

"When you are thirty-five, in man's proudest prime and yet far from the comb of the hill, I shall have begun to go down the other side," she urged. "You might be able to contemplate the contrast boldly, but could I forgive myself? There may be a suspicion of poetry—pathetic but real—in the idea of an old man's darling, but an old woman's pet! *that* is a theme no painter or poet has dared to handle. The suggestion of grotesqueness is inevitable. Both are to be pitied, but I think the wife needs compassion even more than the man she has made ridiculous."

The rising young lawyer was a clever advocate, and he had never striven longer and harder to win a cause. When his triumph was secured Agnes could not quite dismiss the subject. It haunted her like a wan ghost, with threatening beck and ominous eye. Once, but a month before their wedding day, they were speaking of George Eliot's singular marriage with a man young enough to be her son, and an abrupt change fell upon Agnes' visage—a shade of painful doubt and misgiving.

"Dinah Maria Mulock, too!" she exclaimed. "And Mme. de Staël! Elizabeth Browning's husband was some months younger than she. Then, there are Mrs. —— and Mrs. ——" naming two prominent living American authors. "How very singular! There must be some occult reason for what we cannot set down as coincidences. It looks like fatality—or" hesitatingly— "infatuation."

"Rather," said Barton in gentle seriousness, for her perturbation was too real for playful rallying—"attribute such cases to the truth of the eternal youthfulness of genius. These men see in the faces and forms of the women they woo, the beautiful minds that will never know age or change. Time salutes, instead of challenging those high in favor with the king."

"Do you know," Agnes said, her slim white hand threading the brown curls of the head she thought more beautiful than that of Antinous—"that you will never say a more graceful thing than that? You are more truly a poet than I. Don't disclaim, for I am not a bard at all. When I drop into poetry *à la* Wegg, it is *not* 'in the light of a friend.' When I am in the dark or at best in a half-light, sorry or weary, or lonely of heart, my thoughts take rhythmic shape. They are only homely little crickets, creeping out in the twilight to sing by the fire that is beginning to gather ashes. I am a born story-teller, but I deserve no credit for that. Something within me that is not myself tells the stories so fast that I can hardly write them down as they are made. I am no genius, dear. Don't marry me with that impression. I wish for your sake that I were. How gloriously proud you would be of me!"

"I am 'gloriously proud' of you now!" He said it in fervent sincerity. "If you have genius, don't develop it. I can hardly keep you in sight as it is."

Dimly and queerly, the feeling that prompted the half-laughing protest returned upon him to-night. The solemn radiance overflooding her eyes and clearing into exalted beauty lineaments critics pronounced irregular, positively awed him—an uncommon and not altogether agreeable sensation for a bridegroom, especially one of his practical and somewhat dogmatic cast of mind. Rebel though romantic lovers may at what they consider derogatory to the constancy and depth of wedded affection, it is not to be denied that the turn of the bridal pair from the altar symbolizes a reversal in their mutual relation. The bonds that have held the lover in vassalage—very sweet bondage, perhaps, but still not liberty—are with the utterance of the nuptial benediction transferred to the woman he holds by the hand. Barton Ashe was very much in love, but he was a very man. His wife was now his property.

"I feel a wild desire to put my arms around you to keep your wings from unfurling," he found occasion to whisper presently. "I suppose these people would think me insane if I were to yield to the impulse and tell them why I did it."

The luminous eyes laughed joyously into his. With all her intellect and passionate depth of feeling, she had seasons of childlike glee that became her rarely.

"As you would be. I was never farther from 'wanting to be an angel' than at this instant. The life that now is appears to me eminently satisfactory."

A fresh bevy of congratulatory guests interrupted the hasty "aside."

"We find it hard to forgive you, Mr. Ashe," twittered an overdressed, overcolored, and overmannered spinster. "How can you reconcile it to your conscience to change a broad, beneficent river into a canal to serve your own particular mill? I shall not congratulate you upon a private good which is a public disaster."

"Many others are thinking the same thing, but they cannot express it so beautifully," said a plaintive matron, one of the many whose perfunctory sighs at weddings are the reverse of complimentary to their bonded partners. "But we must be thankful you have been spared so long to make us happy and do so much good in the world."

"I am puzzled," Barton observed, looking from one to the other. "If I were taking her out of town, to Coromandel, we will say, or even to New Jersey, there might be occasion for outcry."

"You are robbing us of the better part of this woman," interrupted the hortatory spinster in a dramatic contralto. "My protest is in the name of those to whom she belonged by the right the benefited have to the benefactor, before you crossed her path, in an evil hour for the world. It passes my comprehension, and I know much of the arrogant vanity of your sex, how any one man can hope to make up to his author wife for the audience she resigns when she sits down to pour out his coffee and darn his socks for the rest of her mortal existence. It is breaking stones with a gold mallet to make a mere housekeeper out of such material as this," lightly touching the head crowned by the bridal veil. "But my imagination is not of the masculine gender."

"Don't strain it needlessly," smiled Agnes, before the attacked person summoned wit for a retort. "Soup-making is a finer art than writing essays, to *my* comprehension, yet I hope to learn it."

The matron put in her sentence, sandwiched between sighs.

"You will find the two incompatible. Once married, a woman's life is merged in that of another. She has no volition, no thought, no name of her own."

"The married woman does not possess herself!" cried the spinster in shrill volubility. "She effaces her individuality in uttering the promise to 'serve and obey'—vile words that belong rather to the harem of the sixteenth century than to the home of the nineteenth. Somebody else has reported me in yesterday's *World* and *Herald*, so I may as well tell you that I brought forward a motion in Sorosis last Monday, that the club should wear crape upon the left arm for thirty days, dating from this evening, in affectionate memory of one of our youngest and most brilliant members. Talk of the self-immolation of the Jesuit who changes the name his mother gave him and resigns the right of private judgment and personal desire in joining the Order! He is riotously free by comparison with the model wife. Her assumption of the conventual veil is mournfully symbolical."

Another wave of newcomers swept her onward, still hortatory and gesticulatory.

She was never spoken of again by the bridal pair until the marriage day was a fortnight old.

They were pacing the wooden esplanade in front of the Hygeia Hotel at Old Point Comfort, basking in the December sunshine. The sea air had set roses in Agnes' cheeks; her lips were full and red, her eye sparkled with soft content, and her step was elastic. Barton, surveying these changes with the undisguised satisfaction of a man who has secured legally the right to exhibit his prize, took his cigar from his mouth to say carelessly:

"By the way, I have never asked the name of the painted-and-powdered party who gave a parlor lecture upon Jesuits and harems the night we were married."

"It was Miss Marvel," said Agnes, laughing. "She is an eccentric woman, and as I need not tell you, indiscreet and flippant in talk, letting her theories and spirits run away with her judgment. But she accomplishes a great deal of good in her way and has many fine traits of character. It is a pity she does herself such injustice."

"Humph! Does she belong to the sisterhood of letters?"

"In a way—yes. Her articles upon the Working Girls of New York, written for newspaper publication two years ago, attracted so much attention that they were collected into a volume last summer."

"She is a member of Sorosis—I gather from her tirade?"

"Oh, yes. One of the oldest members."

"What a hotch-potch that society or club—or whatever you may choose to call it—must be! Do you know, darling, I never associate you—or any other true, refined woman with the crew to which you nominally belong? You are a lily among thorns in such a connection. I should rather say among thistles and burdocks and stramonium and the like rank, vile-smelling weeds."

"I thank you for the pretty praise of myself," smiling sweetly and fondly at him. "But I cannot accept it at the expense of fairer flowers than I can ever hope to be, true, strong women who are trying to help their sex to a higher plane and prepare them for better work than they have yet accomplished, in spite of the limitations of sex—"

He caught her up on the word.

"Don't fall into their cant, for Heaven's sake! The 'limitations of sex' are woman's crown of glory. I have done some sober thinking lately—especially since the drubbing received from your Miss Marvel—with regard to the mooted subject of the emancipation of women, falsely so called. My conclusions may not coincide with your views upon the subject. But, perhaps you do not care to discuss it?"

Her face was sunny; her look at once fearless and confiding.

"We are both reasonable people, I hope. If we are not, we love each other too well not to agree amicably upon unavoidable disagreements."

Barton tossed his cigar stump into the foam of the nearest wave; a touch of impatience went with fling and laugh.

"Isn't that like a woman? She presupposes disagreement and forestalls argument by pledging herself to forgive for love's sake whatever she will not admit. The wisest and best of the sex—and you are both of these—will press feeling into what should be impersonal debate. Perhaps it is safer to talk of other things. See that gull swoop down and come up empty-clawed. That is his fourth unsuccessful trip to market within thirty minutes. The *passée* belle upon the pavilion over there has had that rich youngling in tow twice as long. I will wager a pair of gloves against a buttonhole bouquet with you that she doesn't land him."

Neither tone nor manner was pleasant. Agnes laid her hand upon his arm.

"Won't you go on with what you were about to say? I may not be able to argue. I think, with you, that logic is not woman's forte. Perhaps we may learn, with time and education, to divorce thought and feeling. But I am a capital listener, and a willing learner."

"You are an angel"—pressing the hand to his side, "and so far above Miss Marvel and her compeers in intellect and breeding that I fret at the alleged partnership. This talk of woman's serfdom and the need of elevating her, mentally and politically, is stuff from first to last. Vile and pestilential stuff! Heresy against the teachings of Nature and of Him who ordained that man should be the superior being of the two. Those who are pressing forward in what they call Reform of Existing Wrongs are your worst enemies. You should need no champion but your other self, Man. In arraying one sex against the other, you antagonize him. I see this rampant attitude of woman everywhere and hourly. If a man resigns his seat in a public conveyance to a woman, she takes it arrogantly—not gratefully. She pushes him aside with sharp elbows in crowds, jostles him upon gangways, presses before him into doors, always with a 'good-as-you' air which exasperates the most amiable of us. Her voice is heard in debating societies; she sits beside man upon the rostrum; competes with him in business, often successfully, because she can live upon less than he. The devilish spirit of revolt permeates all grades of society. The home—God's best gift to earth—has no longer a recognized governor, no judge to whom appeal is final. Sisters wrangle with brothers for equal educational advantages, instead of making home so pleasant that boys will be content to stay there. Women's Clubs, Women's Congresses, Women's Protective Unions, are part and parcel of the disunion policy. Instead of refining man this is surely, if slowly, arousing the latent savage in him. When that does spring to action, let the weaker sex beware. Outraged natural laws will right themselves in the long run, but sometimes at fearful cost."

Agnes was perfectly silent during this harangue, ignorant as was he of his resemblance to pudgy and pompous Uncle Simeon, while he beat the palm of the right hand with the empty left-hand glove, and rolled slightly from one leg to the other in the slow promenade. The bloom gradually receded from her cheeks, her profile was still and clear as a cameo. Her eyes were directed toward the gray-blues of the meeting line of wave and sky. Once she glanced up to follow the gull, rising from a fifth unsuccessful dip.

Presently she halted and leaned upon the parapet to watch the half-consumed cigar, swinging and bumping like a truncated canoe in the foam-fringes of the rising tide. Barton stopped with her without staying his talk. An impulse born of the innate savagery he imputed to his sex, bore him on. His wife's very impassiveness irked him. Silence was non-sympathetic; white silence, like hers, chilling. Irritation, engendered by piqued vanity, does not withhold the home-thrust because the victim is dearly beloved.

"You do not like to hear me talk in this strain," he pursued. "It is only natural that a woman of independent thought and action, accustomed to adulation, and to whom the excitement of a public hearing for whatever she has to say has become a necessity of existence; who has looked beyond the quiet round of home interests and home loves for a career; who has fed her imagination upon unreal scenes and situations—should——"

He could get no further. Fluent as he was in speech, he had wound himself up in nominative specifications, and the verb climax failed him unexpectedly.

"Should—what?" said Agnes, turning the set, tintless visage toward him. Her eyes, blank and questionless, showed how far from her thought was sarcastic pleasure in his discomfiture. Barton was too much incensed to reason.

"Should—and *does* sneer at her husband's serious talk upon a matter in which, as he is fast discovering, his happiness is fatally involved!"

"*Fatally!* O Barton!"

Independent and strong-minded she might be to others, but he had hurt her terribly. The stifled cry took all her strength with it. She caught at the railing for support, and leaned upon it, sick and trembling.

He lifted his hat in mock courtesy.

"If you will excuse me I will continue my walk alone. It is useless to attempt the temperate discussion of any subject when my words are caught up in that tone and manner. May I take you back to the hotel?"

Agnes straightened herself up. Her color did not return, but her voice was her own. It had always a peculiar and vibrant melody, and her articulation was singularly distinct for an American speaking her own language.

"You misunderstand me. I did not mean to be abrupt, much less rude. If I seemed to be either or both I ask your forgiveness. You need not trouble yourself to escort me to the hotel. I will sit here for a while and then go in. I hope, when you think the matter over dispassionately, you will see that I could not be guilty of what you imply."

He strode off toward the Fort, the deep sand somewhat derogatory to dignity of carriage, but favoring the increase of irritability. Agnes strolled slowly along the beach until she found a lonely rock upon the tip of a tongue of bleached sand, where she could sit and think out the bitterest hour she had ever known. People, passing upon pier and esplanade, saw her there all the forenoon, a slight figure whose gray gown matched in color the stones among which she sat, as motionless as they. The brackish tide rose slowly until the spray sprinkled her feet, whispering mournful things to rock and sand. She saw and heard nothing, while her eyes seemed to follow the stately sail and swoop of the gulls whose breasts showed whitely against the blue of the December sky.

Other wives than Lorraine Loree have wedded men of high degree only to find that "husbands can be cruel," and more than Lorraine or Agnes dreamed of have made the discovery before the wane of the honeymoon.

This bride felt bruised and beaten all over, and suffered the more, not less, for her sorrowful bewilderment as to the exact cause of this, the first quarrel.

CHAPTER II.

SOME women and many men are compounded and shaped into sentient beings without the infusion of so much as a pennyweight of tact.

Many women and a few men combine with this deficiency—which is, in itself, a deformity—a fatal facility for saying exactly the wrong thing when the wrong thing will do most harm.

Miss Marvel had taken all the honors in this line which native bias and feminine fussiness could win, and she wove a new spray into her laurel wreath one day in the March succeeding the winter in which Barton Ashe and Agnes Welles were made one—in law and gospel.

The morrow would be his wife's birthday, and Barton had in his breast pocket a tiny box containing a sapphire ring for her, when he arose to resign his seat in the street car to the dashing spinster, whom he recognized as soon as she entered. He had never seen her since his wedding eve, but she was not a woman to be forgotten or overlooked. She was in great force to-day, gorgeously appareled and flushed beyond high-rouge mark by three hours at a literary breakfast, given at Delmonico's to a distinguished foreigner.

"I am surcharged with electric thought," she confided to Mr. Ashe when she had taken the vacated place with a cavalier nod that might mean "Thanks," or "That's only decent, my good man."

"Ah!" said Barton, in naïve wonderment, for the want of anything else to say.

"Surcharged! bristling! I could fancy that at the approach of the negative pole I should crackle and emit sparkles like a brisk battery. Such a feast of intellect! such flow of soul! such scintillating wit! Three hours of such intercourse were worth ten—a thousand cycles of Cathay. Our guest was superb! such dignity and such graciousness of affability as can only coexist in an Old World product."

She spoke loudly, after the manner of the New World product (*genus homo*, feminine gender). Several solid men peered at her around or over the evening papers. Two giddy girls, who had taken without thanks or scruples seats from weary men, smiled undisguisedly. Barton, standing in the aisle, holding on by the strap, his knees abraded by the jet passementerie of Miss Marvel's velvet skirt, could not budge an inch. He must hear and, hearing, essay reply of some sort. "Ah!" albeit the safest and most commodious monosyllable in the language, cannot go on forever.

"The lunch was largely attended, I suppose?" he ventured in tones studiously lowered.

"By every woman in New York who is worth the notice of an intelligent being. With one distinguished exception. Mrs. Ashe's absence was the occasion of universal regret. As a well-wisher let me warn you that you may be mobbed some day for your unconscionable cruelty to the highest order of created things; for imprisoning the eagle and stilling the song of the lark. At least fifty people asked me to-day why Agnes Welles had disappeared from the literary firmament. For one and all, I had one and the same reply. 'She has taken the bridal veil,' I said, tears in eyes and voice. 'In consequence of that piece of barbarity, and for no other cause, the places that once knew her know her no more.' One woman—I won't divulge her name, lest you should *hate* her—said she 'should as soon think of chaining a thrush to the leg of a kitchen chair as of obliging that glorious young thing to resign her Heaven-appointed mission for the position of caterer, housekeeper, and seamstress.' I shall work that *bon mot* into my next literary letter to the Boston *Globe*. Another delightfully satirical creature advised me to take up the cause of 'Great Women Married to Small Men,' in my next series of papers upon 'Unconsidered Wrongs of Our Sex.' You see the reputation you are earning for yourself with the powers that be!"

Barton Ashe was a sensible man, well educated and well bred. Under favoring circumstances, as when inspired by the society of his wife and her loving appreciation, he was quick with repartee and apt at fence even with a wordy woman. Under the present onslaught he was furious and dumb. Had a man insulted him, and less grossly, he would have knocked him down or given him his card and demanded a meeting elsewhere. This berouged and bedizened old maid compromised him in the eyes of solid men and giddy girls by entering into conversation with him at all. Each shrill word was a prickle in a pore of his mental cuticle. She advertised his wife as one of *her* kind, arraigned him as despot and churl, menaced him with public exposure, and posed as Agnes' champion against the oppressor on whose side was the power of law and tradition—made him ridiculous to all within the sound of her brazen tongue—and he was powerless.

He did the only thing possible to a man calling himself a gentleman, when baited to desperation in a public place by a woman who passes for a lady— he lifted his hat silently and pulled the strap to stop the car. Other passengers than Miss Marvel marked the dark face and blazing eyes, and curious regards wandered back to the offender, smiling to herself at this new proof of her ability to, in her favorite phrase, "drive a poisoned needle under a man's fifth rib."

"Great Women Married To Small Men?"

The most offensive count in the unanswered indictment seemed to be flung after him by the shrieking March wind. Until this moment of intensest exasperation he had never consciously compared himself mentally with his wife. That spiritually she was purer and better he was ever ready to admit. The gallant alacrity with which men yield the palm of virtue and piety to women may be due to the candor of real greatness, but a keen student of human contrarieties is excusable for likening it, sometimes, to the ostentatious generosity of the child who surrenders to a playfellow the wholesome "cookey," while he holds fast to the plum cake for his own delectation.

"Great" and "Small" were explicit terms that threw our hero upon the hostile-defensive. Agnes was a pearl among women, as good, true, and sweet as any man need covet for a lifelong companion. She kept his house well and his home bright, her sympathies were ready, her love was poured out upon him in unstinted measure, she studied his tastes, humored his few foibles, in brief, filled his life, or so much of it as she could reach, most satisfactorily. Her mind was fairly stocked with miscellaneous information; she had remarkable facility in composition and graceful fancies, and, above all, the happy knack of saying, in a telling way, things people cared to hear. Being in "the literary ring," she had secured a respectable audience, and, being a tactful woman, she had kept it.

"Great," she was not, in any sense of the word, except according to the perverted standard of the "Club" gang, the mutual-admiration circle, with whom every poetaster was a Browning, and the writer of turgid essays a Carlyle or Emerson.

He gave a scornful snort in repeating the adjective. Agnes would be the first to deprecate the application of it to herself. Yet—if she had not invited the commendation of the *Précieuses ridicules*—had her name never been bandied from mouth to mouth in public, the antithetical "small" had never been fitted to him. Husband and wife were in false positions. That was clear—and galling. Almost as clear, and harder to endure, was his conviction that the situation could not be altered for the better.

He had not made up his mind to graceful acceptance of the inevitable when he fitted the latchkey in the door of his own house.

The popular impression as to the housewifery of pen-wrights had no confirmation within the modest domicile of which Agnes Ashe was the presiding genius. During her mother's protracted invalidism and her own betrothal she had studied domestic economy, including cookery, with the just regard to system and thoroughness that made her successful in her other profession of authorship. Her computations were correct and her methods dainty. She deserved the more honor for all this because she was not naturally fond of household occupations. If she reduced dusting to a fine art, mixing and baking to an exact science, it was conscientiously, not with love for the duties themselves.

Once, when praised for excellent housekeeping by a friend in her husband's hearing, her native sincerity made her say:

"You are mistaken in supposing that the drudgery connected with home-making is easy or pleasant to me. If I did not feel it my duty to go into the kitchen sometimes, and to arrange rooms, I doubt if I should ever do either. Nor am I fond of sewing."

"Yet your needle-work is exquisitely neat," said the surprised visitor.

"Because I hold myself to the necessity of doing well what I undertake. It is all business, not delight."

After the visitor had gone, Barton gave a gentle and needful caution.

"Don't talk in that way to acquaintances, dear," he said. "I don't want people to report that your tastes are unfeminine."

"Surely there are other feminine tastes besides love for needle, broom, and egg-beater?" Agnes protested, no less gently. "Why should every woman be proficient in baking, when every man is not compelled to learn book-keeping? I am faithful in the discharge of domestic duties because I love you and consider your happiness rather than selfish ease. I love my home, and to enjoy the effect of clean, orderly rooms and well-served meals, I am willing to perform tasks for which I have no real liking. The game is well worth the candle—a good many waxlights, in fact—but I question if you, for example, really *like* to draw up conveyances and make searches."

"Illustration is not argument," said Barton dryly. "You are undeniably a clever woman, my love, but your reasoning would hardly convince a jury. Women's efforts in that direction are what we style 'special pleading.'"

This talk was held two months ago. Agnes knew better, by now, than to attempt argument with him, and his love grew apace because of the forbearance he mistook for conviction of his ability to direct thought with action. She was the dearer for being dutiful. The docility with which she listened to his dicta, never betraying a suspicion that they were dogmas, won him to forgetfulness of the circumstance that she was his senior by six years and a blue-stocking.

She was in the front hall when he got home to-night, receiving the adieu of a spectacled personage whom she introduced as "Mr. Rowland of Boston."

"Charmed, I am sure," said the stranger airily. "The more that I am positive of enlisting Mr. Ashe's powerful interest upon my side, and that of the book-loving public. If Mrs. Ashe will pardon the additional trespass upon her time,

I should like to explain to you, my dear sir, the nature of my petition to her, and now to yourself."

They returned to the parlor, and he had his say. It was succinct and comprehensive. He wished to engage Mrs. Ashe to write one of a projected series of popular novels. Her coadjutors would be authors of repute; the programme was attractive and must take immensely with the best class of readers. His terms were liberal.

In any other mood than that for which Miss Marvel was chiefly responsible, even a prejudiced man must have been gratified by the compliment to his wife implied in the application. It acted upon the chafed surface of husbandly vanity and dignity like moral *aqua fortis*. Barton listened with lowering brow and compressed lips while the fashionable publisher subjoined appeal to statement. When both were concluded the master of the house waited with palpable patience, apparently to make sure that all the pleas were in, then arose with the air of the long-bored householder who dismisses a book agent.

"Mrs. Ashe is so well acquainted with my views upon the subject of her undertaking any literary work whatsoever, that I may be allowed the expression of my surprise at her reference of this matter to me. I believe, however, that the feminine *littérateur* considers a show of deference to her husband a graceful form. Your appeal to me is, you see, the idlest of courtesies. Now, as I have just come home after a wearisome day of business, may I ask you to excuse me from further and fruitless consideration of this subject?"

He bowed and went off to his dressing room.

The man of the world, left thus awkwardly *en tête-à-tête* with an insulted wife, always remembered with grateful admiration the perfect breeding that helped him out of the dilemma.

"Mr. Ashe is very tired and far from well," Agnes remarked, eye and smile cool and unembarrassed. "As one conversant with the fatigues and harassments of business life, you need no apology beyond this for his seeming brusqueness. I dare say—" with archness that was well achieved— "that Mrs. Rowland would comprehend, better than you, what serpentlike wisdom we wives must exercise in broaching any subject that requires thought to our hungry lords. I will appeal from Philip famished to Philip full, in due season, but I think you would better not depend upon me. I am a very busy woman just now, and shall be for some time to come."

"It would give me solid satisfaction to punch that fellow's head," muttered the publisher in the street. "He is a boor and a tyrant, and his wife is an angel."

He was wrong in both specifications. Barton Ashe was a vain man, and his vanity was smarting from a recent attack. His ideas of the supremacy, intellectual and official, that do hedge a husband were overstrained, but natural.

Agnes Ashe was a very mortal woman, walking up and down her pretty room after the departure of her visitor, hands clenched until the nails wounded the flesh, and cheeks so hot they dried the tears before they fell. Her breath came fast between the shut teeth. Women will comprehend how much easier it was to forgive her husband for the slur cast upon her than for lowering himself in the eyes of a stranger.

"I am afraid of myself!" she whispered pantingly. "I am afraid of *myself!* Must I, then, despise him utterly? What right has he to charge upon me as shame what others account as honor? Can it be that he is conscious of being small and fears to let me grow?"

By different roads, the refined woman, who loved her art for its own sake and reverenced it for the good it might do, and the pretender, tolerated by true artists out of charity, and out of respect for the active benevolence that redeemed her from the rank of a public nuisance—had arrived at a like conclusion.

Barton, after his bath and toilet, sat down to dinner, and scarcely spoke until excellent clear soup and the delicious creamed lobster prepared by Agnes' own hands, had paved the way for more substantial viands. Then his righteous wrath was partially cooled by perception of the truth that the still, pale woman opposite meant to enter no defense against the aspersions cast upon her in another's hearing. Nay, more, she made no attempt to cheat him into a milder mood, broached no prudent topics, attempted no diversion. Second thought found fresh fuel for displeasure in her reticence. The double offense of Miss Marvel's tirade and the airy publisher's errand were not condonable by discreet silence.

He slashed simultaneously into a roast of beef and the grievance upon his mind.

"I met your particular crony, Miss Marvel, in the car on my way uptown. She was, if possible, more detestably impertinent than usual."

Agnes beckoned to the waitress and gave her in a low tone an errand to the kitchen. Glancing up at her husband, she saw that he had laid down the carver and was gazing sternly at herself.

"May I, as the least important member of this household, inquire why you sent that girl out of the room? I may be, as your dear friends assert, a small man married to a great woman, but I am credited by others with a modicum of common sense and discretion. I am willing to abide by the consequences of whatever I say at my own table and in the presence of my servants, if I have any proprietorship in either."

Red heat he had never seen before in Agnes' face suffused it now, her eyes dilated and gleamed.

"I sent the girl from the room because she was recommended to me by the matron of an orphan asylum in which she was brought up. Miss Marvel is a manager of the institution and had the girl trained in a school for domestics. Mary is much attached to her. I thought it hardly safe or kind to discuss her in Mary's presence."

Barton met generous heat with deadly coldness.

"When is your waitress' month up?"

"On the fifteenth."

"This is the seventh. Pay her a week's wages to-morrow and pack her off. I will have none of that woman's spies in my house—that is, always supposing it to be mine. I understand this afternoon's scene. She is kept posted as to the status of domestic affairs."

"You are out of humor, Barton, or you could not be so unjust to me and to a faithful servant."

Griselda would not have retorted in a hard, cutting tone, but Griselda could neither read nor write. Diffusion of knowledge has a tendency to breed sedition among the lower orders.

Clubs for the lofty, and lager beer saloons for the lowly, stand, with controversial Benedicks, for the "refuges" foreign cities offer to the fugitive from wheels and hoofs.

"Excuse me for leaving you to digest your dinner and the memory of that last remark in solitude," Barton said sardonically. "I shall finish *my* dinner at the club."

The library was the coziest room in the house. Before Mr. Rowland called, Agnes had looked into it to see that the fire was bright and that Barton's easy-chair, newspaper, and cigar-stand were in place. Upon the table was a bowl of *Bon Silène* roses he had ordered on his way downtown that morning. She had poured out his coffee and lighted his cigar here for him last night. It all rushed over her with the pure deliciousness of the roses' breath, as she returned to the deserted apartment after dinner. As she moved, the fragrance broke into waves that overwhelmed her with the sweet agony of associativeness.

Sinking upon her knees before her husband's chair, she laid her head within her enfolding arms and remained thus until the clock struck nine. Then she spoke aloud:

"What has he given me in exchange for my beautiful ideal world and for my work? A drugged cup, with gall and wormwood in the bottom."

The slow, scornful syllables jarred the perfumed waves and echoed hollowly in the still corners.

She arose, unlocked a secretary at the back of the room, and took out a worn portfolio—also locked. Selecting from the contents several large sheets of paper, she laid them in order upon the table, and drew from an inner pocket a gold pen in a shabby handle. With it she had written her first book. For six years she had used no other. Before dipping it into the ink, she kissed it.

"I have come back to you!" she said.

CHAPTER III.

WITH the first heavy snows of December a little daughter was given to Agnes Ashe.

On New Year's Day her husband proposed to read aloud to her a book "some of the Club fellows were talking about last night." The pale face flushed nervously when he undid the wrapping paper.

It was one of the "happenings" we persist in classing among singular coincidences, although they are of daily occurrence, that he should have selected that particular novel for their entertainment on the holiday he proposed to devote entirely to his convalescent wife.

"The Story of Walter King" had not been sent, as one might suppose would have been natural, to Mr. Rowland of Boston.

"He would guess instantly how matters are," Agnes reasoned. "I am still too proud to run that risk."

She took the MS. instead to a New York publisher in whose discretion she could trust, told him of her whim to establish a new reputation which should owe nothing to past gains, and left the story with him. In a week it was accepted and in the printer's hands. When Baby Agnes—upon whom the mother bestowed the Scotch pet-name of "Nest"—was born, new editions were selling as fast as the press could turn them out.

It was evident, said critics, that the fresh, nervous novel was from the hand of a young writer, skilled in the use of language but unhackneyed by the need of furnishing "pot-boilers." It was as evident, said readers, that the unknown author had fed the pen directly from his heart, and that personal experience had had much to do with the make-up of the "live book."

Agnes had held no communication with the discreet publisher since the contract was signed. She had not corrected the proof-sheets, or had an advance copy of the work. There was, therefore, literal truth in her reply to Barton's query—"Have you read it?"

"I have not even seen the book that I recollect. Who is the author?"

"John C. Hart"—turning to the title page. "What else has he done?"

"The name sounds familiar. Or, perhaps it may be that I am thinking of Professor John S. Hart. You are very kind to think of getting a new book for me! trebly kind to offer to read it to me."

"It is little enough I can do for the best wife in Christendom!" stooping to kiss her and then Baby Nest asleep in her crib beside Agnes' reclining chair.

The languid mother, grateful for his society and loverly attentions, was more like his ideal wife than Agnes had been since the eve of her birthday, when he had almost forgotten (through her fault) that he was a gentleman. No explanations had followed the ugly scene. They had met at breakfast the next morning as if the fracas had not occurred, but then and thereafter he had missed something from his married life. Had he tried to analyze the vague, ever present discomfort, he would have said that his wife was always on guard. No surprise of abrupt or rough speech betrayed her into a show of temper or wounded feeling. No overflow of tenderness elicited a confession of answering devotion. When questioned, she was frank in declaring that she loved him, and sought to make him happy in his home and content with her. She was never sad in his sight. Domestic and society duties were cheerfully performed, she was always ready to go out with him when he desired it and gave him her company at home conscientiously. There was the sore spot! He could not prove that her love and duty were perfunctory, but he never got away from the irritating suspicion that they were. Had she been miserable, pettish, or fretfully exacting, it would have accorded better with his creed of the absolute dependence of a woman upon her lord. In plain English— which, however, he would have been ashamed to put into words in any language—it irked him that his mental and moral barometer could not set the weather for his household. There was a *something* back of Agnes' even temper and equable spirits he could not touch and that told him she was sufficient unto herself. Into this she seemed to retire as into the cleft of a rock when the matrimonial horizon threatened storm.

There was no one to tell him of mornings spent in the library, or of the work done during the evenings he passed at the club. He ought to have been gratified at her smiling aquiescence in his apologetic representation of the business necessity laid upon a man to mingle socially with "the fellows." Some women made it preciously disagreeable for husbands who acted upon this compulsion, but his wife was never lonely by day or night. If he came home at eleven o'clock, she was in the library, reading or knitting beside a glowing fire, ready to receive him and to listen with interest to club stories or incidents. If he stayed out after midnight, she went to bed like a sensible Christian and slept soundly.

What could be more exemplary and satisfactory? He had a model wife. Would sulks, tears, and chidings have been more to his taste? This conclusion reached, he would berate himself for "an unreasonable dog"—and go on missing something he could not define.

An odd conceit came to Agnes as the full, manly voice began "The Story of Walter King"—a fancy that won a smile from her at first, and terrified her when she could not shake it off. She was the unsuspected mother of a foundling. In secret and in fear, she had laid the new-born baby at a stranger's door. He had cared for, fostered, and clothed it, and on this New Year's Day, her husband had ignorantly adopted the waif and led it, a beautiful child, to her, bespeaking her admiration for it.

For her own baby! the thing born of her soul, the express image of her thought, the bright, glorious darling in whom, and with whom, and by whom, she had lived all these weary, weary months! Her husband would introduce these two to one another! Was her left hand a stranger to her right? Was her heart alien to the blood leaping from it?

She could have laughed and cried hysterically, could have snatched the book from the unconscious reader and covered it with tears and kisses. She must touch and hold it once, if but for a minute, or the strained heart-strings would part.

"Can you see well?" she interrupted the reader to ask. The calm tone surprised herself and lent her courage to carry out her stratagem. "Does the light fall right for you? In her anxiety to exclude draughts and the snow glare, Mrs. Ames may have made it too dark for well people. Is the type pretty clear?"

She put out her hand and drew the volume from his. The sight of familiar paragraphs and names was as if the child had laughed, in happy recognition, into her eyes. She passed her fingers lovingly over the page, stroked the binding, raised the open book to her lips, and gave it back reluctantly.

"The smell of newly printed pages is delicious to me," she said, trying to laugh. "Sweeter than new-mown hay."

"They have brought it out in good style," observed Barton carelessly. "One gets no slipshod literature from that house. Their imprint is a title of intellectual nobility."

Agnes smiled brightly in assent, turned her cheek to the cushioned back of her chair, and closed her eyes to keep the happy tears from slipping beneath the lids. Was the time close at hand in which she could safely acknowledge her offspring? To screen the fact of her maternity from possible premature discovery she had refrained from so much as looking upon or speaking of the bantling for these long weeks. Providence had put this opportunity of honorable recognition before her. How should she seize it?

A thought struck her like an icebolt. What would Barton say, even in this auspicious hour, to the systematic concealment practiced before and since the advent of the adopted child? Would he throw it from him as he would a snake? She pictured the possibility of virtuous horror in the regards turned upon her, the aversion a moral man feels for a lost woman. Deception— even untruth might be forgiven; the deliberate disregard of his expressed wish that his wife should never again put sentiment or feeling of hers into print would be construed into absolute crime. He held the desire for literary renown on the part of a woman to be a fault that unsexed her. In a young girl the ambition might spring from the unrest of an unfilled heart, mistaken, but pardonable as a blunder of ignorance. A wife's heart, thoughts, and hands should be *full* of home and home loves, or she did not deserve her high and blessed estate.

She felt, now, that she could never make him understand how the side of her nature which he saw and knew was bettered and elevated by the healthful action of its twin, to which he was a stranger. She *had* "put herself into the book," but not in the lower and vulgar sense in which the reviewers had used the phrase. The aspirations with which others could not intermeddle—least of all, the husband who so grossly misjudged her, the fancies that beguiled Time of heaviness and drew the soreness from her heart while she dallied with them—were there. Her ideals were her real companions; her dream children her only confidants.

"The things which are seen are temporal; the things which are not seen are eternal."

The author who is not made, but born; the idealist whose brain creations are to him almost visible and tangible, while he communes with them—can, of all men, enter most joyfully into the meaning of the sweet mysticism uttered by the Creator of things temporal and things eternal.

It was a snowy day; transient glimmers of white light, shed from thinner clouds, were the precursors of thicker falls of soundless flakes. There was no wind, and as Agnes watched the storm between the slightly parted blinds, a curtain of purest lace seemed unfolding and wavering earthward. The hush of a great holiday enwrapped the city. Baby Nest slumbered peacefully amid billows of lawn and wool; the strong, mobile features of the husband she loved and feared more than any other living mortal darkened and lightened like the snow clouds, with the progress of the story. He read well, and threw unusual spirit into the present task.

Agnes hearkened, with a growing sense of unreality. The disowned child pressed nearer and closer, gazed appealingly into her face, cooed love words in her ear, covered with kisses the hands with which the hapless mother was constrained to hold it aloof from the heart that yearned to take it in.

Sometimes Barton's voice sounded a great way off, and she confused his utterances with the winged ideas she had formulated into human language. Was she thinking it all out? or was *he* enunciating what she *had* thought through the languorous summer days and cool autumn evenings? She used to wonder, amusedly, what he supposed she did during the many hours she spent in solitude. He never asked, but if he had deemed the matter worthy of speculation, he might have reasoned that a woman who did not make her own clothes and had no taste for fancy work, whose house was well appointed and not large, and whose health was good must, with two servants to do housework and cooking, have much time upon her hands.

"How do women occupy themselves who keep plenty of servants and do not write, paint, or study anything in particular?" asked the young son of a woman who kept house, wrote books, painted pictures, and studied with her children.

"They make a profession of *horacide!*" answered the mother.

Barton lowered the book so abruptly that his wife started and clasped her hands involuntarily. She was very weak.

"I should like to know this man!"

"What man?"

"The fellow who wrote this book! He is a New York lawyer—that is plain. His insight of legal chicanery and his apt use of technical law terms show that, if his clever reasoning did not. A Columbia graduate, too! I'll go bail for that. And a society man. By George! that narrows the case down pretty well. I don't know a man at the city bar, though, who has sufficient literary skill to turn out such a piece of work as this. 'John C. Hart' is a pseudonym, of course—but there may be a meaning in it."

He fell into a muse over the title page, knotting his brows and plucking at his lower lip while he scanned the name.

Agnes' breath came quick; her head swam as in seasickness. She shook herself mentally and tried to speak as usual:

"It may be another case of George Eliot, *alias* Mary Anne Evans; or Charles Egbert Craddock, *alias* Miss Murfree."

"Preposterous! There isn't a feminine touch in the book. And no woman of the education and refinement of this writer could know anything of the scenes and motives he describes. Men can paint women faithfully. Women who try to depict men show us up as hybrids, creatures of their own sex disguised in masculine habiliments. Ready-made clothes at that, baggy at the knees and short at the wrists. I should *not* like, however, to know a woman who could write 'The Story of Walter King.'"

"It does not impress me as coarse!" Agnes was nerved by instinctive resentment to say.

"Not a symptom of coarseness about it. But it *is* virile—and that your woman author ought never to be! Any man might be proud of having written this novel. Any true, modest woman would blush to be accused of it. You see the difference?"

"*I* see the difference between the patient I left three hours ago, and the one I find here now!" interjected the nurse bluntly.

She had come in while Barton was speaking, and had her hand on Mrs. Ashe's pulse.

"Tut! tut! tut!" she went on in grave vexation. "We shall have the doctor again if this sort of excitement goes on. Eyes glassy, pulse up, and, I venture to say, headache back of the eyes. Don't deny it, Mrs. Ashe! I know the signs. Here's your lunch—after which, we *must* have the room darkened and try to compose your nerves. It won't do to have a throw-back at this late day."

Barton carried off "The Story of Walter King" with him to the library, a little anxious, but more aggrieved. In common with the mighty majority of husbands, he resented Mrs. Gamp the more virulently because impotent against her tyranny.

"Thank Heaven that her time, like her infernal master's, is short!" growled he, dropping into his easy-chair and throwing his legs over the foot-rest in lordly disdain of appearances. "I suppose women enjoy being hectored, or the sex would rise *en masse* against this order of haggish humbugs. Agnes didn't dare peep a defense of herself, or of me. Great Scott! suppose I had been born a woman!"

He lighted a cigar and reopened his book. A luxurious, if lonely, lunch was served at half-past one. Wine and walnuts went with him into the library after the meal was eaten. The air was blue with fragrant smoke for the rest of the day. He did not take the nap he had promised himself as the chief delight of a lazy afternoon, until the last page of "The Story of Walter King" was devoured. Even after he had stretched himself upon the lounge and drawn the silken and eiderdown slumber-robe over him, he lay looking at the purring fire of sea-coal and listening to the muffled tinkle of sleigh-bells along Fifth Avenue, which was but a block distant—and thinking of the book that had enchained him so many hours. It had taken a powerful grip of his imagination and titillated his intellectual palate smartly. There were passages in it that recalled pertinent and pregnant sayings of his own relative to certain topics discussed in the fascinating pages; theories he had advanced and maintained; his very turns of speech were here and there.

Again he said, "I should like to know that man. He has a long head and sharp wits of his own. Immense knowledge of the world and human nature." Without the least intention of being conceited he subjoined to the silent soliloquy: "If I had turned my attention to literature, I believe I could have written that book. But one man cannot be proficient in everything. The suggestion of feminine authorship is ridiculous. Poor Agnes is a sensible girl, but she is wide of the mark there."

Here his thoughts wandered into the poppied plains of sleep.

Awaking from his siesta to find himself in the dark, he arose refreshed, and paid a dutiful call to his wife's chamber before going out to dine at his club. The nurse met him upon the threshold and stepped out into the hall for a whispered colloquy. Both of her charges had been restless all the afternoon. The baby was colicky, Mrs. Ashe feverish and excited, although persisting that nothing ailed her.

"She has an exquisitely susceptible nervous organization," she continued in the parrotlike lingo of the trained nurse. "We must really guard her more carefully in future. She was talking about that novel in her sleep just now— begging you not to take it away from her and all that, in quite a wild way. There is evidently cerebral excitement. Perhaps, as you are going out, it might be prudent to telephone the doctor to drop in toward bedtime."

"Oh, a good sleep will set her up all right!" returned Barton slightingly. It did not suit his notions of marital rights to be interviewed and advised in a ghostly whisper without the precincts of his own room, by this pretentious hireling. "The book had nothing to do with her uncomfortable afternoon. It was probably the luncheon. I thought, when you brought it up, that it was more like a meal for a ditcher than for a delicate invalid."

Pleased at administering this Roland for accumulated Olivers, he ran downstairs without attending to her protest, and whistled softly while equipping himself for the walk through the snow. The night was sharply cold; the drifts were as dry as dust. He laughed like a boy in plowing through them. The return to bachelor freedom was not bad, for a change, and there were sure to be a lot of prime fellows at the club on a stormy holiday night.

CHAPTER IV.

AT eleven o'clock of that New Year's night the snow still fell, but the wind had increased to a gale, and shook the eastward windows of Agnes Ashe's bedchamber.

Nurse and baby were sound asleep in the adjoining nursery. Even in the well-built house and curtained room, the night-light wavered in the unquiet air, sending fitful hosts of specter shadows scurrying over the ceiling and falling down the walls. Sometimes one dropped upon the bed and made mouths or crooked lean fingers at the convalescent. Now and then they whispered something in fleeing or skulking past. When this happened they spoke of her husband and how he had carried off both her babies downstairs. For Baby Nest's crib was gone. She had been doubly robbed.

The door of communication between the rooms was ajar. Mrs. Ashe had need to move cautiously in arising and wrapping herself in a dressing gown. She had been three weeks upstairs. Mrs. Ames had declared her too feeble to walk across the room unaided, but to-night she felt strong and restless. Her brain was teeming with fledged thoughts, crying and fluttering to escape. If she had pen and ink she could begin another book, now that the nurse was asleep and Barton out. But that was not her reason for getting up and slipping on the wrapper. Oh, no! She drew the door to behind her cautiously, listened with held breath for sounds from the inner room, and hearing nothing, smiled cunningly, crept to the stair-head and down the polished steps. Their chill struck through the slippers into which she had thrust her stockingless feet; she shivered in the wind that drove fine snow under the front door and whistled jeeringly at her as she went by.

The library was void of human presence but warm and murky red with firelight. The vivid glow of the Argand burner, as she touched the regulator, shone upon glittering eyes, scarlet cheeks, and red lips that showed her teeth in the fixed smile of successful cunning. She found what she sought at once. Barton had left "The Story of Walter King" upon the table beside his reading chair. He would be out late. There was nothing to call him home and he was fond of his club. She was quite safe for an hour or two—secure from spy and intrusion—she and her brain-baby.

Clasping it to her heart, she wept and smiled, rocked herself to and fro as she would cuddle Baby Nest, did the nurse allow it. There was nobody to meddle with her here. She settled herself in the easy-chair and, finding where Barton had left off, read on and on, until the type began to gyrate queerly in fantastic measure across the page. Her eyes were getting tired. The tyrant above-stairs had prohibited reading so long that the effort tried her strength.

Still holding the book to her bosom, she looked around. The library was not so orderly as when she visited it tri-daily. There were no flowers on the table, yet she fancied that she smelled *Bon Silène* roses, as she had on that far-back March night when she unlocked the door leading into her beautiful, comforting Other World, where no rough blasts shook buds from blowing, no iron hand pressed down Fancy and held in Imagination with curb and bridle. The ash-cup of the bronze smoking table was filled with ashes, burnt stumps of cigars littered the hearth. Seeing them she bethought herself of the truncated brown canoe tossing in the foam-fringe of the tide on the Old Point beach. By shutting her eyes she could reproduce the scene with the minuteness of a photograph; could see the floating and swooping gulls, silver-breasted against the blue sky, and hear the swash of the waters between the rocks.

She was dreaming! It would never do to fall asleep here and be discovered by Barton or Mrs. Ames! Rubbing her eyes, she forced herself to note that one slipper lay on the rug, the other under a chair, just as Barton had kicked it off.

"Fie! fie! what would people say of a literary woman's *menage*, were these things seen?"

Presently, when her head stopped reeling, she would pick them up and straighten the slumber-robe, all crumpled together on the foot of the lounge, the pillow of which was indented by Barton's head. Sitting bolt upright, she stared at robe and cushion, so eloquent of her husband's recent presence. Her eyes were dry with misery, her features worked into sharpness. She looked, not six, but twenty years older than the hale man who had lain there, indolent and at ease, while she turned wretchedly upon her bed throughout the tedious afternoon.

Oh, the dead Past! Oh, murdered Love!

"He said that no pure woman would have written that book," she murmured. "He must never know! Why, he would turn me into the street to-night, if he found it out."

She crossed the room, catching at the furniture as she staggered along to the secretary. The key hung upon a hidden hook under the drawers. She felt for it, opened the central compartment of the escritoire, and took out an old, roomy portfolio. There were papers in it that must be destroyed. She meant to do it before she was taken ill, but everything had been so sudden. It would never do to leave them for other eyes in case of her death. While she fumbled in the pockets and drew out the MSS. she checked herself in repeating irrelevant rhymes:

"That husbands could be cruel,

I have known for seasons three,

But, oh! to ride Vindictive while a baby cries for me."

"If only my head would be steady and clear again for five minutes!"

The portfolio was nearly emptied into her lap when an awful voice from the doorway said:

"Mrs. Ashe! what am I to think of this extraordinary proceeding?"

Mrs. Ames, portentous in flannel gown and curl-papers, confronted the affrighted culprit. Through the open door and down the stairway came the wail of the hungry baby.

"I only came down for her brother," tremblingly clutching her book, and letting the portfolio slide to the floor. "I felt so strong! so well! I will run up to the little sister now—at once. Poor little Nest! she wants me, I suppose?"

Mrs. Gamp's severe eyes softened into anxiety. She spoke soothingly, in passing her powerful arm around the shaking form.

"Yes, dear. She wants mamma. Lean on me and don't hurry too much. The stairs are a steep climb."

Upon the upper landing Agnes, stopping to breathe, smiled piteously into the compassionate face.

"You see"—showing a corner of the volume hidden in the folds of her gown—"this is as much my baby as the other one, and I knew he was downstairs all alone. You will let me keep him—won't you?"

"Certainly, dear! We'll put him to bed with you, right under your pillow."

"And not a word to Barton?" Putting her lips close to the other's ear, she whispered fearfully—"You know he would turn us both out into the street if he knew."

"He shan't hear a lisp from me!" asseverated the nurse stoutly. "We'll have the two of you sound asleep before he comes in."

She always humored delirious patients. In such cases veracity courtesied to expediency.

The prime fellows made up a theater party after the club dinner and ended a jolly day with a jollier supper. The silvery tongue of the French timepiece upon the library mantel said it was one o'clock as Barton, entering, was amazed to see that he must have left the Argand reading burner up at full height. A second step showed traces of other occupation than his and of later date. His wife's secretary was open, a portfolio lay wide upon the floor, and the rug was strewn with papers. Before the suspicion of burglary could cross his mind, he trod upon something hard. It was a heavy gold hair pin of a peculiar pattern, which Agnes wore constantly. He had noticed it in her hair at noon to-day, as her head lay back against the cushions, weighed down, it would seem, by the heavy coils.

Had that hypocritical hag of a nurse allowed such outrageous imprudence in his absence? He examined the lock of the secretary. The key which he believed was kept upstairs by Agnes was in it; a survey of the apartment revealed no other signs of unwonted disorder.

"Oh, these women!" his face, florid with champagne, hock, and righteous choler, crimsoned apoplectically when he stooped for the portfolio. A sheet of paper, covered with his wife's neat, compact chirography, fell out.

It was in verse, and bore no caption.

"So-ho! poetry!"

As in a dream, he seemed to hear Agnes' voice:

"I am not a bard at all. When I am in the dark, or at best in a half-light—sorry or weary, or lonely of heart—my thoughts take rhythmic shape."

At the bottom of the third page of the rhymes was a date.

"*October 5, 188—.*"

He recollected the day. He had gone off to join some friends for a week's hunting, leaving her in a quiet mountain inn.

"And she was lonely of heart—poor little wifie!"

He sat down to read:

"He turned him at the maple tree,

To wave a fond farewell to me.

The burning branches touched his head,

Tawny and ash, and dappled red.

Behind him, in still fold on fold—

As painters lay with leaves of gold

The ground on which they mean to trace

Some favorite saint of special grace—

The chestnuts floored and roofed and hung

Niche for my hero saint. Down-flung

From cedar tops, the wild woodbine

Lent pennons brave to deck the shrine;

Barbaric sumachs straight upbore

Their crimson lamps, and, light and hoar,—

Like votive lace bestowed by dame,

Repentant of her splendid shame,—

O'er withered shrub and brier and stone,

The seeded clematis was thrown.

I thought my heart broke in the rush

Of tears that blotted out the flush

Of draping vine and burning bough.

'Oh, love of mine!'—thus ran my vow—

'Let Heaven but stoop to hear my prayer,

But lift the cross I cannot bear,

This lonely, living death of pain,

And give my darling back again

To longing heart and straining eyes—

To grief and loss in other guise,

Silent I'll bow, and, smiling, see

Sweet dawn in gloom that's shared with thee!'"

The champagne had been heady, and there was a good deal of hock. Tears of maudlin sentimentality suffused the reader's eyes at the metrical tribute to himself as his wife's "hero-saint." So long as she published nothing of the sort, it was pleasant to find, accidentally, that she wrote love verses in his absence, dedicated to him. He had not suspected how much she felt their parting—she had borne herself so heroically. Brushing away the soft moisture, he read on:

"To-day, I stood and saw him stay

His horse upon the woodland way,

And toss to me a gay farewell.

The chestnut leaves about him fell;

The royal maples burned and shone,

Veiling misshapen branch and stone,

The misty clematis lay white;

The woodbine from the cedar's height,

The sumach's crimson cones, the breath

That amber hickories yield in death—

All were the same. October rare

Held sway divine o'er earth and air.

The horseman's port was kingly—yet

My lips unwrung, my eyes unwet,

My heart recoils in cold despair

At memory of that granted prayer.

            .   .   .   .   .

My beautiful dead dream! The Spring

Beyond Life's winter, which will bring

Earth's buried ones to love's embrace,

Will hold for me no quickening grace.

Summers may go, Octobers come;—

Deep out of sight, and pale and dumb,

Lies the hope that never was to be.

My saint who lived not—save to me!"

He went over the second section of the poem twice before the wine-warmed brain accepted the significance of the lines.

Then, he swore a little. He would be no-matter-what-ed if he could make out women's fantasies. He supposed this was a fancy sketch, an impersonal rigmarole, altogether, but it was no-matter-what-ed (again) disagreeable stuff for a fellow to read who recollected that he had ridden away last October from a dry-eyed wife into the burning heart of such a wood as was here described. He did not remember turning under the maple tree, it was true— if indeed there were a maple tree at the top of the hill. There might be some mistake in the whole thing, but it went against a fellow's grain to admit the possibility that his wife had another man even in the eye of her imagination.

He renewed the business of collecting the scattered papers. He would read no more poetry to-night, but an unsealed law envelope, without address, lay under the armchair. It was white and fresh, and the folds of the instrument inclosed were crisp with newness. He pulled it out:

"MEMORANDUM OF AGREEMENT made this 6th Day of August, 188—, between AGNES WELLES ASHE of New York City, and RHINE, RHONE & CO., Publishers of New York City.

"Said AGNES WELLES ASHE being the author and proprietor of a work entitled, 'THE STORY OF WALTER KING, BY JOHN C. HART,' in consideration of the covenants and stipulation, etc., etc., etc."

The shock cleared the lawyer's head on the instant. He perused the document to signatures, seals, and witnesses, refolded and restored it to the envelope, put it back into the portfolio, and the portfolio into the escritoire, turned the key in the lock and took his stand upon the rug, his hands behind his back, his back to the fire. His face was purple, his eyes glared.

"So much for marrying a literary woman! They are a *bad* lot!"

He spat it out viciously and a bitter, sounding oath after it.

The door-bell rang loudly, attended by the sound of stamping feet upon the mat outside. The master of the house answered the summons. The family physician crowded in past him, pulling off his overcoat as he came.

"How is she?" he demanded, without preamble.

"She! Who?"

"Mrs. Ashe! One of your maids telephoned for me at half-past twelve, from the nearest station—'Come at once! Mrs. Ashe is dangerously ill.' Can there be some mistake?"

Mrs. Ames called him from the top of the stairs: "Come up quick, please, doctor. It takes two of us to hold her in bed."

The doctor rushed upstairs. Barton walked leisurely back into the library and shut the door. A woman who had sat here reading old MSS. and new contracts until she heard her husband's latchkey in the outer door, then rushed off up a long flight of stairs to avoid him, in such frantic haste that she fell into a fit at the top, might come out of it without his help. He would never be fooled by her again, so help him God!

Half an hour went by and he had not moved, although the stealthy rush of feet overhead bespoke excitement and yet caution on the part of the attendants, and twice a faint scream penetrated the ceiling. At last he reached out his hand for pen and paper and began a letter.

"MY DEAR UNCLE:

"I said to you, jestingly, thirteen months ago, that I would employ you to draw up articles of separation in the event of my needing——"

The pen stopped. He could have sworn that someone passed him, so close that he felt the wind from floating garments, and that there was the odor of *Bon Silène* roses in the air. It was strangely still overhead. Cold sweat broke out all over him; when he strove to resume his writing, his fingers were nerveless. Slow, heavy feet came down the stairs and to the library door. It was opened without the ceremony of knocking, and the physician appeared.

A withering glance took in the details of the quiet figure at the table, the paper, and the pen arrested in the hand. He went through no form of merciful preparation.

"Mr. Ashe! your wife is dead! A severe shock of some kind—the nurse thinks you can explain it—brought on convulsions and suffusion of the brain."

Baby Nest survived her mother but a week. Her father married again, eighteen months afterward, a beautiful society girl with a tolerable fortune.

She said a good thing in my hearing the other night, which I offer here in the place of the conventional moral, my story having none.

"What have you been doing with yourself all the winter?" she asked of a fine-featured, dainty little old lady, whose blue blood adds nameless finish to the fair product of brains and breeding. "I have not seen you for an age."

"I have gone out to few large assemblies this season," said Queen Mab. "But I have greatly enjoyed certain conclaves of choice spirits, to which I have been admitted. Evenings with the Laurence Huttons, the Edmund Clarence Stedmans, the Brander Matthewses, and Mr. and Mrs. William Dean Howells are something to be remembered forever with pride and delight."

"Ye-es?" the priceless lace on bust and sleeves swaying in the languid breeze of her fan. "I have heard others say that *some of these Bohemians* are really very, very nice—don't you know?"[B]

THE END

FOOTNOTES:

[A] Literal report.

[B] A verbatim report.

Milton Keynes UK
Ingram Content Group UK Ltd.
UKHW020239250424
441687UK00004B/270

9 789357 957908